Kind-ness: of, belonging to ... the self is not something one finds, it is something one creates.
　　　　　　　　　-THOMAS SZASZ,
　　　　　　　　　　-The Second Sin

A Cup o' Kindness

By
George Nilsen

Copyright © 2009 George Nilsen
Al Rights Reserved.

ISBN: 1-4392-3915-0
ISBN-13: 9781439239155
LCCN: 2009904119

Visit www.booksurge.com to order more copies.

Dedication
To Jean, who told me what she thought

Chapter One

Early in the afternoon of Thanksgiving Day, November 24th, 1932, Hans Lederhof, engineer of Engine #37, DSS&A, struggled to open the sticky side door of the depot at Bergland, Ontonagon County, Upper Peninsula, Michigan.

The nose-drip icicle on the end of Hans' beaky nose quivered as he raged at Edwin Borseth, depot agent,

"When are you going to get this god-damn door that you always say 'It'll be taken care of' fixed!" he bellowed in the deep bass voice with which some small men amaze.

"Well, what's wrong with Old #37 now, Hans?"

"The same god-damned thing that's always been wrong— I set the throttle for the scale of logs you say is on the cars, and she groans like bejesus before she can get up that first shock that jars her link to the first car that jars its link to the second car and so on down the line to get that first roll of all the wheels—"

"Puh-leeze close the door," whined Ed, his arms spread out over his desk in a vain effort to keep the dozen freight orders from flying to the floor in twos and threes, while keeping the point of his pencil where it had been on the top sheet.

Hans fought the door every inch back toward closing. Ed watched the engineer stop for a couple of deep breaths, felt sympathetic: "Have a seat over here," pointing at the plain kitchen chair Hans always sat in while complaining about something, the seat pad retaining the imprint of Hans' bony little butt from before now.

"Old #37 is a Shay 2tr, that's the most reliable engine today. Well, we've checked all the bolts and gears and oiled every g.d. movin' part, there ain't no holes in the steam lines, BUT what there must be is somethin' fishy about the scale you're handin' me."

Hans broke off to put his grease-and-oil-stained hands over his ears.

"Can't you shut off that g.d. clackety-clack machine!"

"And get fired if the inspector drops in? You want me to get fired, Hans?"

"Inspector—on Thanksgiving Day? You think there's anybody else at work today but us two fools on turkey day and gravy on yams, cranberry sauce, choice of punkin or mincemeat pie? I still got some gravy on my vest—look, there—and for sure everybody but you and me is sleepin' it off at home!"

"All right, Hans, get it off your chest."

"There's more, I swear, on those flat cars than the scale says, somebody's doin' somethin' fishy and somebody's gonna pay for it, you mark what I'm sayin'!" Hans tossed back over his shoulder, fighting the door again to get it open enough for even his thin self.

"I have the order right here," wheezed Ed, "Right from Levi Skantz, the office boss down in Milwaukee, name says signed by, right there, and type of log is 'Pine/Hemlock', 75,000 board feet of logs. How many cars have you got in that train?"

"Fifteen—ten yesterday afternoon and five more this mornin'. Good bye!" and Hans slammed—tried to slam!—that sticky door.

But Ed had to drag himself up out of the swivel chair, nearly stepping on the papers that had blown every which way, lean against the door, kick it shut, finally.

"I just tell them what's on the shipping request, I don't haul the logs," he muttered, making his tottering way back to the desk.

Going out the gate from his shack August Schmidt, ferrule-tipped applewood stick—peeled, sanded, shellacked—in hand, known as 'Dutchy' to all of Bergland Township, tossed a few chicken bones for Zwei, his little 'hund' to chew on over the weekend while his master was in Milwaukee. Zwei could snarl to his doggy heart's content at all the one or two passers-by on the Mile Road, exactly one mile north of Bergland (whence its name) which ran its grass-centered gravel-tracked two-mile length west of M64.

Dutchy was in a jovial mood, as he often was, but not because this was a day of Thanksgiving. Like many immigrants, he knew his own country's days of celebration—the Palatinate was his point of origin. There, on the day of the Erntedankfest, people brought food, thankful for having it, to church for the altar, taking it to poor people after the service. But the day the American Pilgrims chose to celebrate their thanks for surviving in their new country held little special meaning, since most of the immigrants were pilgrims themselves, but not from religious persecution.

No, Dutchy was jovial, and his playful swiping his walking stick at a piece of gravel here and there as he strode along demonstrated his carefree joy, for he was on his first leg of a trip to Milwaukee to check in with his August's Applejack Brandy distributors there. The brandy he had made from his own apples, plus some of his Mile Road fellow bachelor Jonas Amundsen's. His inner coat pocket, though made of denim, held an envelope thick to splitting open with fifty-dollar bills. The profit was partly from local sales, too, but the trip to Milwaukee had a perhaps secondary purpose as well:

For some years now, local folks in this Great Depression era had had to live with penury. The only jobs had been at Gunlek Bergland's sawmill and the other aspects of his lumber business—building temporary railroads here and there into the virgin white pine riches covering the Midwest North, sawing down the millions of board feet of lumber the white pine provided, hauling the logs to the Bergland depot. These the DSS&A hauled, as demand dictated, to other mills. But liquor, though Volstead's Act of Prohibition shared timing with the Great Depression—some claiming that Prohibition *caused* the Great Depression—was always in demand, *especially* in ego-bruising times of penury!

So Dutchy intended to flaunt his personal riches at the man in Milwaukee who'd forced his flight, accused him of cheating on freight billing while employed in Gunlek Bergland's Milwaukee office years ago, just when this German immigrant, who had shown such promise for his intelligence and quick grasp of his office job, could likely have been tapped to be the office boss. That man was Levi Skantz.

So Dutchy's greeting to Edwin Borseth, when he finally got the depot door open, was the opposite of Hans Lederhof's grumpiness.

"Happy Thanksgiving Day to you, my good friend Edwin," caroled Dutchy. "what trains sometime before tomorrow west are going?"

The depot agent glanced left at his wall calendar. "There's a five-car passenger/freight coming through to Marengo. I don't know how many of the five are passenger cars. They won't be here until well after dark. You can flag it down. The ride may be free since it doesn't show on their regular runs.."

"That suits me fine," replied Dutchy, "though broke today I am not."

He eased down into the chair, obliterating the indents made by Hans.

After more than an hour of the clackety-clack machine, Ed grunted something that may have been a good-bye, turned the telegraph off, fought the door until Dutchy helped open it, and left, stepping carefully down the two steps to the end of Pine Street and off homeward.

Dutchy heaved the depot door shut. 'Dark' would come about seven p.m. The little pot bellied stove contents, slowly subsiding to glowing bits and then to mere ashes, let more of the chill from outside infiltrate.

Time to begin his own light-up. From an outside pocket Dutchy retrieved a tin of Prince Albert; from an inside pocket his meerschaum, the huge bowl once white by now stained the appropriate dull brown glowing yellow. Into the yawning maw Dutchy poured a load of Prince Albert, tamped it down with his thumb, s-cr-at-ch-ed a kitchen match along the edge of the chair seat, held it up while the sulphur in the match head burned itself away, then sucked the flame into his pipe bowl, the rich tobacco smoke into his lungs, then sent the gray-blue exhale up to the ceiling. The next few puffs dimmed the hanging single bulb of light as what he inhaled with each breath correspondingly dimmed his brain until at the last exhalation a tiny light went on in that nearly somnolent brain:

He was alone in a freight shipping office near a desk top with freight shipping requests and orders not five feet from him. The old habit of this former worker in a lumber business office took command. Dutchy stood, moved forward, in the dim light sat in the chair Ed had sat in, put the Meerschaum to rest, mouthpiece against the desk top hinge, to study, elbows on the desktop, what sorts of freighting, what kinds of carloads, were departing Bergland.

On the very top of the thin sheaf, so neatly restacked after Hans' breezy entrance, was an order labeled 'Friday a.m.' on top and, on the bottom, 'For Hans on #37'.

It took a few seconds to soak into Dutchy's tobacco-clouded brain.

That must be the train of logs sitting on the siding right now, keeping the through tracks open for all night trains.

Ed must have had some reason for looking at it before I came in Dutchy read the few words left: Type of logs: Pine/Hemlock. Total Scale: 75,000 bd ft.

Things had not changed. The weight of the load was not stated. Railroads didn't weigh logs, actually. Such machinery wasn't available. Conifers, less dense than hardwood, were assigned less weight per board foot. The DSS&A, like all railroads, charged for moving logs according to type of wood by board foot total: Scale. Conifers cost less to ship, same scale.

What Dutchy saw was transporting him back to his old office work days in the Milwaukee office of Gunlek Aslak Bergland, lumber baron.

Was Levi Skantz still working that old dodge of which Dutchy had been falsely accused, dismissed to the far north, seeking a place like the Mile Road on which to hide?

Cheating the DSS&A on hauling fees, billing Gunlek, pocketing the difference?

But there was more to it all than that!

Dutchy picked up his walking stick, heaved the depot door open, yanked it almost closed behind him to step down two steps—tap, step, tap, step on the first yard of Pine Street.

Bergland downtown was dark. No homes with windows casting beams here and there to lighten the night. The Peterson Hall across Pine Street was dark, though its upper floor had been busy on Thanksgiving morning with feast preparation, the meal eaten by the town's destitute. Much the same as the Erntedankfest, this time ladled out by the Ladies' Aid of the St.Paul Trinity Lutheran Church, the feast had been well lighted by daylight.

Now the Hall, as was Rosberg's Mercantile on the lower floor, was dark. Both saloons, Big Marko's halfway up the first block of Pine Street, and Lackie's, across from Marko's and further up Pine at its junction with Center Street, were dark, all the usual clientele at home or asleep somewhere.

Only the single shaded bulb above the Bergland Hotel, a block away along Railroad Street, cast a dim yellowish coloring on the frost-sparkled air.

With his ferrule-pointed walking stick, tap, swing left and right, step; tap, swing, step Dutchy moved his portly self across the pair of through tracks to the siding. Against the gap of trees the gleam of Lake Gogebic was partly blackened by–yep, that's a locomotive and a line of flatcars, loaded with logs.

He forgot to breathe, thoughts churning, nearly overcome with what might, what just might, be the outcome of what he would or would not discover.

Would this day of Thanksgiving, with some few hours yet to run, be such a day for him, here in America? Or would hoping for justice, for payback, for re-establishment of self-worth, by itself defeat the effort?

Tap, swing the stick left and right, establish the location of each tie-end of the siding on which this train lay; tap, step, swing until the end of the last flatcar, the fifteenth, was immediately to his left, his shoulder touching the ends of a few saw logs.

Grasp, with the left, nearmost hand, the end of the log, press the sharp end of the stick ferrule into its sawed wooden end.

Hardwood or conifer? Conifer, fairly soft. Feel the bark: smooth, but only atop each raised rib.

Punch the ferrule end into the next inmost log's end—AHA!—the ferrule end skidded over—HARDWOOD!–and feel the bark: Not smooth, but no ridges like conifer bark.

This car carried a mixed conifer/hardwood load.

So with the fourteenth, the thirteenth as he moved back toward the depot. Not just one log, but a half-dozen heavy hardwood on each flatcar.

The bill of lading was wrong.

Deliberately so by the signer, Levi Skantz.

But the intent was not merely to bilk the railroad of its due transportation fee.

His intent was to claim payment from Gunlek Bergland for a mixed load, with the true nature of the mixed load on the office file version of the bill of lading; pay the DSS&A, in this instance, for the lighter conifer load specified, then pocket the difference.

Back in the warmer, lit depot, Dutchy reviewed how he had been duped, then accused, threatened with disclosure:

One day, years ago, Skantz had suddenly absented himself from the office, claiming a sudden fit of malaise, thrusting a bill of lading at Dutchy, "You sign for me, I have to go to the hospital!"

And next day, holding the bill of lading, admitting it was false, but Dutchy's signature right there, with Skantz' terrible smile; Gunlek to know or not up to him, August

From far east down the track, a faint short, then longer, train whistle. If it had light from windowed cars, it would be his train!

Dutchy thrust the carbon in his coat pocket, put the original back on the slim stack on Ed's desk, hurried out to look down the track.

The light streamed from inside the last car. Dutchy scratched a kitchen match with his thumb nail, waved the flare crosswise to flag the train. At its blast of air, the screech of the steel wheels on the steel tracks, he forced himself back inside for his Meerschaum witness, yanked the stubborn door CLOSED with both hands, turned to await the last car stopping even with the Bergland depot loading platform.

Once aboard, the sole passenger in the single car trailing the dozen or so boxcars, he stared out the left window, left arm over the worn back of the uncushioned seat, left knee- and thigh resting on the seat.

Through the coal-smoke flecked glass the evening star, sometimes called Venus, or Latin Hesperus, from the Greek Hesperios, 'western' star, sulked reddish and low over the dark glimmer of Lake Gogebic.

Hesperios—he himself, before turning south for Milwaukee, was headed west—as had Odysseus returning from the battle of Troy. Dutchy—August, in his youth at the Heidelberg University, in Doctor Pudendorf's English Literature seminar, the good Doctor always going back to the original word, its original meaning:

"Always behind the present meaning the original meaning find," his oft-repeated admonition to the select group around the large round table, itself, as the good doctor explained, a lesson learned from Malory's Morte d'Arthur. "Then the current meaning has undertones, like the harmonies of Bach, making the meaning richer than before."

"See," he'd said, gesturing around the table, "I sit at one place, just as we all do herein, to make more meaningful my first day's claim that I am one with you, you are all one with each other, there is no seat to be sought after, envy, jealousy to cause. At the same time I make clear I learned it from reading of King Arthur's Round Table."

And he'd grinned at the too serious faces of his students,—I was there, August nearly said aloud—"I ignore for the moment the Siege Perilous!"

The Siege Perilous, empty, reserved for the Knight who would find the Holy Grail, and fatal to any other knight. Then he would ask around the table for any comment that might delve into the allegory, some meaning Christian perhaps, or just meant to encourage each knight to seek the Holy Grail, or 'merely' something about knowing one's place and better stay in it rather than die?

Now his passenger car had left Lake Gogebic behind. After shifting his seating, Dutchy dwelt still in the memories of his youth and young adulthood.

Since attempts to sleep promise to be miserable failures!

Before the good Doctor, there was his father, 'grand' in the meaning of 'august', his father's huge powerful body making the anvil ring in the Count Palatine's estate forge. A quiet man of few words, a pleasure to obey, who'd taken him before the Count, who'd been impressed as much by his smith as by the smith's son's scholastic record.

I learned to stand straight in quiet confidence from both. In vastly different livelihoods, each sure of his worth in his place, they agreed that this lad, me, should live and study at the 'hoch schule', hone his mind and his knowledge of philosophy and literature, with a reasonable grounding in Greek and Latin from the best at the Heidelberg University, from 1346 a citadel of highest learning.

And what a rich field was learning! The Bible, in both German and English, seeing the huge popularity, the love of Shakespeare in his own German country, Hamlet the Dane, the castle on a promontory, Hamlet himself purportedly a student here.

And more: The works of Emmanuel Kant, of Carlyle and his *Sartor Resartus,* usually translated as 'The Tailor Re-clothed'—and that outer clothing, witnessed as his father and the Count faced each other, spoke volumes about the men themselves.

But not only books, ideas, history. Around and about the Palatinate flourished many state-supported distilleries, the goal being an empire eschewing fossil fuels when horses would become superseded by machines, driven by alcohol!

For the tenth time, the train now headed south away from Hurley, Wisconsin, Dutchy sought a different position on his seat. Though not six feet tall, somewhat bulky in the same appearance as his sire, if he attempted sleep it would have to be with his legs from knees down hanging in the aisle, or, on his side, bunched up on the hard seat.

He recalled the huge casks, one called the Heidelberg Tun, so huge as to be immovable, capable of over 58,000 gallons of wine. But never used, except for a dance floor atop it.

And then the post-war depression, revolution, the Nazi party taking the funds from both other parties, the Social Democrats and the Communists, the Brown Shirts rampaging on the streets, Kristall Nacht, the NY Times reporting the pogroms in Galicia, by Germans, might their own land be next? my incipient professorship I had expected, been promised, given up, as intellect became a liability, as professors became targets for the prisoner camps and the hundreds of railroad cars packed with 'enemies of the Third Reich'! So I took my books, a thick bottom layer in my trunk—the mark was valueless—and off to America.

And not too far ahead of the Depression which hit America, I reached the German enclave in Milwaukee in 1924, my goal.

A long night of patches of sleep in the unheated car, jerked awake by screeching stops.

In the years—was it eight?--that August had been away from Milwaukee that city had changed so much as to be wholly unfamiliar. None the less, at the railroad station a taxi driver said he knew how to get to the Merrill Building, in which number 22 was Gunlek Bergland's main office.

And get there Dutchy did, a wild ride in a Model A Ford sedan much the same as the one Aslak, Gunlek's nephew, Dutchy's neighbor on the Mile Road, was known for in Bergland. Wild because the car had to miss all the traffic coming the other way, and some detours had to be taken because the new trolley line work messed up the streets.

But the building hadn't changed. To pay the taxi driver, though, Dutchy had to cross the street to a bank—the driver couldn't make change for the fifty Dutchy first proffered.

That done, Dutchy, alone in the largest city in Wisconsin, figuratively hitched up his suspenders and marched into the building he knew well.

The door to #22 stood open, and Dutchy stood in that door—but it was no longer the office of Gunlek Bergland's Lumber Company only. In Dutchy's time Skantz had been the office chief. Now, the room was stuffed full with desks at each of which a man or a woman hunched over a clattering typewriter, in divisions the name posts he'd never heard of, but there was no Levi Skantz patrolling as he had in years past, his lanky, slouching body, topped by a full beard under heavy black brows, eyes darting intimidating glares at his subordinates.

Oh, there was Levi Skantz, all right. But he was just one of the hunched bodies over a typewriter. After a full minute he raised his head to stare at the door, perhaps feeling the hostile stare directed at him.

The intimidating presence, though, was just as plain as ever. Skantz stood, walked in that same concentrated coil of enmity to the connecting glass-windowed side door, jabbed a thumb to summon Dutchy to hallway privacy, went through without waiting to see if Dutchy would follow.

Dutchy waited, standing weight on rear foot, front leg bent at the knee in a casual style, waited until he saw Skantz' surprise that Dutchy wouldn't take the same bullying that Skantz had habitually practiced.

Then he went through that door, stopped a full step from Skantz.

"What the hell are you doing back down here? Didn't get the dismissal get through to that dumb German head yet? Or should I say dummkopf so you'd grasp the meaning?"

Dutchy let a slow smile uncover his large teeth. He reached inside his inside coat pocket, pulled out the envelope of fifty-dollar bills, plucked out one, held it up.

An involuntary twitch in Skantz' right shoulder signaled his desire to reach for the bill, more than he earned here, probably, in a week. But his hand didn't move.

"You've managed to work some other nefarious scheme, a crooked one no doubt, and you came all the way down here—oh yes, I know where you are!—just to flaunt it at me?"

Dutchy replaced the bill in the envelope, stuck it back inside his coat. Kept the smile out where Skantz could see it.

"I owe much of my fluency in English to your own eloquence, Skantz,"—who bristled at the familiarity—"but I thank you for it, without admiration."

He stepped closer; Skantz shifted backwards.

"When you sent me off, maybe you feared I might oust you as the chief here, you did me a great favor. I was forced into producing a product that has made me rich"—he patted his coat over the pocket-"while you have lost out as a chief of anything to be merely one of the clerks chained to a typewriter."

"You can just dig back into that pocket and I don't have to reach for it. You can take a step closer and tuck it into my shirt pocket right now, and keep sending one each month from now on. I still have the phony order you signed, and my word is still worth more than yours."

"Oh, I'll reach into my pocket all right!" Dutchy pulled out the carbon copy of the freight bill of lading for #37, held it up close to Skantz' eyes, watched his face break up into fear, surprise, and hatred. He thrust out his hand but Dutchy snapped it back.

"I doubt very much you have that phony order you tricked me into signing! You long ago thought you had me taken care of for good"—seeing his guess strike home—"what you just saw was proof in writing…and you may know that I live right next to Gunlek's nephew on the Mile Road out of Bergland."

Skantz's face distorted with pure hatred; Dutchy drove his point home.

"In the future, I'll know if you are sending up fake bills so you can continue to skim by taking money from Gunlek's pocket. Then you won't even be a clerk typist—you'll be in jail!"

Dutchy found himself standing outside of the Merrill Building, with no recall of walking out the door. Half afraid, doubting, he looked down to reassure himself that his feet *were* on the ground. His elation was a sense of his new, freed self, not a physical fact!

This taxi trip was to be to a place where Dutchy could be washed off and August Schmidt assume his rightful place.

"Go to the best hotel inside of a mile from here," Dutchy said loud and clear. "I want new clothes, a soaking bath, a good night's sleep!"

"Right-O!" responded the driver, 'I've got a live one here' to himself --and got the big tip he'd hoped for when August-to-be debarked at the Knickerbocker-on-Lake, East Juneau Avenue.

First, at the desk, where one of the bills secured him the weekend suite on the top floor. A tub of hot water his aching portly self raised just under the brim; he drained it down to half as it began to cool, refilled, Lake Michigan (or wherever the water came from!) in sight, scrubbed the dirt from his knuckles. Leaned back, eyes closed…aaaahhh!

Next, at the men's clothing shop on North 76th Street, from which he emerged an hour later in a worsted gray suit, narrow white striped, vest plain gray, solid deep red tie, gold tie clasp, white shirt, gold cuff links. No hat—be different!

For an hour or so that Friday afternoon, August paraded his new outfit, matching his new infit, on the streets near the Knickerbocker. Milwaukee could hardly differ more from Bergland, his town of exile. There, the only car visible, and that not daily, was Aslak Bergland's black Model A sedan chugging past on the Mile Road; here, on Juneau Avenue, the noise of the trolley track preparation, cars by the bunches going both ways, shops like his source of his clothes, also shops for ladies, with clientele sucked in and pushed out in steady streams.

Then a sumptuous evening meal, Bratwurst, fried potatoes, corn on the cob, green beans, apple pie—all steaming hot, with vanilla ice cream melting on the slice of pie—in the dining hall—'room' was too small a term!—then up in the elevator, 'whoosh'—slide in between smooth white sheets to mix deep sleep with dream visions of coming back to live in this stimulating city—say goodbye to the Mile Road?

Saturday:

At times afoot—the applewood stick befitting a suited, dignified man—at times in a taxi, when the distance demanded, August re-acquainted his new, independent identity, free of the black cloud of malfeasance-in-office threat , with as much of the city's parks and sights as the day would allow.

Could even his lately more portly body, his expanded sense of self: August Schmidt, sole proprietor of *August's Applejack Brandy,* contain the joy?!

Would what he visited, understood, today, teach him how? Going by Dretzka Park he marveled at men walking along in mown, undulating at times, at times flat, green swards, stopping to hit a little white ball, then following it to hit it again, sometimes on an extremely short-mowed green small area, whereon the white ball dropped into a hole, to be immediately picked out and carried (by a small person laden with an open-topped bag, clubs for striking the little white ball protruding) to a nearby flat area to be struck again, to the accompaniment of cheers, praise, or groans!

Then up 92nd Street to Hales Corner, where the 1,000-acre Whitnall Park Arboretum housed the Boerner Botanical Gardens, where, except for a lunch at Henry Maier Festival Park, August spent the remaining sunlit hours of the day.

It was awesome. Everywhere were landscaped collections of perennials, herbs, and annuals splashing vivid reds, yellows, blues, whites; a Rock Garden; the largest ornamental Crab Apple Tree collection in the *nation*; over five hundred varieties of roses—all still open in the unusually warm late November on the west shore of Lake Michigan.

Saturday evening, reconstituted by a sixteen-ounce sirloin steak, rare, with Pabst (near beer, 3.2 in the strictures of Prohibition), August enjoyed incidental piano tunes in the club atmosphere, with, served in an unobtrusive style, a small brandy that he recognized as a bit of his own apple decoction!

And so to bed. *August's Applejack Brandy!* Not 'Dutchy'. *August.*

Sunday:

The late morning, August at Captain Frederick Pabst's mansion, West Wisconsin Avenue, but called the 'Grand" Avenue because of all the mansions lined up along it. It was not open yet—not until twelve noon—but August was there to see the outward aspect. His intent was not clear in his own mind, not clear enough to state clearly and precisely, but it had something to do with his own new suit of clothes.

The initial vision, coming up 'Grand' Avenue, was of a cylindrical stone tower with a conical cap on it, some vague hugeness behind it spreading out to nearly the size of a small warehouse. August walked around it slowly, craning his neck, tilting his head back to take in its entirety. It wasn't private anymore; the city had cleaned up the surrounding lawns, redone the entire inside with carefully matched furniture and fittings to its 1892 erection.

August in fact felt a kind of bond with the whole mansion.

He and the Captain, both brewers, one of beer, the other, brandy; one, of course, much smaller capacity, but in the same creative act. Both had taken what they did seriously enough, adeptly enough, to profit by their ventures. And both had chosen to 'dress up' for others to view the success they'd had: one, huge, a mansion; the other, new clothes. The mansion was forty years old. So am I.

Neither had the Captain, August realized, been able to contain *his* joy. Once inside, he read a plaque alleging that its interior was an authentic replica of a Victorian mansion.

August was no expert, or even familiar with what a Victorian mansion should look like, but he accepted the claim. What it meant to him was that the Captain felt that his rank among brewers elevated him to a sort of royalty among them, so the house in which he lived should look like that which Queen Victoria had when she was the ruler, the royalty, the top person, in the United Kingdom.

With a bit of a rueful smile he wondered if in fact King Arthur's castle, rumored to be at Tintagel, could have been more impressive in the putative 9th century.

August realized that his decrepit shack on the Mile Road was a far cry from this mansion; this mansion resembled the others along 'Grand' Avenue, and his shack was worse in both exterior and interior than any on the Mile Road—all of them were wooden homes, more or less painted, while his was a yellow-rusty tin. All of them were reasonably large and fairly neat inside; his was small--one room!—and a dirty mess.

Except for his stove.

He'd have to go along with Aslak's recommendation: Blow it up and start over, from the ground up. He smiled, remembering Aslak's disclaimer of any extra charge for the cellar!

The rest of Sunday afternoon August spent wandering around in the Milwaukee Art Museum, especially in the Collection of American Folk Art. Soon he saw a connection in these items—drawings, furniture, sewing, animals, people, even the old 'home place' to the Captain's Mansion in that each, though often crudely done, simple in technique, and minor, were reflections of how the creators of the art saw themselves. Many of them showed an appreciation of Nature—waterfalls, trees, grass, lakes, wild animals. They seemed to August to be more in tune with his Upper Peninsula, his Mile Road surroundings. People in his environment up there, and the folk artists, had little time or energy to spare to create vastand or intricate, polished works of art. But the sentiment was the same: Record something that doesn't last forever by itself, such as a season, a short time, a happening—especially a fame or reputation!

August imagined the neat, functional order of his own 'brauhaus', where he processed raw apples into brandy. A painting of that would not be out of place in this folk art collection!

Finally, body tired, mind abuzz from his return to his first American city, to bed.

Sleep. Whether spurred by the late thought of his own 'brau haus', or the confrontation with Skantz triggered it—

who can explain why a dream comes?—that night August rose from his bed and traveled to Bergland for an audience.

In Marko's Saloon, of course, the lumber baron a heavy, heavy drinker of moonshine. August, not the first time facing a local 'baron', professing his desire to remain employed, in the mill or the yard, giving him an opportunity to find a place with orchards, to give him a start in his own business, be a brandy maker.

The generous Viking avatar, laughing delightedly, telling him to settle on the farm next to his brother Ole, on the Mile Road just north of Bergland, acres of apple trees planted by earlier employees, now dead or gone in the way of those days.

Unaccountably, for such is the nature of dreams, he next eyed that same Hesperus, Venus, viewed through the train window three nights before, 'amo, amas, amat' and how he'd gloried in his venture into that new, classical language, dancing in joy atop the Heidelberg Tun, flinging high his hands on strong young arms ...

... banging his headboard in his room in the Knickerbocker Hotel in Milwaukee.

Chapter Two

Next morning, time to get to work. August checked out of the Knickerbocker, went to the Central station, bought a ticket north on the Soo Line for just after noon, then out to the Pabst Central office, next to the huge blocks of the brewery, to discuss his brandy with the purchasing agent: Were they content with the brandy's sales, his delivery system, should we modify anything about the whole deal? On his way to the office, August noticed the air of near silence—naturally, conveyor belts, dolly wheels, etc., were noisy—but the workmen who tended the moving parts and items went about their jobs with attention solely on what they were doing, with a minimum of frustration and movement. They took the time to do their handling of bottles, kegs, sacks of hops, and so forth with care but without strain. From his own experience in Bergland's office in the Merrill Building years ago August knew what tension looked like. Here in the work areas, where all the materials and the finished products were moving, and in the office spaces as well, through the top halves of glass of most closed work places, he could see only the same air of purposive action without any signs of anger, tension or boredom.

In sum, the work force showed ideal dedication to the quality of the end-product, the beer being produced.

I feel—probably show—the same about my own brandy, and how it should be produced. These beer brewers and I, we are alike.

Nor was he disappointed in the purchasing agent's office. There, he was greeted with a hearty handshake, a clap on the back that demonstrated this man recognized August, once he had re-introduced himself to a busy man, as an equal, some kind of expert, or at least knowledgeable, man in the same field.

Moreover, this important man in Pabst, who decided entirely what other producers Pabst would work with, would allow only the best products not made by Pabst to issue from their control in a huge city with brewers and brews drunk and handled by many, many self-acknowledged connoisseurs, would discuss only *in*creasing the size of August's delivery each month:

Customers praised his brandy, the Pabst stocks of it ran out well before the next shipment came in.

So August promised that, sole proprietor and worker in his own 'factory' as he was, he would see if and how much he could increase Pabst's quota of brandy. He felt sure enough to claim he wouldn't try so much for quantity that it might affect its quality; sellers who ran out would just have to adjust their sales, increase its price, do the best they could with what was available. It shored August's confidence no end to see the buyer agree that quality was to be the sole deciding factor!

At the Miller Brewery office, things were nearly identical. The same air of quiet aptness and dedication not to work hours, or 'perks', but to the excellence of the final product by taking due care of each stage of its production everywhere evident. The reception and conclusion in the buyer's office was the same, as well. August left in time to get aboard his BNSF train with the recognition of, and future increase in product delivery to, if possible, both of his outlets in the city of Milwaukee.

While seated in the diner, elbows on the snowy white linen, toying not with the gleaming silver, but watching the growing depth of snow along the tracks and attempting to sort out the sum of all of his impressions, results, of his business trip, he found himself trying to put them in words, get some specific clarity, from those impressions.

'I truly enjoyed the sheets, the hot water baths, the food, the lounge music—all of what people call 'the good life'—that, and the clothes, are what I should have as a prosperous business man. I feel comfortable in that group.'

August felt his neck hairs rise at the next recollection.

'I feel elated, sitting here, because I got that Skantz off my horizon; always behind me I dragged that possible ball and chain of a convict gang sort of thing. Now that's tied up; if Skantz makes a move toward legal action against me, he can expect a counter action. That would be more harmful to him than to me. Besides his job, he'd lose the trust of Gunlek and any future job, even if after time served, would be out.'

A tiny cloud: How keep an eye on the bills of lading in Ed's office, the actual make-up of a flat car's load? Tip Ed off? Would the old agent actually go out and check as I did? Do I want the word to get out about this whole mess, why Skantz kicked me out of Milwaukee, get the whole township relishing, laughing, maybe some angry, all that?

Why not let DSS&A in on it, partly, hint they should check lading bills, actual loads, at Bergland depot?

Time enough after I get back, maybe get Aslak, Jim—he lives close to the depot—to keep an eye out, talk it over, anyway.

A waiter—called 'steward' as if on a ship—brought him his roast beef, noodles in gravy, green beans, coffee. August wondered about the features, the black skin. What 'elation' did he feel, sense, rationalize about his station in this world? Was this a promotion, and if so, from what? What next step might give him hope?

From what he had seen and done on the weekend, August felt he belonged now to men who were achievers, like Pabst, like the buyers there and at Miller's since he was doing what they had done, and successfully. Most citizens felt that Prohibition was on its last legs, and when repealed, brewers, moonshiners, fermenters, would lose whatever cloud of illegality they now shivered under to bask in the sun of legal alcoholic beverages once more.

'So I'm not only 'up' but face more elevation when that comes."

The monotonous, rapid clicking of the train's wheels hitting the rail joints suggested his journey through the years to come.

'Now I'm forty, prosperous, content with myself, single, going home.'

A last little bit of impression not yet realized, nor yet amalgamated with his current thinking: What if 'home' turned out to be someplace in or around Milwaukee?

A spate of doubt gushed over him: Where, possibly, would be a place good for him, for his brandy making, lots of apples? An opposite flood of yes, buts: Good food, good comfort and ease of personal care, lots of people for friendships,…

A tidal wave swept him away, inundated him, he choked a gasp, cleared his air way: *Marriage. MARRIAGE*

The steward, returning to pick up his dinner ware, refill his cup, sounded worried:

"Are you all right, sir?"

And stepped quickly away, stopped; August realized his hand waving dismissively at the steward still held the knife—European by birth and early years, August ate by using knife and fork at the same time.

He gestured the waiter to close in again. "No, I just got something stuck, I guess! Yes, I'm done, and it was good, too!"

But for the rest of the trip, while he feasted in mind on his growth in self-estimation, how at the beginning the trial and error, learning, persisting, gathering the bushels and bushels of apples, developing a hand-cranking tool such as the machine driven ones in the Palatinate to core and peel the apples, to grind them into pomace, store the cider, waiting for the ice-cold nights to form the ice. Then picking off the ice in the mornings, until the hygrometer indicated the proof was at or near 38%, finding the red oak barrels, nearest to the Limousin used in Europe, making the local sales to the multitude—yes, good for business!—with Aslak's help in that Model A, his uncle Gunlek, proud of me, helping spread the word not only in Ontonagon but opening up the Milwaukee distributors...coming back to the present, his daily duties—Zwei, more brandy, the house—the thought of marriage kept thrusting itself back into the midst of those cerebrations!

Near dark was sliding its mantle over the chill air of Bergland as August stepped down on the depot platform, aware of the last car of the Soo Line train getting smaller as it speeded up east toward its home base. The depot windows were blank; Ed Borseth had gone home. He had a wife, August thought aimlessly.

There were lights, though: The single bulb illuminated Anna's Hotel sign; windows at Marko's and Lackie's Saloons were blazing.

"First, sign up for a bed, get a supper, at Anna's, then see what if anything is new at Marko's," August—not quite yet 'Dutchy' again—decided.

Most of the tables at Anna's were empty—her clientele, mostly working men, ate as soon as their work day was over; a few 'traveling men' were still at table, most with a cigarette or cigar thickening the air.

Anna herself was at the desk, overlooking the dining room, when August walked in.

"You're back at last!" Anna greeted him. "Are you staying with me tonight?"

"I'll need a bed, yes," cautious August replied, leaning his apple-wood walking stick against a chair back. No lightweight, though of average male height, he, as were many men even taller than he, was somewhat unsettled by Anna's physical presence, though she was noted for her gracious manner, usually smiling as well. She was not a woman, probably never had been, a female men looked up and down to estimate her sex appeal in a totally masculine manner! In fact, some men looked up when addressing her, literally.

But August was aware 'staying with me tonight?' from a woman could be taken in different ways! It could be taken as the typical *witch's, or enchanted lady's invitation!*

"Done!" Anne answered immediately. "You'll sleep up in the crow's nest, the cupola over the sign out front. Are you hungry for a good meal?"

"You know I never turn down a meal when it's offered," August rejoined, showing those huge front teeth.

"It's pork roast, boiled sweet potato, apple sauce," said Anna over her shoulder, striding toward the kitchen. "Take any table; I'll be right back with your meal!"

When August drained his cup, Anna was there with a refill from the pot. No decaf in those days.

"I think you ought to wear a suit more often, every time you come to town," Anna began, sitting at his left, "Aslak tells me your brandy is doing well in the township."

"True, it is selling well," August admitted, lifting the fresh coffee. Hot and sweet. Why not open up?

"I was asked by both Pabst and Miller, my distributors there, to ship them more, as much as I could make of the same quality"—he dipped his head, put his cup down—"so when I went out on Grande Avenue to see Captain Pabst's mansion, I felt like a captain of brandy, and maybe even like King Arthur!"

"I've heard the name, know next to nothing about him and his Round Table. I wonder if the school library…"

"Bound to," August allowed, raising his cup, fully at ease now. "You might find him to have been much like your husband Rudolph—a large, strong man, looked a lot like Gunlek Bergland, was popular in much of Europe. Dig into it, why don't you?"

"Sounds very much what I like. Did you visit any personal friends in Milwaukee?"

August shook his head. "I saw a man from before I came up here, but he wasn't a friend. He had created a problem for me; so I came up here."

Anna could see not to press for details.

"It's a nice city, with lots of things going on, and not hurt much by the Depression, nor by Prohibition, being a port city, they say," Anna continued.

"You're right there," agreed August. "I got a couple days' view, but I just barely touched the surface."

He paused, looked Anna straight in the eye. "I might go back, who knows? The brandy is doing very well down there!"

Smiling in approval, Anna rose. A couple was waiting at the desk. "Just keep us locals supplied first, old friend!"

August laid five dollars on the table, picked up his applewood walking stick, went out the door, that thought of a loose end flickering like the dancing shadow of the hotel light.

Who could be the watch dog on the lading bills, the flat cars? DSS&A? Ed Borseth? He turned west around the Post Office, up Pine, and into Big Marko's.

For the first hour of August's stay, a slowly sipped near beer in front of him, a few who knew him sitting down with him for a few minutes made the evening quite what he had hoped for: A relaxing time with friends before his morning hike out to the Mile Road and getting the next few batches of apples ready for the procession toward brandy.

Last time—early spring, it was—that wild woman, Gallopin' Lil, Tiger Lil, works out in the woods with the other lumberjacks, took a swing at me for not laughing at that joke about–whatever it was. And Nick Anderson, Constable, put her in jail in Ontonagon!

'Galloping Lil from the Norwich Mine;
Hair on her head like a porcupine.'

From her first days in Bergland, that was how Lillian Eunice Ryan was described, tagged.

Abrasive. In one word.

A laugh at her own jokes like a siren stuck on the high note, like a pig squeal's effect on the ear drums: Acute, actual pain.

One hundred ten pounds, two inches at the most, over five feet.

A match for this old saying: Dynamite comes in small boxes.

Because no matter your size, or gender, if you offended her, she'd explode at you.

Around Bergland, Ontonagon County, she worked in the woods. Drove horses hauling logs or pulpwood, sawed, chopped, helped camp cooks, in the company of Jack Ryan, not much bigger than she was, or by herself.

Another old saying: Drank like a fish—but not water!

The joke Dutchy didn't laugh at: To a barkeep refusing her a free drink: "You're tighter than a bullfrog's ass, and that's water tight!"

So Gallopin' Lil swung at Dutchy, missed. Nick Anderson locked her up in the county jail, an hour's drive away.

Her story about the next morning, when she showed up in Marko's (never there without her alleged husband Jack) the next Saturday night:

"I told him I needed a Kotex and he said, 'You'll get cornflakes like everybody else!'"

S k r e e c h!!!!!! of laughter.

And the quick stare around to spot and glare at a sober face!

Where did she come from, how did she get to Bergland, why was she ......?

Born in 1892 in Antioch, Illinois, on the seventh of December, the last of five daughters in the twenty-first year of her mother Flora Rebecca (McClellan) Ryan's 1871 marriage, at the ripe old age of twelve, to John Ryan, a drummer boy in the Civil War from August of 1862 to December of 1863, when he was discharged with a disability, Lillian Eunice Ryan lacked a few days of her fortiethth birth day on that 1932 Thanksgiving weekend.

Mother Flora, aged thirty-three when Lil was born, in her same decade as Lil now, had begun child-bearing when scarcely past puberty. Lil, more like Mrs. Hubbard's dog, had none.

She came to Bergland following employment by Gunlek in Cadillac, where he'd begun on arrival from Norway, to Sidnaw in the Upper Peninsula.

She'd escaped competition with four older sisters by starting out at age ten in Cadillac as a cook's helper. Independent. Like her mother, who'd wed at twelve.

How did she, a child in most people's eyes, get from Antioch, Illinois, to Cadillac? Antioch is a few miles south of the Wisconsin border, some forty miles from Milwaukee, Gunlek Bergland's main office even when his sawmill was up and running in Bergland.

So, reasonable.

Nobody knows that part of the story. Lil never told. Nobody ever asked. In those times in that area *all adults were from somewhere else. 'Venturesome'?*

In those times in that area all of them were. Hopeful, following good jobs, not worried that Bergland's surrounding timber would one day be down, turned into boards, nailed up somewhere, logs left Bergland most every day!

And when the logs went, so would most everyone who came there because the timber was there.

But take a look at Lil's forebears:

Mother Flora, as we go back through her ancestors, a descendant, from mother Eunice (Weeks) Avery McClellan whose great-grandmother, Eunice (Weeks) Avery was a descendant John & Priscilla (Mullins) Alden. From *somewhere else* on the *MAYFLOWER*.

People not afraid to leave their parents behind, play entirely different roles.

Flora wed at twelve; Lil ? Flora branching out with five children; Lil none.

Barren, involuntary? Voluntary, a reaction to...?

August's first beer, 3.5 according to Prohibition law, sat going even flatter as the nightly hubbub in Marko's Saloon buzzed amongst the relaxing sawmill laborers and friends.

It must have been after eight when a party of two came in. It was Gallopin' Lil with a sort of puny middle aged man with a greasy billed cap and a bit of a stagger.

"Gimme what you got for beer, and the same for this piece of cow-plop who drove me up from Chicago, Marko!" Gallopin' Lil shouted over the easy, good-humored buzz of talk at the tables.

The saloon was full; not odd for a Monday night, since there was only one other saloon in town, and drinkers and just plain socially starving people tended to stick to their usual places in a small town where jobs were scarce.

"C'mon, chug-a-lug, driver, make this one last 'cause it is your last one. I been buyin' 'em for you at every stop all the way up the lower peninsula.!"

The other patrons turned away from their companions to watch what kind of a show Gallopin' Lil was going to put on this time. Her reputation, gained by her common habit in the last few years, was to get louder and louder as the quaffs went down, and either resort to jokes, ending with her own loud guffaws—SCREECHES, some named them—to be followed as like as not by some insult real or imagined, which would make Gallopin' Lil take offense, which always wound up with Lil winding up and blasting some man who, in Lil's loud estimation, had insulted her—a man's sort of reaction for what woman was left in Lil to take as an insult 'not fit for a 'jack to put up with' as Lil would decide, and after such decision would come an attack on the insulter.

This is how this one went: The driver (never named) thumped down his emptied glass on Big Marko's bar top and asked Gallopin' Lil, to his right at the bar, in a slurred voice heard clearly by the now hushed fellowship:

"You promised to pay me some money for drivin' y'up here all way from Chi—I wanna see fifty dollars from you right now!

"…kissed a bull on the ass a mile up the road!" Lil ended the story about how fast her first car had been, SCREECHED HER LAUGHTER, *then turned on her driver with an unholy glitter* in her two pale blue middle-aged eyes.

In the dead silence after her screech, not a glass being lifted in Marko's, she hissed,

"What did you say you wanted to see right now?"

The driver lifted up his empty glass, thumped again on the bar, thrust his face into Lil's—a short, slight woman, in lumberjack overalls and boots, spiky hair a mess in all direction, and repeated:

"Fifty dollars from…"

And his nose spouted blood as Gallopin' Lil, who'd worked in the woods as a 'jack', for years, planted her right fist in his threatening face.

Down he went, banging into his bar mates on the way down.

"You goddam bloodsucker, I bought you more than fifty dollars in drinks all those times we stopped you never bought a one!"

Driver, drinkers, including August, silent; Marko, behind the bar, leaning on it in his "Not again!" droop; Yaga, serving tray in hand, motionless by the table next to the door.

Lil was the first to move. Bending over the prostrate, stunned driver, she grabbed the front of his shirt with her left hand, his belt buckle with her right, knuckles white on the left, red-splotched on the right.

"Here's what you need, whatever you want!" the SCREECH now in anger; she lifted his upper body just off the saloon floor and never mind her size of body, her size of anger let Gallopin' Lil drag him toward the door with such speed that Yaga by the door opened it out of habit and Gallopin' Lil heaved the driver sliding, tumbling down the two steps to sprawl in the freezing slush of Pine Street.

"Come back if you want more," Lil screeched. 'Otherwise, don't"

And turned to Big Marko, behind the bar, now, head up.

"I just saved enough for drinks for the house. Double 'em up, Marko!" and sagged into a booth, head sinking into her arms on the table top.

Yaga roused her, and at Marko's nod, started Lil toward the stairs to an extra bed.

Frank Cutler slammed his beer stein on the table.

"Damned woman is a disgrace to this town. Somebody ought to lock 'er up 'n throw away the key!"

"Bar's closed!" announced Marko "Drink up, folks! I'm closin' up!"

August followed the rest out the door past the driver trying hard to stand up; August gave him help to his taxi.

Went around the Post Office to Anna's and a night's sleep. He hoped.

First step: Lift your foot.
Pause.

Why?

We're going up to your bed for tonight. Lift your foot.

Whissh one?

Either one. We're going up to your bed for tonight. Lift this foot.

What foot on?

The first step. Now push up on that foot and lift your other foot to the next step.

"Are her eyes open?"

"I don't see but one; it's closed."

"I've got her. Let go."

And Marko carried Lillian up to the spare bedroom, Yaga pulled off her boots, Lillian crumpled on top of the covers.

Out.

"I'll pull the other edge across over her. She won't know anything until morning."

Chapter Three

At six a.m. Tuesday morning, 29 November, 1932, her guts rumbled in warning. Somebody was thumping on a huge drum. What was wrong with her throat? That 'whoomp, whoomp' was coming from ... where she was? She was ... where?

Her eyes had sand ... She tried to move, then to move her arms; finally, in near terror, she was able to wiggle her toes, moved her feet, THREW THE COVER OFF HER LEGS! Get up on one elbow, stare at the half-dark blur all around her. Lie back, free of the grasp of...what had it been?

Again

Her own arms were crossed in front of her, hands cupping her ribs on opposite sides.

Only she herself was holding herself.

Something in with her. Ham smell—somebody frying ham. Lil sat up.

In her stockings, rough work wool. Ham smell, sweaty socks smell, too.

Going the wrong way, no door on this side. Oops, those my boots? Not now.

When she stepped off the last step down on the first floor, kitchen light showed where to go—GO! The first door handle she found was the bathroom.

Lucky. She'd taken in a lot of liquid. Out both ends.

Heaving even after there was nothing left to come up. *PAIN!*

Yaga, Big Marko, Mary, Marko, John, at the table for breakfast, heard a soft, muffled version of the sounds. John, due in an hour at third grade, looked at his father, at his mother, who shook her head 'No'.

After breakfast, the three went off to school. Big Marko went out into the saloon part. Yaga cleared off, heated some dish water, piled some cups, knives, forks, into the dishpan with a few shavings of Fels Naphtha.

Lillian tried to stand, helped herself up by hanging on to the towel rack.

Who was that—witch—over the sink? Duck, cover that face with water, hold the towel up in front of it, open eyes toward the door.

Sometime, somebody has to see you today

A flash of the old Gallopin' Lil *guts*.

Now.

She opened the bathroom door, kept her head up high enough to see the kitchen table, Yaga sitting on the far side, looking straight at her. Not smiling, just looking at her.

Lil let go of the bathroom door knob, moved a foot toward the table, no power in her legs, sagged to the floor.

Yaga didn't move.

Someone in the saloon rattling glasses, running water, moving chairs.

An old-fashioned alarm clock ticking—in the kitchen?

Lil rolled flat on her belly. Now her arms were free. Up on one elbow, up on both elbows, move one ahead, push with her stockinged toes, no help there; lunge somehow from her hips, bring up the other elbow.

Again. Yaga didn't move.

Some more, again, over the doorsill.

Rest.

Clock ticking. Kitchen floor warm.

Now toward the table, this end.

Big green and white squares of linoleum up close.

Chair in the way, turned partly toward me.

Left hand, fingers, around the bottom rung. Pull, it comes to me, upandturndon'tfall!

Knees underneath me, big HEAVE hang on to the table edge!

Legs sideways pointing the way I came, but elbows on table, butt on chair!!

Lil looked up at Yaga, smiling kindly at this wreck of a human being. Lil bowed her messed-up head of hair on her hands, the first and next and next shuddering sobs wracking her already agonized body.

Slobbering on the table, choking her intake of air ...

Dimly aware Yaga had left the other end, a hand now on her forehead, lifting her out of the table mess, dropping a soft towel down, holding something—black coffee!!—under her nose, touching her lips; some spilled down her chin, she opened, sipped, sipped again.

The sobs gone. Yaga set the cup on the towel, pot on the stove, went back to her end.

"When you can pick up the cup and empty it, then we can talk."

One end of the towel, careful, don't spill the coffee, wipe your face.

Breathe, open your eyes, breathe, straighten up, your back, try to smile at wonderful Yaga. Breathe. Bring your hands to your lap. Swing your legs in—first!

With a bit of *guts*—must be the coffee!—Lil reached both hands out to clasp the cup in her hands. Smiled at Yaga, whose eyes now had a bit of shine.

A time of silence, people silence. The clock ticked loudly now, as ignorant, uncaring, as when Lil had been dragging her vacationing body across the linoleum. The noise in the saloon stopped.

Silence.

Yaga silent, not moving. The clock ticking away ...

Carefully, Lil bent over, just a little, toward the cup, lifted it slowly, could she do it without spilling any, not a drop?

Her lips, the cup rim, touched; Lil opened up, tilted the cup, some spilled down her chin, more tilt, SWALLOW it in three gulps,

SET THE CUP *DOWN* let go.

"Now   I   can talk."

Yaga put her arms akimbo, leaned a bit on the table.

"Why you come back up here from Chicago?"

"I didn't have any friends down there. I didn't make any friends down there. I didn't go anywhere to meet anybody! Jack wouldn't take me to meet his friends—his whole family is down there—he's workin' for a big company down there, somethin' with ore or metals but he said I was too rowdy, too loud, I talked dirty"—Lil's hands rose to cover her face.

Yaga waited.

A mumble: "All my friends are up here!"

"Who friends up here, our place last night?"

Lil stared at Yaga. "You, and Big Marko, and Dutchy—no, he's not my friend—I—"

"You what?"

"I swung at him the other night—last summer—and and Nick put me in jail for it!"

"You swung at somebody last night, yes?"

"He wanted me to pay him for the ride up here, and I told him I'd paid for all the drinks on the ride up here. So I slugged him—he had it comin'!"

"So you make him friend?"

"I don't want him for a friend! My friends up here are lumberjacks, they don't sponge drinks off me, want pay for the trip anyway. So I hit him, threw him outside!"

"So you do what friends—lumberjacks—do, you smack him."

Yaga considered, voiced her thought:

"We all know you work alongside lumberjacks, are good one, even you not man. Why act like man?"

Lil's whole body tensed. Her hands made fists, she pounded the table. The empty cup tipped over, the handle pointing back at Lil.

"When I was a girl and the other girls started bleedin', their butts got wider, their chests started t' stick out, they looked at me sideways 'cause I didn't look like them! I didn't bleed, they talked about how they were changin', getting' t' be women, interested in make-up and hair color and I had nothin' to say t' them I saw them lookin' at me and talkin' behind their hand to other girls! One girl told me they were all sorry for me I still looked like a boy and I was good at battin' and fieldin' and throwin' the ball and the boys would pick me first when choosin' up sides in softball and the girls smirked at me and the boys liked me so I did what they did and when I came up here to work for a livin' and I could do what lumberjacks did I didn't WANT to be a woman I hate girls feelin' sorry for me, I hate anybody bein' sorry for me or tryin' t' gyp me like that taxi driver…!"

"What 'deal' when you start from Chicago?"

Lil's bloodshot eyes snapped back to Yaga's.

"What 'deal'?"

"What driver get for giving ride up here?"

Lil's gaze dropped. Yaga pressed:

"Did you stop, fill gas tank? Add oil? Check tires?"

No answer.

"How many times you stop for drinks?"

"I didn't count…."

"The saloons, right along the highway or you go, look for them?"

"Driver use up all day driving up here? What time you leave Chicago?"

"You tell driver on way up, drinks his pay?"

"You think driver willing to drive, you ask him again?"

"Who pay gas, oil?"

"Your friends, you come here to be with, they see you slug driver when he ask for pay, will be your friends still?"

Lil's head tipped forward into her hands.

"I thought you were my friend, Yaga. Why are you….?"

"Last night you flop in booth, Cutler, he say, You skinny little bitch, you not even bitch, pretend you lumberjack, they should put you in Newberry with other crazies!"

"Look at cup, here on the table!"

Slowly, Lil's fingers parted.

"Now tell me, what cups for?"

"To… drink out of?"

"What must be, first?"

"This cup?"

"Any cup! What must be before, you drink out of cup?"

"It has to have somethin' in it first?"

Yaga's face softened; she reached across the table, took Lil's hands in hers, brought them down and toward her so that their four joined hands bracketed the cup lying on its side.

"This morning you in terrible shape. I right?"

Lil nodded once, her chin stayed on her collar bone.

"But you want, sit in that chair across from me bad enough, drag that body, body you live in, right?"—Lil dipped her bowed head—"across floor."

In the silence, the clock kept on going.

"I sure, I see you crawl, you make it or die along way. Lil, I know you have mind made up, you come to me. I make up mind, make that crawl worth something. Look at cup."

Lil obeyed.

"I take you on path, I hope you willing, walk with me, so no more mornings like now."

"Path maybe hard, like crawl. You willing?"

Tears slowly slid down Lil's unwashed face.

"Help me Yaga."

Yaga spoke softly, slowly. "You that cup between our hands, Lillian."

No sounds from the saloon; the clock ticked, ignored them.

"What is cup's name?" Yaga continued.

"Lil—Lillian."

"Is cup any good, can do what it meant for, tipped over?"

"No."

"Can you, me, tip cup back up, put cup how should be, do what is meant for, right now?"

"No."

"Why not?"

"Because we're holdin' each other's hands."

"We let go, I turn up, show I think you no can do by yourself, you want me sorry for you?"

"No."

"If I help you get to table, this morning, you think I sorry for you, you no get here by yourself?"

"Yes."

"So who must turn cup right side up?"

Head up, Lillian spoke: "*I do!*"

"How cup get tipped over?"

Lillian dipped her head just a bit. "I pounded the table with my fist."

"That part of be lumberjack? Is punch the taxi driver part of be a'jack?"

Lillian's head dipped a fraction lower.

"Is what you go through in the bathroom this morning, crawl to this table, is that what happen again you keep thinking you can be a lumberjack?"

No answer.

"Right now you no can get drunk, hit anybody, because I hold both your hands. Do lumberjacks have somebody hold their hands?"

No answer.

"You think you some different from other girls, bodies change to women's bodies, you not let stop you, you deny and be like man, real tough man, lumberjack. Look at cup, you are cup. Husband ashamed of you, no want be seen with you. You hold him back, not help. And you not help taxi driver. And you not help yourself think well of Lillian Eunice Ryan."

Yaga released Lil's hands, sat back in her chair.

"I ask you question, Lillian Eunice Ryan. If answer no, you free to, get up, go. I no hold you. You want me stay, with you, with this, turn cup over. Cup still be empty. I not know how much you can put in cup, I not talk now about coffee, but leave cup tipped over means you want keep on way you are now. Turn right side up, tells me you want be *ready for your right use, this world.* I will say what might help you do right, not be lumberjack."

Even Yaga could not hide her surprise, her pride in her charge at what happened:

Lillian Eunice Ryan painfully levered herself erect, up and out of her chair, took three forced, laborious steps to the stove, grasped the coffee pot in both hands, carefully lifted it to waist height, shuffled her feet around until she was facing the table and an awe-struck Yaga.

Then, the coffee pot held out in front, both hands, like a shield, Lillian Eunice Ryan inched her way to Yaga's left, tipped the spout over Yaga's cup to fill it nearly to the rim, pushed her feet sideways to put her even with her tipped-over cup

Yaga didn't move, said nothing.

Lillian Eunice Ryan set the pot on the hotpad, tipped her cup upright. Picked up the pot, poured her cup half-full, turned a bit more easily, moved to the stove, put the coffee pot in the identical spot it had been INHALED slid her feet back, turned without touching the table, sat.

"If we can come up with my intended use in the world, I will do my d—I will do my best to practice it, the most serious effort of my life."

"What other woman you know, imitate be a lumberjack?"

Lil bridled.

"I *am* a lumberjack, not an imitation, I do every part of the work they do!"

"You do *only work* they do, you like this any morning?"

No answer.

"If you not loud, talk dirty, drink too much, hit people, Jack Ryan take you with him in Chicago, you meet, make new friends?"

"Yes," very quiet.

"Is not true, that it seem to you not become woman like other girls, you not want their be sorry? Not less full woman?" "Yes."

"And what you decide to do, if not full woman?"

No answer.

"I take guess, you tell me if wrong: You decide, show them you not care, not woman they become by become what they no could become: Tough lumberjack!"

"Yes, and I did it, too!"

"Now think before answer. This no trick question, but you must be most honest to yourself and to me. Answer in way that let me help you. You have to come up with something to put in that cup that is worth keeping to drink. We must find your right use in this world. You say 'the most serious effort of your life', remember?"

"I did. I will."

"Besides 'them', those girls, who you going show you not care not be woman?"

Silence. Clock ticking. "What if I don't get the right answer the first time?"

"I ask again—so I give you hint: When you crawl over to me from bathroom today, was to prove to me you not care, not be woman like others do?"

No answer.

"Okay, I ask again: Jack Ryan marry you, he want loud, dirty-mouth, drunk for wife?"

Lil's eyes filled.

"No."

"Okay, this is last hint. What goes in that cup, what has to be inside you, so you not need me, anybody else, become what you want be, do, has to be true: Besides those girls, beside me, beside everybody else, who you try make believe you not care, not be woman, like other women?"

Mumble: "I was pretendin' I didn't care. To myself."

"You lie to yourself, is what you saying?"

"Yes."

"And you believe, do every last little thing lumberjack men did—not just work they do—everything be fine?"

Yaga leaned close:

"And is fine?"

"No."

"Do you know, know of, women married but not have any children, never give birth?"

A pause: "The Post Office woman, Cynara; the music teacher at school...."

"So. Some women can be happy, childless, what left for you to try, than do the things those women do, that way *be what you do*, a woman, if do what lumberjacks do not make you man?"

Lillian was silent, as if she were sorting out some words to fit.

"Not have three children, let's say you can't do that, what do I do, you can like a lot of other women—not all, maybe—but lots other women do, that makes women, most women, different from most men?

"This to—too important for me to guess at—tell me!"

"I do *for* people, not *to* people. This morning, feed my family; this afternoon, just as I do yesterday afternoon, I help my husband in his business by serving what drinks our customers want. He want me do that, so I do it for him, and our kids, and first and last, *for myself, what I do for others make me the person I want to be."*

"I see," Lillian agreed.

Yaga opened her mouth to speak.

Hastily, Lillian raised her hand, palm outward.

"I get it, it doesn't have to be a woman's own family; I can do *for* others, any others."

The clock 'b-r-r-r-ed', ticked on.

"Pick up cup, drink dry, now in you. Again, I not talk about coffee."

Yaga rose, her face a smile, eyes warm.

"Clock eleven. Help get bar sandwiches ready."

That same morning, the same gut rumble, but it was of hunger, wakened August Schmidt, who tumbled out of bed and down to breakfast, intent on getting on with his business of apple brandy, and feeding a hungry Zwei, too.

Again, Anna was his waitress. August looked around, didn't see Grace Hill, nor any other waitress in a crowded breakfast horde.

"Anna," he sympathized, as she tipped his cup, splashed the steaming coffee, "You look a little harried this morning. Has Grace disappeared?"

"Oh, she wants to be some kind of CPA or something; I paid her tuition for the semester. She's busy being a student, living in Marquette."

"Who is her place taking?"

Anna grimaced.

"You'd think I could call on a list, wouldn't you, the Depression, and all, but listen: Her replacement can't be a school girl, they're all in school in fall, winter, spring. I have a bar, so they have to be eighteen or above anyway. And every one of *those* are long gone to Detroit, or Chicago, or someplace for steady jobs, already." Anna raised her apron, wiped her face, smoothed down the apron.

"What'll you have?"

"Meat and potatoes, Anna. You decide!"

"Waitress!"

Anna tossed back, "If you hear of a girl, tell her to see me!"

When he turned back to face his table, Jim Ferguson was slipping into the opposite chair.

Over his proffered hand, Jim grinned,

"Just finished the woodshed delivery out back. Took me halfway across the room to recognize the man in the coat and tie was you, Dutchy! Tell me all about it!"

August filled in the long wait with increasing enthusiasm—the way things in Milwaukee showed fearless bounty—of flowers, of people moving, the soon-to-be reality of an electric trolley line, the Grand Avenue of mansions, the air of Prohibition and even Depression not the crippling state of mind as up here—finding ways to be proud and joyful as in Pabst's Museum and especially in the hum of worthwhile work in the two breweries—3.2 beer will do us until we get back to honest beer—winding up with the 'We want all you can send us' attitude about his own product:

"August's Applejack Brandy."

Jim's eyes, trying to catch busy Anna's, focused sharply on him.

"So." He made a point of noticing the gold tie pin, the gold cuff links.

Slowly: "The old name—new clothes—the polish—new name—new man."

August nodded:

"We, you and me and Aslak and what we've begun, what we're making work, we don't have to think of as the law breaking, that we crooks are,…we're on the track of something that will in size grow and in respect from the rest of the Township."

He hesitated, took it further.

"Asking customers their drinking to limit to one a day or time maybe as far-fetched as the knights of King Arthur for the Holy Grail questing, but I hope not!"

Anna stood smiling at the two. "More King Arthur! August said 'Meat and potatoes' Jim. You too?"

"Me too, Anna!"

While they waited—their own feeling of growing elation not speeding up the service one iota!—Jim ordered his thoughts, then:

"I've gone a little ways on that sort of line, idea, over at my place, too, D-August."

Anna came by with the coffee pot.

August, seeing the time on the clock now past nine, didn't let the resurgence of his elation of yesterday diminish by worrying about Zwei. Probably sleeping in daylight now, his custom after a night of vigilance and paying attention to the animals—and night birds—enjoying their freedom from observation—*their* custom.

The men of his class in Milwaukee didn't rush through a meal. May be it would be a good thing to start up here.

Of course, some would scoff.

"Still the same man inside!" they'd claim.

What would his answer be?

Jim was leaning over toward him, in a voice of confidentiality:

"I decided to freshen up"—he pointed at August's suit—"the look and the reception at the pick-up point in my cellar. Like your suit, your different name, show an attitude."

He waited, saw that August was interested, fresh from the brewery atmosphere in Milwaukee.

"But I'd like your opinion of what I've done, from what you saw in Milwaukee."

Anna, easily handling the tray, slid both plates of bacon and country-style fries expertly into place.

"Dig in, men, dinner time's still a few hours away!"

"Waitress!"—and she was gone.

So they dug in—no change in that hunger!

When they left, they were the last. Anna had moved round the room, collecting dishes, carrying out the trash, and was sitting at the desk up front, in the check-in/out area, her hair freshly combed, calmly considering a column of figures.

"A good breakfast, Anna!"

"We'll come back for more soon!"

Her composure restored, now the county-wide persona of vigorous, competent business woman, Anna nodded graciously

"Don't let my need for a waitress slip your minds. Like Grace, if she doesn't live close by, she can have a room, eat her meals, right here—part of the wages, which are on a percentage basis—the more customers, the more she makes. And I'll teach her the ropes, no problem. Of age, and willing, fairly presentable, is what we need and I want."

August replied, "I the word pass to Marko; he meets a lot more people than I do!"

August, head up, applewood stick finding the gravel of Cedar Street through the light glaze of frozen snow, walked north with Jim talking about the movie theater soon looming up on their right, just south of the junction of Cedar with Center Street.

A theater in Bergland! Not even Ewen, to the east, had one; Wakefield, twenty miles west, had been the closest.

They stopped even with its hangar-like immensity, certainly large enough to contain the viewers' dream during each showing—tonight was to be *The Adventures of Rin Tin Tin*—but, compared to even the largest home on North Pine Street, huge.

"Does it make money?" August wondered.

"I see people coming down past my house on Center Street, right behind us, every Saturday night." Jim answered. "I see many fewer people, and I'm told it's true, coming to

Reverend Zoet's Northlands Gospel Mission, on Sundays. Same building, different dream."

Both men, mulling this over, stood conjuring in their two minds the picture of the two Congregations: the one passive; Zoet's, by word of mouth a much more vibrant, active, bit of co-production—Zoet reputed to have no hesitation approaching loungers outside either of the two Pine Street saloons.

August found the words forming, gave them voice.

"I don't think they are that different, the dreams—though the Reverend's congregation more active is, takes part."

Jim found a bit of bacon his tongue had been working at, chewed, swallowed. "How are they the same?"

"The theater owner—Wallen's his name?—a dream of a life he sells, not this one here in Bergland, but some other place. So Zoet does."

Jim worked that over in thought as his tongue had wriggled the bacon till it finally came loose so he could work it over, send it on.

"Most folks say a bit of time spent on a dream can't hurt."

August hesitated. Was it his reading, discussions with fellow-students, teachers, in the Palatinate, that lay comatose in his brain, cued onstage at times like this, like the Samarian woman at the well thing, his recollection of 'ouisque beatha' for the WCTU women? 'Known first in German,' he glowed at its present resurgence in English—'I am starting to think in English' surfaced ahead of these words:

"'… a man travelling into a far country, who called his own servants, and delivered unto them his goods.

And unto one he gave five talents, to another two, and to another one; to every man according to his several ability;' Matthew 25. 14-15."

Jim moved his feet, crunching the still-frozen wheel tracks on Cedar Street.

August half-turned, spoke softly to his fellow-American, fellow believer in the policy of restraint in the use of alcohol as a beverage.

"It seems to me most folks say that have a dream–wishing it were true. Most ministers claim the Bible says our time on this earth is short, that we will spend Eternity in either Heaven or Hell, so spend this life earning Eternity in Heaven."

Jim nodded."That's Zoet!"

August heard himself formulating *his* belief: "That same Bible, in Matthew Chapter 25, says the best of the life we now have to make, since that parable says that if we bury whatever talent, gift, that we now have, out of fear of loss or lack of ambition—for whatever reason!—we 'unprofitable servant(s)cast into outer darkness' will be!!"

Wind it up and the knot tie, August thought.

"Jim, what I said about what we are doing is in keeping with the parable. Whether or not a man in the literal truth believes, word for word, of the Bible, surely that advice is good: Do what you can of what you believe is well for us all to do, not only for their good but for our own feeling of satisfaction in our own intended purpose in this world fulfilling."

During August's statement Jim's feet remained motionless.

"Come and see what you think of the pick-up point."

They moved as one up the softening snow-ruts of Center Street.

His words sound odd, at the end like that, Jim thought.

But they surely have more force there. His sentences don't die at the end!

CHAPTER FOUR

Jim's house on Center Street wasn't fancy. Two stories, it sat lengthwise to the street, the front door in the middle, no front porch, just three steps up to a landing; a chimney-block chimney, no brick veneer to dress it up, bisected the east end; a slanting lift-up door behind the house over the steps down into the cellar.

In the cellar, planked floor to all walls, the four shelves for the moonshine and applejack brandy—it was the pick-up room for the salesmen of the Luna Light Gang—lined the northwest quarter on one's right. When Jim bought the house from the town on a tax sale, the cellar was bare-walled; he'd added the shelves for the liquor when the first pickup-point, the crawl-space under Deputy Nick Anderson's house, showed wear and tear to the public eye at its entry/exit way. And it limited pick-up and stocking to Saturday nights when Nick was on duty at the Sandy Beach dance pavilion.

Also, it improved the privacy of the pick-up point: The platted but undeveloped lots behind Jim's house on east-west Center Street were on a steep, heavily-wooded slope. All of the ins-and-outs, ups-and-downs, happened only after dark, but could be on any night, so there was no heavy traffic all happening on Saturday evening to alert nosy parkers.

Inside the house, the front door opened to a kitchen with small table on the right, dining and living room on the left of the entrance, with a stairway-hall to two bedrooms upstairs, an attic under the roof rafters. A shower-stall-toilet-wash-basin room took up the northeast corner of the kitchen next to the cookstove. The sink backed up to the shower stall wall.

But August and Jim went around to the back, down the steps bare of snow—Jim, like all of the Mile Road residents, was a bachelor, who kept floors swept, steps clear, dishes put away, and so on. Normally quiet and quiet-spoken, this day Jim stepped aside in the narrow passageway down the steps after flinging open the cellar door (on well-oiled hinges!) to announce "Ta-Da!" as he flipped on the outside-the-door-switch inner lights.

With an expectant grin at the announcement, August's mouth fell open at what changes Jim had fashioned in the previously bare, business-like, load/unload-get-out atmosphere.

"Jim, I know people swear by you as the best mechanic up at Piper's Garage, but this is something I'd never guessed! What gave you the idea—and the cash this to do?"

For what he saw would have graced any Western saloon (except the soiled doves) to draw cowboys off a drive to have a drink and socialize.

"I noticed that when a couple of men came in for their gallons, they'd stand around and chat for awhile, about family, jobs, fishing, like that, so I got hold of a few old rocking chairs and easy chairs for them to sit in; one of them said he had an old oak table or two in his attic, so when he brought them in, I splurged for some green velvet for the tables, stuck in a few brass tacks to hold them smooth, a couple of decks of cards showed up, I tapped into the chimney against that wall over there, found a little potbelly, and that's what it took. And the gang is now more like a club, specially on Saturday nights."

Jim paused, enjoying the amazement on August's face. "O'course, one drink is all any of them take on what we call 'product night' on Saturdays when you, Herman, and Aslak stop by with that loaded Model A."

"Well, I have the last month or so missed," August admitted. "Is that your bar over there?"

Jim nodded. "I put that up there so I could have a writing top with a few shelves underneath to keep track of what was coming and going, who got what, who brought in what cash—sort of a business desk—so it was easy to stick a gallon, one moonshine, one brandy, there on Saturday nights. Mrs Bailey, you know her, member of the WCTU, then they changed it to WARS—Women's Alcoholic Restraint Society—ha! She brought in that shelf up behind it with those shot glasses in it, said they needed only one at home now!"

August put his right hand up to his chin, thumb on one side of his mouth, fingers on the other side, squeezed in just a tad.

"You mentioned what I saw in Milwaukee, maybe give you a hint or two for the pick-up area. Jim," he put his hand firmly, affectionately, on this Irishman's pudgy shoulder, a man of such qualities as made him a natural in-town leader of the Luna Light Gang, who, if they had not joined in this common endeavor, would never have met, much less formed a bond deeper than either would have imagined, "in Milwaukee I saw monuments to men who giants were in the brewery business. I was privileged to observe men and women working in active breweries whose air of competence, of quiet pride in doing their job well, made me feel that a group of men I had joined who were my kind, who a call had answered."

Jim felt a slight tremble in the hand on his shoulder, matched in August's voice:

"You've gone them one better, Jim. This is a place where of what they do they can feelproud , enjoy member camaraderie. I saw nothing this good in Milwaukee. This could like the fellowship of the knights at King Arthur's Round Table become, where the seating places showed all to be equal in honor and seniority, just like we in the Luna Light Gang are!"

Jim flushed with pleasure; his glance fell, then rose, sensing something awry in Augusts' manner. He saw a tightness in his friend's mien, his lips pressed hard together, as if holding something more back, hesitant.

He tugged August toward one of the easy chairs. "Let's have a brandy, relax."

Both seated, Jim tipped a tiny brandy into two small snifters, raised it: "Here's to us, August!"

The musical chime of the two glasses was like a bell in a boxing ring to August.

"Jim, to Milwaukee I went to Gunlek's old office, with a bill of lading I picked up in the depot office that showed me, when I checked the flat car, my office boss down there up to his old tricks of cheating the DSS& was , and worse, Gunlek himself, with what he tried to pin on me, forced me to come up here or maybe to jail."

He felt Jim's intent focus, met his wide-eyed stare.

Let it all out.

At the finish, he took a deep breath, straightened.

"Jim, I cannot here be in town my discovery to repeat, nail Skantz, myself redeem doing it. I need to figure out some way to know if Skantz again tries. Or, DSS&A alert. "

Jim, steady as always, grinned, tapped August's knee. "I've known Hans Lederhof most of my life. He's complained about the scale for years—not lately, though, I've been busy here for a couple of weeks. Of course, there's not many logs going anywhere these days. I'll get with him, make sure he keeps what I want to himself, and he'll tip me off when there's something fishy about the bill and the scale on the flat cars."

"What a relief!' August rose. "The same I feel as when I left Skantz down there—as if I'm up in the air!"

Jim stood, took the empties to the sink. "You're on firm ground, for sure. Hans will be glad to know he's been right; he'll be happy to cooperate!"

Slogging west on Center Street, August shivered at the sense of danger from afar he'd voiced to Jim. Coming to America to stay ahead of the omens of pogroms he feared, would he always be so apprehensive? Would his dream, not the dreams of the movie-goers nor those of Zoet's ministry, be viable here in Bergland? Surely America remains 'the land of the free'!

That mention of King Arthur's Round Table had flashed him for a moment back in the good Doctor Pudendorf's seminar at Heidelberg, from which he'd left at the pogroms threat.

And Jim's little haven, fostering community, fellowship, was the best way!

At the first step crossing Pine he remembered to swing left down to Marko's, ask him or Yaga to put out the word for a waitress at Anna's, live and eat in, of age, fairly presentable.

Although the noon mill whistle had been silent for over a year, the memory, the old habituated expectation of the hoarse vigorous blast from its throat woke every dozing creature, widened the eyes of all awake, as August stepped up to Marko's Saloon door.

No bell tripped by an opening door announced entry to Marko's Saloon. One (A) gave the door a sharp double-tap, (B) opened the door, (C) pulled it shut behind one, (D) advanced, at noon-time beer-and-sandwich offering, to the table or booth of one's choice.

August had no problem with (A), (B), and (C). After all, here was a successful business man, an entrepreneur able to make his way from Bergland to the largest city in the State of Wisconsin, contact his business associates there with great success, maneuver himself on and around the bustling Milwaukee streets, reside over a weekend at one of the leading hotels, dress in a suit and tie, white shirt with gold cuff links.

But today the last bit of routine for the beer-and-sandwich noontime offering at Marko's Saloon wasn't as simple as (A), (B), and (C).

No, indeed.

Oh, surrounding him was the crowd he'd expected, a swift backward glance assuring him of friendly faces, chomping on sandwiches, raising steins or bottles, brushing foam from mustaches, relaxing, talking—until they noticed his turning from closing the door.

Then it all stopped as, with grins growing, they all turned their heads to watch his reaction to the small woman standing not a yard in front of him.

August, at forty, had never worn, never needed, glasses. But he couldn't be sure he was actually seeing what his eyes told him.

The woman had hair just long enough for a helmet of small, tight curls making her tall enough to reach August's shoulder height. Not tall, not quite six feet, August was solid; this woman was—well, slender? Sort of ...wiry...

The face, though tired, he knew. It showed a slight, tentative smile. However, the last time he'd seen it she'd been calling to Marko to 'double 'em up!'

And the curled hair wasn't the only odd thing about her. On her feet were shoes, not lumberjack boots; from her ankles to her knees was some sort of light brown thin covering.

But what kept his mouth open, silent—gaping, even!—was that in between the knees and the face was a

D
R
E
S
S

of some winter-weight fuzzy wool colored grey just like his worsted suit with thin white vertical stripes just like his suit

And the roar of laughter that greeted his obvious consternation confirmed what his eyes told his amazed brain.

This had to be what once was Gallopin' Lil who, tray heaped with plates of sandwiches, moved to his left to the row of booths where patrons helped themselves as she moved decorously, smiling moderately now, along the row away from August. Then, empty tray dangling from one hand, at the kitchen door she curtsied to the wave of applause.

August shambled to the booth where Aslak sat facing Haywire Johnson, propped the applewood stick against the table edge.

With his hallmark chuckle, Haywire welcomed a somewhat dazed August.

"Here's a spare stein, grab a sandwich on us!" chortled Haywire. He tipped the pitcher, poured down the inside to minimize the foam, held the beer out to August.

"Welcome back," from Aslak. "How'd it go in Milwaukee?"

August downed half of the stein's contents, downed the stein on the table, stared at the open kitchen door, empty now of any person.

Aslak gave August, sitting next to him, one of his 'taps'. August's applewood walking stick slid off the edge of the table, crashed full length on the wood floor; August tilted out after it as if to pick it up, tilted back in.

"What?"

"How'd things go in Milwaukee?" Aslak grinned at Haywire, across the table, winked, turned back to August, who was looking vacantly at his interrogator.

"How come you and Haywire aren't out on Section Thirty? Who's tending…."

Haywire chuckled, "We brought in the last of the corn we planted there, nearly fifteen bushels, this morning, so this is our treat today!" August looked from Aslak to Haywire, at the kitchen door, back at Aslak.

"That *was* Gallopin' Lil I just saw, wasn't it?"

"You are more right than you know," Aslak asserted, "That WAS Gallopin' Lil, but just before you came in Yaga presented her as Lillian—Lillian Eunice—so, different outside, I guess different inside. Yaga didn't say, but who she WAS would tell us to get our own sandwiches, don't you think?"

August nodded slowly. "And with a few colorful words in for free thrown." August ran his left hand along the table edge; looking at Aslak, he queried:

"What was it you asked me?"

"What about your trip—see anybody you knew down in Milwaukee?"

August ran his left hand back along the table edge, looked down, bent, brought the stick back up, laid it across his lap, ferrule tip well outside the booth.

"I some things straightened out down there, my old boss, anyway." He brightened up.

"I got both Pabst and Miller brandy orders up to all I can send them! And some ideas I got about a new house, and how nice it would be in Milwaukee to live, too!"

Haywire leaned over to rub the suit material between thumb and forefinger.

"Where'd you get those fancy duds?"

August smiled, back in touch. "At Napoleon's, nice place on North 76th Street. They one off the rack pulled, a seam here and there let out, like a glove fits! makes me feel like the Mile Road I never saw!"

He took a first bite of the roast pork on brown bread, just a touch of mustard.

Aslak nodded. "We might take a hint from that, ourselves, quit coming to town in work clothes if we're not working while we're here. Look what a bit of dress-up does for Lillian!"

He turned to August, "And you too! By the way, did you notice how you and Lillian are both in gray with white stripes, wool?"

As if he'd said an 'abra ca dabra' out through the kitchen door, sideways with a second tray piled high came Lillian: shoes, stockings, curled hair, the dress. Down August's, Haywire's, and Aslak's side first, the steam from her tray rising in the barely heated saloon.

While she was in profile at the booth ahead of theirs August, sitting on the outside next to Aslak, swallowed, lifted his stein for a sip, found the table top with it while he focused on the face.

The curls and collar on the fringes of his vision made what had been a blank face when her hair and clothes were a lumberjack's rough cut above and denim below it—plain, nondescript, gender-less—now seem womanly. Little if any color showing in the semi-lit smoke-laden air of a saloon; three squint-creases suggested behind the light brown short eyelashes.

Straight nose, compressed lips, chin even with nose tip, firm neckline under chin to dress collar.

She turned to move to his booth.

To his yellowish-brown eyes her faded blue eyes, over dark half-moons, locked.

The clink of steins touched, the dozens of medium-to-loud exchanges of words heretofore clamoring in the thick air, the feel of dozens of fellow-patrons surrounding him, rushed from his awareness.

In what seemed infinitely slow milliseconds Lillian's eyes neared his. The rest of the face he'd stared at in profile, now face on, blurred.

Her nearly colorless, faintly, faintly blue eyes widened, rounded ...

August pushed both hands against the table edge to stay there, not disappear into Lillian's direct gaze.

The applewood stick rolled off his lap, clattered on his and Aslak's toes.

Haywire rapped his fist on August's white knuckles.

"She wants to know if you want more sandwiches!"

In Lillian's slightly upward curved upper lip there were no vertical lines.

Aslak spoke up. "I guess we've had enough, Lillian!"

He handed the applewood walking stick to August, with his usual half-grin. "That's for when you try to get up and walk out of here!"

Haywire slid August's stein to the edge, close to the red tie, with gold tie pin. "Drink up, we'll give you a ride out to your house."

"Where did you stay last night?" from Haywire brought August back into reality. He turned back at half-way to the door, applewood stick in both hands.

"Leave word with Marko," he mumbled.

Yaga lifted the bar flap, met him halfway.

"Everybody talking about suit! What you forget?"

August mumbled; Yaga, the clatter of lunch-time noise too much for her, put her hand behind her ear in that universal signal.

Louder, August spoke his promise to Anna:

"Anna says Grace at school is in Marquette, she a waitress needs at the Hotel, eighteen or over, willing to work, fairly presentable, live-and-eat in if needed, right away!"

Yaga's face lit up. "I hear you!"

August wheeled, strode toward the door. Lillian was at the other side, back to him.

He hadn't forgotten he loved riding in a car. Free at least of his promise to Anna, but fighting a different desire to stay, he burst out the door to jump into the back seat of the famous black Model A sedan, Aslak and Haywire enjoying the purring vibration of the marvelous little four-cylinder engine.

Back to his applejack brandy business and Zwei.

Wonder if Aslak has blown up my house? Hope not; that stove is still perfect!

After all that pavement and cement in Milwaukee, good to hear gravel under the wheels again!

And even better when Ein, returning, greets awaiting Zwei!

While his 'hund' chews, gulps and gnaws, August inventories, still standing in the middle of the kitchen/dining/sitting/bedroom, the hovel in which he still lived.

What would Captain Pabst say, seeing this scrap heap? (Except for the kerosene stove!)

But too late this year, freeze and snow and Christmas coming any day. Fire up the little stove in the apple jack 'factory' and….

Tomorrow.

Have a seat.

Next morning, November 29th, 1932, August carried the heavy black spider two steps from the gleaming kerosene stove to his half-table, slid out the slices of cooked, then sliced and fried spuds atop the bacon, no shortage of grease to flip over the two eggs atop the pile, on his heavy white plate, hiding the filigrees of brown cracks in the plate, steaming a victory over the winter chill in his cramped one-room kitchen, sitting room turning to bedroom each night he stretched out on his couch, dragged the Hudson's Bay blanket over him.

Today was work! Comforting routine, after comforting sleep in his own house, after his comforting meal! Zwei, his own breakfast of potato slices in grease gulped down, whined at the door, went out for his morning constitutional, check the bulletin boards at his height above the ground.

That was his work.

Once the apple corer/peeler/slicer began its work on the new batch of apples lifted from their fragrant winter bed on the straw-bottomed hole in the corner of his 'factory', August, from long habit a thinker in this nearly automatic task of preparing apples for his trademark August's Applejack Brandy, dwelt on his present situation, past discoveries/actions, what he might expect in the near future.

Lil. No, Lillian.

No, there is wasted time. No trash; she soon back will slide! The evening star, Hesperus, Venus, 'amo' et cetera!—I go over the edge of the ocean into nothing with Odysseus!

He stopped, filled the tray from which the unpeeled apples fed, started the handle turning.

It was the small references to the bad times in Germany, the Round Table, the Polishpogroms, that would not go away. Still as clear in his mind was Nathan Strauss' reply to Polish official representatives, M. Gorski, in the Polish Information Bureau, and M.Smulski, the President of the National Polish Department of America, who had earlier denied reports of pogroms against Jews in Poland in the New York Times of May 27, 1919:

"The only wish of the Polish Jews is that Polish Jewry be allowed to live side by side with their Polish countrymen, to share the burdens, the responsibilities, but also the rights of citizens of a democratic, free and humane commonwealth. If, however, bands of robbers and murderers are let loose on them, if the Polish authorities countenance outrages and the Polish military forces commit them openly, it is the right and bounden duty of the Jews here and abroad to call the attention of the world to such unspeakable horrors ..."

Appended to Nathan Strauss' letter were AP bulletins beginning with June 6th, 1918 'agitation against Jews increased'

Nov. 14, 1918 '6 Jews killed in Sielice'

Nov 28, 1918 'pogrom in Lemberg by Polish army; authorities refuse to interfere'

Dec 3   1918 'massacre of Jews spreading in Galicia'
Dec 6   1918 '950 victims of Galicia pogroms buried so far'

His hands still, the sweet perfume from the apple pit, and from his own work making the pomace for eventual brandy thick in the constrained air of the warehouse, August had heard that Germans had participated.

How long would it take for Germans, using the excuse of the mark so nearly worthless that stories of a wheelbarrow full of marks would buy a loaf of bread, that age-old rumor of Jews sacrificing a Gentile boy as part of a ritual, to bring pogroms into Germany itself? First the Jews, then other non-Aryans, then the rich and propertied, the academics protesting such violence...

All herded into the trains head for internment.

August cast his eyes around his source of wealth. Saw in his mind's eye the hidden caches of fifty-dollar bills here and in the still shack on Section Thirty, there hidden at the bottom of the corn barrels for the moonshine mash.

All built as a means of building himself a niche in this America, solidifying his stature in his own mind, demanding work, needing skill, attention, perseverance.

Make him a target for the likes of the fanatics in Poland, in Germany, desperados?

Keep at his work. Winter was a time for applejack making.

Night and day, storm and sunshine, the primeval forest bordering Bergland Township ran its miles of pine and hemlock timber north up to and over the Porcupine Mountains to stand silent sentinel over the southern shore of Lake Superior, while the white-crested waves ran up the sandy shore, ran back, leaving the off-white foam of each on that sandy strand.

Chapter Five

In the middle of December, 1932, they stood on the first slight rise of the Mile Road, their skis pointed north, gazing over Aslak's Lake. At the northern limit of their gaze the tiptop of the Bergland Fire Tower marked their horizon. That entire northern expanse was one solid white blanket, a myriad of tiny glittering points of snow keeping their eyes just a tad covered under the lids.

The beaver house near the northwestern corner of the five-acre, spring-fed deep lake, now frozen over, just as white as all of the surrounding open field between the lake and these two, could be taken for an Eskimo igloo, minus any entry way.

No one else was visible.

"We could be all alone in a wide world of white," Cynara murmured pensively. "It reminds me of when we were sitting at Anna's—I squeezed your hand thinking none of the others sitting there with us would notice, but I think Hattie Walker did notice. I still feel a little like keeping how I feel about you to myself, not letting anyone else in on it."

"I wouldn't mind the whole world knowing how I love you," Aslak responded. "Nothing else I've done, or earned, or ….whatever, is as big as wanting to share the rest of my life with you."

Cynara side-stepped over to nudge against him.

"What we are doing together right now is so simple, so casual, but I feel it is so meaning-full, too—this snow covering makes everywhere we can see, all around us, a new world, and we are travelling in that new world, not just here over the new snow. We are—I don't suppose you've read Milton's *Paradise Lost*?–but when they leave the Garden of Eden, the poet describes how vast and new their world is, for them to make their way, the first two people."

Aslak shook his head. "I've heard of the poem—but I think that in the Bible they didn't simply leave Eden—they were dismissed by God for disobeying his one command: Don't eat the forbidden fruit. I'm not an intellectual, but most people think that having seen their nakedness, and, from eating the fruit of the Tree of Knowledge at the serpent's urging, now know the sin of carnal coupling, they were justly driven from the Garden of Eden by the flaming sword of the Archangel Michael!"

Cynara shivered, not from winter's cold alone. She gave Aslak's arm a tug.

"C'mon, let's drop in on August. If he knew about the Gaelic 'ouisge beatha' maybe he can talk to us about the Garden of Eden—or at least talk with us about it."

She raised her face close to Aslak's.

"I don't know if you know how important, for most of my life how *all-important the* Bible and all that's developed from it was, and is still somewhat, I believe. Would you like to—want to—or just would agree to talk over the Eden thing with Dutchy, in a warmer, more relaxed setting?"

Aslak flipped his off ski around, joined it with his inside ski and miraculously, she thought, the rest of him followed to place him pointed back up the slope.

"I'd be happy to, my lovely lady. That's your well-known world, new to me, but as you guessed when we looked at the stamps in your Post Office the other day, it's a new world I'd enjoy exploring."

He grinned that half-grin she knew. "Now if you can edge your skis around without falling down or knocking me over in this first new world you just declared, we'll get ourselves in where Dutchy just might have some apple cider heated to warm us to your subject!"

Cynara giggled: "We can mull it over with some mulled cider!"

Turning took a few minutes, but they made it to Dutchy's gate. Zwei heard them approach, and they heard his warning to his master, who opened his door to shush his hund and shoo in the two skiers.

"I just opened a gallon of apple cider—it's not alcoholic yet—would you like some?"

"Cynara just mentioned mulled cider—can you show us how to do that?

"With pleasure," August (he was wearing his 'factory' clothes—overalls and rubber boots) showed those really outsize teeth. "I've even got some hot water on the stove. We can stick a huge mixing spoon in there, stir the cider with it, and be drinking mulled cider!"

He motioned the two skiers, their skis and poles leaning against the rusty yellow-brown outside of his shack, toward the couch taking up all of the west inside wall.

"Warm up a bit while I dip this huge mixing spoon into the cider!"

While August busied himself with mugs and cider, Cynara nudged Aslak, pointed at Zwei staring at them from where he crouched protectively behind his master's knees.

Sotto voce: "I'd hate to have him think we meant August harm!"

Aslak nodded, the half-grin present.

"So what did you like about the skiing, out there?" August asked, carrying over a tray with three mugs of steaming cider.

"I felt as if we were Adam and Eve in an Upper Peninsula version of the Garden of Eden," Cynara responded. "We were gazing at a whole newly covered vista of white, the lake in the foreground, the cutover behind us, the timber in front, and not a soul like us to be seen!"

August smiled, those exceptionally huge teeth visible. "In gymnasium—your highschool, I think, yes?—we studied English using the Bible, beginning with Genesis, of course."

Cynara's eyes widened. "So you didn't stop learning with the concept of 'water of life' and the Gaelic-Scot 'ouisque Beatha' Aslak told us about!"

"Here's to present company," Aslak proposed, and all clinked the heavy white porcelained mugs and drank.

"That's a good warming," Cynara decided. "And I did feel a chill looking out north over the lake. I felt a bit fearful of calling it our Eden—it didn't last long for Adam and Eve. I hope what Aslak—Pikey" she poked Aslak playfully—"and I are enjoying doesn't rush away as the wonderful beginning of Adam and Eve did—flaming sword at the gate and all."

Aslak looked for a place to set his mug on; let it rest on his thigh. "I wouldn't let it discolor my delight; that was long ago and far away."

He turned more to Cynara. "I learned a bit of Latin to match your translating Mediterranean the other day: Carpe diem!"

August leaned back, ran his forefinger around the rim of his empty mug. Looking up at Cynara kindly, he ventured:

"We also discussed whatever else came up while we were translating…" he shifted his glance to Aslak-"because there was another reason for dismissing Adam and Eve from the garden."

August reached behind him to a shelf of battered books, pulled out a Bible.

"See, it's in English!" he smiled wryly, "It's become the language I catch myself thinking in nowadays. In fact, lately I've even been speaking in English—without the verb at the end of my sentences!"

"We've noticed the other, the former sequence!" Cynara laughed.

"I don't remember chapter and verse that well, so I want to check for the other reason—yes here it is, Chapter Three, verse 22:

'And the Lord God said, Behold, the man is become as one of us, to know good and evil; and now, *lest he put forth his hand, and take also of the tree of life, and eat, and live forever:*

23. Therefore the Lord God sent him forth from the garden of Eden …'"

August closed the Bible on his forefinger. "See, there was the first reason—Eve, and then Adam, broke the first taboo, eating the fruit from the Tree of Knowledge, which made the two of them just what the Devil had promised—like God and the heavenly beings—and the second reason was to keep them from living forever."

Cynara was about to speak, when Aslak blurted, "So since we're already out of that Garden we don't need to fear a repeat, for us, for here!"

August nodded. "Your Latin—'seize the day'—was apt. All of us, never having eaten of the Tree of Life, will one day die. Another poet than Milton put it this way:

'The grave's a fine and private place,
But none, I think, do there embrace.'"
–Andrew Marvell

"I was about to say, a minute ago, when Aslak reminded us we're not in the garden, that I wished that we had some sort of law-giver in this garden—all that newly covered vista we stood looking at—to tell us what not to do—then I realized that the Lord gave us not a prohibition, but a positive law; 'Be fruitful, and multiply'"—a quick glance at Aslak—"and not too long ago talking with Hattie Walker and Anna Stindt I said I had no children, and I felt guilty about that."

Aslak winked at August. "I repeat, *Carpe diem!*"

August spoke quietly. "Cynara, most people in Bergland Township are well aware that you and Pikey are 'keeping company', as the saying goes. Everybody is in favor of you two getting married. If neither of you is past the age, then you have another chance to obey the command you just quoted."

Aslak returned the poke given him by Cynara.

"August, we've already decided to marry as soon as we can convince Reverend Seeliger to work with us on the ceremony details!"

August rose, seized the mixing spoon, swirled it around in the still warm water, mulled some more apple cider, returned with the three filled mugs.

"I propose a toast to the issue of this marriage's consummation!"

Several more toasts followed, and when Aslak and Cynara went out the door darkness ruled.

So, too dark to venture on skis up and then down to the empty house-being-revamped, they walked up and down and into that house.

Imagine what you will.

For August, a few moments, meerschaum re-lit, seeing in his mind's eye the two nearly-weds leaving their present-day Eden (or at least that part of Eden Cynara had described); the mind's eye picture calling up the Biblical departure.

What he hadn't told Aslak and Cynara was that that reading he'd just reminded them of, why God had dismissed Adam and Eve from the garden, called to mind the so-called Hegelian triad of Thesis-Antithesis-Synthesis really so stated earlier by Fichte and was suggested to him by that very reading of the dismissal:

Thesis: God created Adam, that famous painting of the finger from the heavens giving life to the supine human form in the garden.

Antithesis: God denying, modifying that life to eventual death, so that mankind would not be as the gods, who lived forever.

But the command to 'Be fruitful, and multiply', so important to Cynara, how is that the third part of Fichte's triad: Synthesis—finding a commonality in the two previous statements?

Which created a newly-whetted thirst: first, for a refill of mulled cider; then, for a close scrutiny of Genesis dealing with the garden of Eden.

Why not?!

Man does not live by applejack brandy alone!

He lit the kerosene lamp, adjusted the wick for most but smokeless light, sat at the kitchen table for a slow reading, thoughtful, for the first three chapters of Genesis.

Ending that first perusal, he pushed the Bible away, summed up his gleanings. Two general characteristics: One, Genesis reflected the supposed 1400 B.C. composition date-culture; two, there were obvious ambiguities if not contradictions.

The advice of Adam to husbands, to 'leave mother and father'. Surely, since the Eden pair had neither, understood only in terms of the then culture—1400 B.C. More, to explain the reality of each generation, in 1400 B.C., dying, the punishment of death for disobeying the commandment not to eat of the fruit borne by the Tree of Knowledge of Good and Evil, implies that Adam and Eve were intended to live indefinitely, yet the second reason for dismissal from the garden was 'lest he put forth his hand, and eat of the fruit from the Tree of Life, and live forever'!

How can the Almighty, never mistaken, be reconciled with petulance?

Most of the reflections of 1400 B.C. culture occur in the creation of God in the image of a then king—jealous lest subjects try to escape into a higher caste. In Ch. 3-22, 'man is become as one of us…' i.e., 'royalty' for learning the difference between 'Good' and 'Evil'. Nor was Man to disobey God—without question—as a king likely also ordered.

Other ambiguities or contradictions are frequent. At the end of the creation of the Earth, God saw 'it was good'. Then, no reason given, 'Let us make man'. Why, was his first effort not 'good'? Again, if after being dismissed from the garden, Adam and Eve were to 'replenish the earth, and subdue it' the implication was that it really wasn't 'good', *or it reflected the culture of 1400 B. C.* when that was true of the then earth.

He remembered the Collection of Folk Art in the Milwaukee Museum of Art, how its simple rough-hewn creations reflected how those creators saw themselves.

As far removed from Biblical times as were the Middle Ages, it was still the idea of 'saving the appearances' that men followed in explaining what the earth was and did. For example, the sun appeared to move up and over from the east, disappear down in the west. So, it was a 'fact': The sun moved! And even then, though it was admittedly archaic, it was common to think of the sun as a 'person': Apollo drove his golden chariot across the heavens daily!

How ironic that in Ch. 1, after Adam and Eve were 'created', God 'blessed them'—in a garden where a Tree of Knowledge and a Tree of Life grew to tempt them to disobey! What were, specifically, the 'blessings'? No mention.

August had forgotten, in his intensity, to keep his Meerschaum going.

What could he say to himself was his conclusion, how wrap it all up? The thin cloud of tobacco smoke suggested an answer. Just as smoking his meerschaum alleviated whatever need, whatever anxiety might at a given time be troubling him, so the people of that time, in that place, given their culture, created a Being in *their own image* to explain the trials of their time and place, a system that they could say no one could change, so accept what was inescapable.

For each of those people, it must have met the need. "And in that way, I find nothing wrong with it," August told the kerosene lamp. "Only when it becomes a structured institution, with ranks of officials controlling it, that it becomes restrictive, authoritarian, punishing, demanding, hierarchical, do I deny it."

Zwei whined at his knee, sensing perturbation.

"We get along, mein hund, the two of us, don't we," he answered, stroking Zwei's furry neck.

A vague sense of disquiet remained with him about perhaps a too-quick resolution: A sense of some question remaining unaddressed.

Other cultures, other gods, yet the same anomalies?

What was it? Something about fruit forbidden? Apples Brandy Wealth?

Outside the wind had stopped. August blew out the lamp. And so to bed.

Aslak and Cynara on snowshoes, August on skis, they proceeded in early afternoon on the 24th of December, 1932, down the Mile Road extension where, once past Jonas Amundsen's acres of apple trees, they moved over hip deep snow toward Pendock Road.

August glided over the snow packed first by Aslak, then by Cynara following. He fell behind periodically as they trudged straight up the far side of various gullies and dips, while he side-stepped those steep rises. He caught up easily once up those obstacles to a skier.

Once on the former railroad grade now called Pendock Road, and reaching south all the way to M28, August glided along, rusty from the long absence from his youthful days on skis near Heidelberg.

For Aslak and Cynara, the going on the grade, though a full two miles, was easy once the rhythm took over and the feet didn't need constant admonition to 'swing wider'. Aslak's stride stayed the same; Cynara found it nice to stretch out hers as long as was comfortable.

August glided effortlessly in their checkered packed way.

They came to a junction: Straight ahead it continued south; to their right it swung due west. Aslak held up his hand in the cavalry gesture: Whoa.

"I hope he's home today?"

"No question," Aslak pointed ahead, then west. "No fresh tracks on the snow; see that chimney smoke out there? Here's where we turn west."

A hundred or so strides on, Cynara, leading now the way and path were clear, halted.

"I smell a roast, but it's neither beef nor pork."

She raised her right wrist, pulled back the cuff.

"It's almost eleven!"

"Sherm never leaves things to the last minute. He makes a fine venison roast—onions, a bit of garlic, some of his own potatoes in the oven with the roast—we'll have a fine meal as he promised a week or so ago."

On a slight breeze in their faces the aroma quickened their pace.

They topped a small rise to see an older man leaning against a porch post of his two-story wood frame house, waving an arm.

Aslak waved vigorously in return as a second man, his face turned toward them briefly, remained turned away as he strode vigorously south toward Meriweather.

"Who—wasn't that Frank Cutler?" Cynara asked.

"Oh, ja," Aslak replied, his genial half-grin vanished. "He's not one to celebrate, even Christmas."

Then the half-grin came back.

"Today is Sunday, we're here for Sherm Pendock's Christmas Eve dinner! And we are the first! of a house full!"

Sherman Pendock, stood straight, beckoning them to enter.

"It's not fancy, but it suits me all the other days and nights of the year, so I hope it is okay for this one half-day of the allotted twelve for the season."

Inside they were in the presence of the source of the aroma they'd sensed out on the snow.

Cynara bosom swelled.

"This aroma is nourishing in itself! I can identify the onions, the garlic, but the base—this is a first for me. If that's venison, then I'm all for deer season in Ontonagon County!"

At one point in the early afternoon, just before the fixin's and the roast were ready, the lower two rooms were so tightly packed that Aslak raised his glass to suggest:

"When I say the word, everybody protect your glass and turn to face another person; Ready, turn!" and not a drop was spilled (so all claimed on the break-up!).

The many exchanges going on were not the result of alcohol only. In fact, all there knew of the restraint policy: Leave the second drink in the jug, and all (except Aslak) had that first and last drink on arrival. The jug was corked and stuck away out on the porch.

Exhilaration ruled not from alcohol. Each and every one there was a vessel of new hope, of rejuvenation from an inward sense that, while times still might be said to be hard, a new sort of life was in the offing.

All each one had to do was to keep going in the direction they were now moving: Self-respect based on accomplishment *in spite of hard times.*

Though each showed outward evidence of that inward sense.

All had come on foot—some, as had Cynara and Aslak, on snowshoes; the rest, riding shanks' mares or on skis from M28 at Merriweather, a mile distant over unplowed grade now called Pendock Road, those on snowshoes packing down a trace for the rest. None wore shabby clothes. The lately popular snow suits were without rents, discolorations, scuffed knees; some had gaily-colored woven scarves off-shoulder now inside a soon-overheated small house; all were well-enough-off for dollars to have new-looking boots of all kinds: Rubber bottoms, leather bottoms alike glistened.

But the chief outward evidence was in the expressions. All heads were up, backs erect, smiles on every mouth, all eyes shining.

Who was once Gallopin'Lil, now Lillian Eunice Ryan, haggardly-thin face newly contoured to glowing health, spoke in moderate tones barely audible over the Babel of voices to August Schmidt,

"The pay depends on how many people come in to be served by me, the waitress at the Hotel, just like the board feet of the logs I used to cut, but I can dress as a woman, use a bit of makeup, and the pay is better every week, I feel good about myself—I haven't had one drop until just now this"—holding up her tiny shot glass—"and my hands—look, I have ..fingernails!"

To which August returned,

"My brandy"—holding up his snifter—"buys me what I need and as soon as the snow is gone a new house will start by my orchard."

August leaned a bit down and closer to hear Sherman Pendock, the oldest and host, invoke his sense of the forest spirit.

"I used to stand here on my porch, staring at the timber, sad that so much of the land once covered with virgin timber was now covered by second growth, brush and poplar,the trees cut down, sawed into boards to house Bergland and wherever."

He paused, the old man catching his breath, while August thought, 'Timber, thesis; cut down, antithesis.'

"Then, while I didn't have the tall pines, to somehow whisper to me their history since the last glacier, sense their spirit, when I walked out into what's replaced it, saw and heard the deer, rabbits, once in a while a coyote or a bear."

Sherman looked into August's eyes.

"Am I a fool saying a fool's crazy thoughts?"

August smiled, reached out to grasp the old man's thin arm.

"If you are, you have hundreds of years of history up to now saying what you are actually telling me. Centuries ago a Greek named Heraclitus claimed the only reality was motion, that all is in process of alteration. Its names changed. A German named Johann Fichte called the first state Thesis, its opposite, Antithesis, the conflict arising out of those two, combining like aspects of each, Synthesis. The trees as timber, their absence its opposite, the second growth the third stage."

Sherman Pendock stared for a moment.

"So I am not first to think of change. But I like it better in my own words. The spirit of the trees still speaks to me when I walk out there."

He swung a feeble arm toward the north.

"Some of those pines now hold up sails, the spirit traveling everywhere across the seas, to my own old Wales, surely. Now the same spirit with the wild game I sense, the same spirit though different to look at. Even when sawed, nailed in buildings, people live inside, factories, that spirit is strong, my trees are not destroyed, they still live!"

Though his eyes were watery, Sherman drew himself up a bit.

"You see me, old, what happens to my spirit I do not know. But I know the spirit of the timber goes on and on even when it rots and new life grows from that rot!"

The 'old man loquacity' not just tolerated nattering but a respectable cure for the Depression depression.

Anna Stindt, imposing in stature as always, listened, interrupting here and there, as Jim Ferguson spoke of the future of his collection-point home on Center Street. It might well be a government-licensed package liquor store, moonshine only one of its alcoholic beverages once Prohibition was finally over with.

"Whether or not I keep the by-the-drink aspect, or stop competing with you and Marko and Lackie—"Good idea," inserted she—or just keep it a package store, with a chat place for a few who want to sit for awhile, not rush off—"Another good idea," inserted Anna, above most in height but easily above the hubbub—"I can foster a relaxed atmosphere I feel is needed. Slow things down a bit," concluded deliberate, solid Jim Ferguson, a single shake of his head in passing to August:

"Hans says no bills of lading from Skantz, no logs."

Hattie Walker, past counselor to Cynara, patted Aslak's intended in congratulation: "I can see you are once more the happy, bright woman we all admired. You are the envy of all the former WCTU women—who wish you well always!"

"In which well-being you shared a part with Anna when I needed some wise counseling," Cynara confessed. "The closed mind is now open!"

When the roast came steaming brown out of the oven to dress one end of the side table, surrounded by the heap of baked potatoes, the canned tomatoes and canned peas, the two kinds of pie—apple and mince meat—a line formed arming itself in turn with warm plates, 'silver' ware, self-serving each went by, loading up to quell the hunger and fortify each for the approaching trudge back home before the short winter day receded into the dark.

All found a place to sit, perhaps a surface other than their laps to rest the plate. Grace Hill could fill in Lillian Eunice about *her* waitress experience in Anna's Hotel; August could describe what he intended his new home to look like to Cynara, who listed some of the improvements now to be found in hers and Aslak's domicile on the other side of the hill. Earl Brismaster of The Trading Post exchanged with Bill Piper of Piper's Garage hopes for better business once Prohibition ended; Jim Demaray, coyote trapper, agreed with Game Warden Limpert, Hattie Walker's son-in-law, that cutover land was much, much more what wild life preferred; all of the members of the Luna Light Gang exchanged opinions with all of the WARS members about the restraint policy of both organizations, and how once the 'doom of the Eighteeenth Amendment promised by FDR' took effect, both might receive praise in the *Ironwood Daily Globe* for trend-setting in spite of the mistaken Prohibition.

Only when the subject shifted throughout the rooms to tomorrow's observance of the Christmas Day did the sun's nearing the horizon break up the group to don outside gear—clothing, snowshoes, boots for those in stocking feet.

To a chorus of 'Thanks' Sherman held open his door, as he had for their arrivals; sank into his chair by the stove when all had gone.

Silence was once more his.

Why had Frank Cutler left? He'd seen who was coming?

The stillness inside the lately-pulsing walls of Pendock's house mocked the churning thoughts inside that old formerly-active moonshiner's brain.

Lying under his winter bed covers, eyes open to the second-story bedroom ceiling lit by the moon in its sly way leaping off the snow outside, he sensed the utter silence, the empty rooms, no dog, no cat, locked in bitter battle with the joy, the health, the hope, the past accomplishments of his feast partakers that day.

For all the years since 1920 when Michigan had enacted its own Prohibition, when he'd made his present life fortune disobeying that law, selling moonshine made near the lake to alocal clientele, then by huge loads on trains, mostly, to other communities, doing it all—the making, the nearby transporting by horse and wagon, the keeping of records—he'd had no time to ponder 'life's questions'—just keep the wheels rolling, store up cash for the future.

But in the years since, his bank account assuring him of his future material well-being, he'd given it all up, he'd had time to wonder.

In preparing against the needs of the rest of his life, he'd made all of his then life busy itself with the future.

Now the future was here, he was financially comfortable. But the empty house was a perfect symbol of that future, now present, life.

Alone.

Until today.

Old, yes. In his sixties. Was he too late? Bible reading made him aware that three-score-and-ten years might well be his allotment. Lately having accepted God as his partner, he knew it was too late to follow the 'be fruitful and multiply' command.

Before his religion had become Christianity, he'd sensed the 'spirit' of the forest. First, in its pristine reality as the virgin timber of the ages before he was born far from here in Wales, then as sail-holders across all the seas, then lumber, as Gunlek Bergland established this part of the Upper Peninsula as his domain, and 'demesne' as well; then, but not all, as cutover to second-growth in part to swell the teeming wildlife with its low-level greenery for food, he'd kept up with that forest spirit, glorying in it.

But even as the years crept, then walked, and now sped on, he'd listened to the Reverend Seeliger a few times at Trinity Lutheran, heard the choral with organ music, reminding him of the famous Welsh choristers, saw the glow on the faces, the gleam in the eyes, the vital joy in the way they spoke to each other on departing the church, offering to share with him their found salvation, their present joy in preparation for that heaven.

How like that indomitable forest spirit, that congregation spirit, that same spirit in his former land's anthem:

Hen Gymru fynyddig, paradwys y bardd
Pob dyffryn, pob clogwyn, i'm golwg sydd hard;
Trwy deimlad gwladgarol, mor swynol yw si
Ei nentydd, afonydd, I mi.

Old mountainous Cambria, the Eden of bards,
Each hill and each valley, excite my regards;
To the ears of her patriots how charming still seems
The music that flows in her streams.

So he had spoken truly when he'd answered Aslak's quest for the stills. He'd given them to the new venture on

Section Thirty mostly to save his initial total religion, the forest spirit, from the arsonists burning up the forest to earn livings fighting those fires.

To Aslak's offer to pay for the six stills, he'd declined, saying that saving the forest from the fires—Aslak's reason, himself a non-drinker, for forming the Luna Light Gang, for men to earn money with moonshine sales—was payment enough.

And to Aslak's making him a silent partner, he'd confessed the Lord was already his partner, all he needed.

Was that all he needed? Did anything, anyone, need him?

Each day of his later years, he had refreshed his forest spirit with the sight of it stretching all its wide miles toward the Porcupines.

His prayer to pave his way to sleep:

Lord, if I can be shown, as I see the forest, a way to share the labors, the joys, the community I fed today, while I fed on their presence, I pray you open my eyes to it.

While Sherman Pendock did join that township community in their blessing of sleep, the forest's thousands of acres maintained its cover up to and over the mountains to guard its verge, sentinel over the ceaseless waves of Lake Superior's southern waters, each wave in turn thrusting its off-white foam crest upon the sandy shore, leaving it to join its fading predecessors, ran back to join its source.

Christmas Day.

On his front porch, coffee cup in hand, staring into its steam, though the sun was warming his world, Sherman realized nothing he needed would begin out here.

Later, shaved, in modern, clean outdoor ski pants, top, billed cap to top it off to stay warm, he strode down the packed Pendock Road to M28.

Somewhat over an hour later, the sun well toward its winter zenith, he entered Anna's Hotel rather quiet dining room to find the holiday brunch table well stocked, a line of loners like himself moving past it slowly, to head for tables with Christmas decorations—a tiny tree here, a sort of mini-crèche there—creating the atmosphere of celebration most had at one time seen while growing up, but missed for the later years.

The first item on the table was a huge ham; then a browned turkey, followed by white potatoes, mashed; baked yams, raisin sauce, gravy, biscuits, cranberry sauce, cole slaw, a pumpkin pie, apple pie, minced pie, a coffee urn.

At the table, behind the ham and turkey, stood a comely small woman, huge slicing knife and long-tined fork in hand, looking at him expectantly from pale blue eyes, the slightest of smiles, lips only.

"Which would you like?" she asked.

He found some words. "You were at my house yesterday?"

The smile showed a bit of teeth. "Yes, but I didn't get a chance to talk with you."

"I guess a slice of ham, and….some of the dark from the turkey."

Lillian Eunice deftly carved and placed neatly on his extended plate, already warmed, two slices each of ham and turkey.

"Help yourself to whatever you want, come back for more when you want."

She turned to the couple behind him.

"Which would you like?"

Half an hour later, Sherman stood outside the dining room door. Decided that, since he'd already walked along Railroad Street to get to Anna's, he'd turn left up Cedar, go through town on Center, hit M28 for Merriweather and Pendock Road.

Nothing ventured, nothing gained. Something ventured, nothing gained, either. He'd known none of the others dining at Anna's; had no conversational entrees to what was a largely nondescript, largely silent, largely downcast group of likely duplicates of himself:

A nobody with nothing to offer, no place else to go.

Bergland Township, December 25th, 1932.

Except for the lone elderly man headed along Center Street past all the closed doors, saloons included, the town seemed deserted. Right on and north on Ash Street to M28, turn west past Lakeview Cemetery on his right.

"Probably know more in there than alive in the whole township," Sherman realized.

Friday afternoon Sherman had a thought: Maybe going into town is the wrong place and in the wrong direction.

Where else to go? There was the snowshoe trail heading toward Amundsen's Creek, made by Aslak and Cynara Sunday. And it went into his mystic forest. Maybe a bit of silent wrapping in the forest spirit, not human company, would lift his despondency?

He jabbed his toes into his snowshoe loops, stepped off. Faint sunshine above wispy clouds, no wind to speak of, and even less light now under the tall pine and medium tall hemlock.

Maybe I'm turning into some kind of … I feel all the same magic of the forest spirit, talking to me of the centuries they and their forebears have grown and fallen and no trace of what the ice age onslaught destroyed, redistributed, left behind ... but there's something not the usual ...

I hear voices?

Human voices, a man and a woman coming up toward me from the east...

Could only be ... Aslak and Cynara. What a name, what a woman! None other like her ever here.

He waited. Now they were a bit behind him; then they broke out onto the grade, waving their hands in greeting as they swung along, at home on the squeaking snowshoes, not needed on the packed snow, really.

"You two are happy people today, to be perfectly honest," Sherman smiled. "What's the good news?"

"We were eventually going to come to your place, we just like slogging around in this beautiful forest," Cynara burbled, "especially when there are no flies, as in spring, and the white snow just keeps getting higher and higher."

Aslak moved up beside Sherman, put a huge hand on his shoulder. "We still talk about the great feast you gave us, Sherm! Anna's hosting a New Year's Eve celebration so that's where you have to be!"

"And if you aren't we'll come out and huff and puff and blow your house down!"

"What's the dress code going to be?"

"Ladies get to wear their dress of choice, as many beads, bracelets, as they want. We men will wear coats and ties if we've got them, something better than work overalls if you don't want unfavorable comment!"

"What about alcoholic restraint?"

Aslak wore that half-grin. "I'll be drinking coffee and orange juice. Other than that, we are going to have a big sign with 'RESTRAINT' on it hanging over the liquor table; the toast at midnight will be in addition to the 'one' we've kept insisting on this year. Just after midnight that toast will be the 'one' for that day, celebrating the policy against abuse of liquor as a beverage."

"I'll drink to that!"

"Who's going to be the counter?"

"Each does his or her own counting—the whole idea of the 'one' drink is that restraint has to come from inside each one of us. If you can't trust yourself, whom can you trust?"

Sherman shook his head. "That's a wonderful ideal, but people are only human, not perfect!"

Cynara smiled, melting Sherman's fallback into pessimism. "But if it isn't stating something that's better than 'reality', it isn't an ideal, is it?"

"Can't argue with that!" Sherman agreed.

"So will you be there? Luna Light is providing the 'shine'; what you prefer is up to you."

"I hope to be."

Cynara glanced at Aslak, who nodded.

"Come with us now—we're headed for Demaray's cabin, then back up to the Mile Road."

Cynara, Sherman, Aslak in single column in that order, they set off.

Cynara took longer steps than usual, Sherman took his normal length step, and Aslak, longest legs, shorter steps than usual.

Thus they all three stepped in unison, in a cadence, as if they were marching to the same drummer.

With a good fire going in the big cookstove at the front end of Demaray's cabin on Amundsen's Creek, Cynara looked first at Aslak, then at Sherman, decided to say what she'd felt moving through the timber on snowshoes.

"When we'd been hiking for awhile after we left the grade and were coming between the trees, especially once we hit the foot trail along the creek to here, I felt something—I don't know what, how to describe it, as if we were not just three people on snowshoes—as if there was a kind of echo, maybe?...some kind of perception, maybe—does this sound crazy?—a kind of communication between us, why we were walking to a cadence, between us and the trees."

Aslak nodded, put his coffee cup back down on the red-and-white checkered oilcloth table cover.

"I've had that same feeling, and Sherm has his idea what it is. Try it on us again, Sherm?"

Sherm turned his gaze from the ice-prism bands of afternoon sun colors on the window.

"It seems to me, Cynara, and I know you've experienced something of this kind in the Trinity Lutheran Church in Bergland, from what you've said over the years about your being raised 'in the church', as people say. There—and I've been there a few times—the minister says directly or indirectly that when the people are in church honoring God, demonstrating their belief, God is there with them."

"That's exactly right, Sherman," Cynara agreed. "Some of it comes from the colored bits of glass in the windows, too, of Biblical scenes. And Reverend Seeliger always makes a point of leaving the Bible open after reading from it, too, saying God's Word is always open for all to see and read."

"And especially on Communion Sunday, or Easter, it seems God is there when the words 'Take, drink, this is my blood, This do in remembrance of Me' are offered with the consecrated wine," Aslak added.

Sherman continued: "Though nobody expects to see God step up to the stage. The same is true for me when I'm in the timber, or even just thinking of it, picturing the rows of trees in my mind. I call it the 'spirit' of the forest. It wasn't too long ago that the people who lived in our forest, the Indians, had a whole bunch of spirits in all living things, trees, which are alive."

Sherman stopped, looked for doubt or questions in the pair of faces.

"Nowadays, we think people who believe that trees are alive, that there is something going on inside a tree just as there is something going on inside us—not in our body, but in our minds, our thoughts—are a bit batty."

Aslak nodded, "There are people right here in Bergland township who swear my mares can do what I want them to do right at the exact moment—and I haven't said a word, or pulled one way the other on the reins."

Cynara took it further. "Also, we put our trust in trees—to keep us sheltered from the outside while we live in houses made from trees"-hearing her own words gave her a further insight—"and even when we burn wood up in that stove we trust it to warm us, boil water, and a whole lot of things—cook food to keep us alive, even!!"

Aslak rose, lifted a lid, dropped two more sticks on the coals.

"So," Sherman ended, "That's what I felt on our way here, that the trees recognized me as I recognized them, their 'spirit', that they were responding to my gentle worship of their growth, their support of my life, talking to me in return."

Sherman stood, slipped his lined overall jacket back on. "I've enjoyed visiting with you, and I suppose you're ready for more tramping in these woods. I'm heading back south to my place."

Cynara offered the polite denials, but, when Aslak asked her,

"Have you ever heard of Dutch John's cabin?" a twosome once again, they went on exploring the world new to her, new also to Aslak when with Cynara.

And Sherman, after closing the draft and damper of the cabin stove, reached his empty house, sure of his bond with the forest spirit, wondering if it would be enough to fill this seemingly empty spot in his being.

Would there be some kind of connection, spiritual or real, found or to grow on New Year's Eve at Anna's?

Chapter Six

Saturday night, December 31st, 1932.
The eve of the New Year.
In the center of the tables in Anna Stindt's Hotel restaurant something for the celebrants to admire:

Two upright four-by-fours eight feet tall on broad iron rings for stability crossed at the top by two two-by-sixes with a huge hook in the middle from which hung a bell. On each side of the bell, at its top, and welded to the bell, was a half-circle of iron, closed at its top.

On the floor under the bell lay two ten-foot coils of half-inch new rope. On one end of each rope was an iron hook the size of one's hand; on the other, a like-sized loop.

Only those who emplaced the bell had any foreknowledge of its existence there; the restaurant had closed, locked out admittance, after the noon meal.

But Anna and all of her conspirators had a chuckle or two or more as they imagined not only the would-be celebrants surprise on arrival, but their joyous use of the bell at the right time!

At the announced time of opening, ten that evening, among the first to arrive were the august members of the Bergland Town Board. Ed Erikson, by any definition—plain age, or seniority on the Town Board, or just plain esteem by all Bergland Townhip residents—was the most august.

Ed's first words to Anna, greeting the first arrivals at the open door:

"Don't know if I can last until midnight, but I'm going to try!" with his habitual stroking of the white, drooping mustache.

"And I'll prop him up even if he does fall asleep!" promised his son Peter, in his first year as the County Attorney of Ontonagon County, his hair still a bright golden above his clean-shaven pink face.

The rest of the crowd, eager to see who else would be there, eager to be seen by who else would be there, most of all eager to partake of the rise in hope were prompt to file in, share greetings with Hostess Anna, so that in less than a half hour all tables were taken.

Packed!

There sat Anna with Cynara and Aslak; the seven Town Board members, with Peter, took two tables; Jim Ferguson, Hattie Walker with her daughter Carol and her husband Warden Limpert rounded a table; others garnered two of the Finn farmers from Matchwood, Art Ahonen (Helvie home with TWINS!) and Wilho Jakkola, with their mentors M/M Jerome Brown and M/M David Kooker, sheep and wheat sponsors of the Finns (they shoved another table over to add Einar Latvala); the merchants Brismaster and Newberg, and wives gathered at another; Reverend & Mrs Seeliger joined the Baileys; and at the extra table from the entry way there were Jim Ferguson, August Schmidt, Sherman Pendock, and Lillian Eunice Ryan.

The last arrivals, Herman Hill, with Bill and Mrs Piper of Piper's Garage, took the last three seats at the two joined tables with Einar Latvala.

"If Frank Cutler had come as we asked, he'd not had a seat!" Herman said.

"Which, lately, would have suited Frank just fine," Bill answered. "He's been sort of stand-offish since just after Thanksgiving."

Just the same, Anna saw, maybe this would be the last time, but it was good to see:

PACKED!!

Anna arose to deliver the group welcome:

"I'm glad to see you all here. I'm glad to see the last of 1932. Lately, what with the Prohibition and Depression I'm glad to see anything new—especially a whole year!"

Loud applause forced Anna to wait, smiling.

"You can see the snack table is loaded with goodies, and there you all can help yourselves—no waitresses here tonight, and no busboys—so when you leave, clear your own tables into the container at the door."

All turned their heads to confirm she spoke the truth.

"At five minutes to midnight I'll have some instructions for a special event. We'll all take a part in making it happen."

A murmur of anticipation rippled over the room.

"A last word of advice: I hope we all have taken to heart the 'restraint' policy of the Women's Alcoholic Restraint Society and others here.

A sudden hush while most nodded in agreement; a few showed wonderment.

"On the snack table is a variety of liquor intended as a beverage, and for the toast to the new year. Remember the sign above the table: RESTRAINT!"

Anna beamed as she swept her glance over the listeners.

"For the toast and the surprise event we'll all need to be able to stand up unaided!"

And she sat down.

Einar Latvala was the first to rise and head for the snacks.

"Come join me," he roared, "We have to build up our strength for the surprise event!"

And this skipping pebble broke up the still water of attention to Anna's welcome.

In the hour remaining of 1932 most but not all eventually returned to their original tables; but the event was truly a mixing as impromptu greetings and conversations resumed.

Cynara sought out Lillian.

"I'm Cynara."

"Lillian." Old habits die hard; Lil offered her hand; Cynara, surprised, grasped the hand firmly.

"I saw you sitting with Pikey, I wondered why."

Cynara smiled, "We're going to marry next month, we hope! You were sitting with Dutchy and Sherman—friends, I suppose?"

"I know them—August better than Sherman. But we're three loners tonight, sitting at the same table because we are 'singles', I guess," Lillian laughed. "I heard you and Aslak—Pikey—waiting for Congress to get rid of Prohibition before you are married?"

"We hadn't really discussed it. It just sort of popped up when Jim Ferguson asked us. Maybe it has some connection to our discovery that—well, my discovery, not his, he had begun the 'restraint' thing before I changed my mind about alcohol—anyway, that we got acquainted somehow because of Prohibition, so…."

Lillian waited.

Cynara looked away, saw Aslak talking to Sherman and August, standing, plates with goodies in one hand, a glass in the other, grinned at Lillian.

"I guess it was somewhat of a whim. We're having such a good time being together when I'm not in the Post Office, out in the woods around Amundsen's Creek, remodeling his house for us," her voice trailed off.

"Maybe we shouldn't wait any more," she giggled at Lillian. "Aslak's new favorite saying is 'Seize the day.'"

Aslak joined them. "Let's go back to your table, Lillian, it's empty right now."

Lillian stared enviously as Aslak held a chair for Cynara, then blushed as Aslak came around to hold a chair for her.

"How come a pretty woman like you is by herself, Lil?"

"I *used* to be Lil, now I'm Lillian Eunice Ryan, and I'm the waitress here except for this party."

Cynara gaped, recovered.

"Sorry, Lillian," Aslak, with the usual half-grin, laid his huge paw over Lillian's hand.

"I'd heard you'd moved here from Marko's."

"I live here, work here. I'm not a lumberjack anymore. And this"—she held up a glass of what looked like water—"is Anna's water by special request."

Cynara smoothed out a near-frown. "Special request?"

Art Ahonen tapped Aslak's shoulder. "Pikey, I talk to you a minute?" He tipped his head away from the table.

"Sure thing, Art. Excuse me, ladies?"

Lillian smiled. "Water by special request has one shot of moonshine in it."

Cynara made the connection. "Aslak's Luna Light Gang is Anna's supplier?"

Lillian nodded, sipped, tabled her glass. "And if Anna lets anyone take a second 'special request', he won't sell her any more."

Cynara stared into Lillian's faded blue eyes.

Hesitantly, "Can I ask you a personal question?"

Lillian stared back. "Probably, if it's what I expect. I've been asked a few times lately."

"Did you used to be—Gallopin' Lil, the lumberjack, and so forth?"

"And with a lot of so forth. Yes. And you're the post mistress."

Cynara swung her glance toward Aslak, deep in serious talk with Art Ahonen and Peter Erikson, the county attorney.

Cynara impulsively grasped Lillian's hand, smiled.

"We have more than you might think in common."

In turn, Lillian gaped, recovered.

"Not exactly," Cynara corrected. "Tell me about Gallopin' Lil, I'll come back with what used to be me."

Lillian rose, moved her chair over to Cynara's side, so both were facing the front, the bell frame.

"When I was in my teens I didn't develop into a woman. When it got too bad for me to take I decided to show everybody I didn't care, I didn't want to be any woman, so I came up here and went to work in the woods with the lumberjacks. I got to be as good with the axe, with anybody on the other end of a crosscut saw, I didn't faint, I took all the bad food and the cold and wet and wound up a hard drinker and a foul mouth just like all the other ones. I showed all the girls I could be even better than them—they were gettin' fat and havin' babies and I was Galllopin' Lil. The hard drinkin' lumberjack!"

Cynara sipped a bit from her glass, straight water. "Did you ever think of quitting that rough tough life?"

"Quittin' it for what? I wasn't a real woman! I be da—dgummed if I was goin' to be a NOTHIN'!"

"But here you are—a cleaned-up nice-looking slender woman in a dress."

Lillian relaxed, leaned back, leaned forward.

"One mornin' I had to crawl from Marko's bathroom on the floor to get to the kitchen. Not on my hands and knees. On my belly I thought I'd left behind. You've probably never worked up to the dry heaves?"

Cynara shook her head, awed.

"When I got to the table and could hold up a coffee cup and drain it Yaga would talk to me. Answerin' her questions showed me I was lyin' to myself. No matter how hard I tried, heavin' out my guts the morning after would be as close as I'd ever get to bein' a true lumberjack."

"Yaga proved to me that if I wanted to quit lyin' to myself about not wantin' to be a woman, and did the things a woman did—*for* people, and not *to* people, I could have a home and even a husband—and not be vomitin' from abusin' whiskey."

Cynara, now on familiar ground, got her smile back. "Anybody you have in mind for that husband?"

Lillian looked down, picked up her drink, tilted it.

Put it back on the table.

"Okay, I started in the middle. Here's the first part. Jack Ryan is my husband. He was some kind of minin' inspector for some big outfit down in Chicago. He evaluated the copper mines around here. When the sawmill quit I went with him to Chi. He wouldn't take me anywhere, he said I was too loud, talked too dirty….So I came up here 'cause I didn't have or make any friends down there. So I drank all the way up here in a taxi, slugged the driver in Marko's when he asked for his fifty dollars, dragged him to the door and threw him out into the slush. Marko carried me up, put me in the spare bed."

Lillian looked at her glass, left it on the table. "Now that's the whole story."

"Will you go back down to Chicago, to Jack?"

"He said 'Don't come back.'"

Cynara glanced up to the front, saw Aslak sitting by old Ed Erikson, that half smile on his face, old Ed nodding, listening. Pikey telling one of his stories!

How can any woman be so lucky?

Lillian prodded her arm. "Your turn."

"I see you've not had a drop from your glass in a while."

Lillian nodded, smiled, her eyes beginning to shine. "I'm tryin'!"

"I was another kind of drunk," Cynara began. "I was addicted to what the Bible said, word for word, while I was growing up. Drinking was an abomination, so it got to the point where I was in thick with the WCTU and with them for Prohibition. I was a believer that if it took a law and force to keep people from abusing liquor, becoming violent, and so on, then I was for it. When it was plain that Prohibition was worse than what went on before, I was shown by that, and by other examples—Pikey's 'restraint' of his Luna Light Gang, and by Anna and Hattie Walker and others about wine in the Bible and so on—that it was the abuse of whiskey, not the whiskey itself, that was to blame."

Lillian nodded vigorously. "That's what Yaga showed me. It's the person, what the person has inside, that has to be worked on. Prohibition treated drinkers like children, so they were childish, not grown-up about drinkin'."

"And I don't have a husband, either. My husband…"

"I heard about the funeral, and about Jesus at the well."

"So now the local WCTU is…"

"Anna told me. Women's Alcohol Restraint Society!"

"And I've not had any children, also like you!"

A bit of the old 'Lil' shone in Lillian's eyes.

"But you are plain to see, a woman, and with Pikey…!"

Cynara lifted her glass. "Here's to our future, no matter what today is!"

Lillian's glass clanged against hers. "To our future!"

Aslak thrust his glass against the two in the air. "I'll drink to that!"

And they did, all three!

"What did Art Ahonen want?" Cynara asked.

"He wants me to help him pick out a team from Dave Kooker's horse farm—your one-time brother-in-law. His wheat did well, he's got a few extra dollars, but he wants to stay away from machines, go with horses, in the summer."

"You should come out and see Pikey's mares," Cynara gushed to Lillian, "they are …"

August watched the others milling about the goodies table, groups and twosomes forming, breaking up. Sherman sat like a stone beside him.

"Come and get a bite, with me," he urged.

Sherman hesitated. "I see everyone I know busy with friends; I don't want to break in…"

"I'm in need of a bite or two; I'll be back!"

Standing on the far side of the goodies table, August could watch Sherman. If I ever saw a man looking lonesome… August brought a plate heaped with a few pickles, some tiny sausages, rolls of ham on toothpicks, a piece of yellow cake with a thin chocolate frosting.

"Here, taste the ham! How's life out on Pendock Road?"

"No one but me, August. Once in a great while somebody comes by. Just a few days ago Aslak and Cynara came out, we met up north of my place, went down to Demaray's cabin and talked for an hour or so. Then they went on, I guess out to Dutch John's, and I went home."

August chewed on a sausage. Sherman broke the silence.

"Sounds crazy, maybe, but there's a kind of talk out in the timber, or some kind of connection, I feel—in the timber I feel I'm in kind of company."

August swallowed, thought 'What can I say?'

Pressured by the silence, Sherman kept on: "There's a kind of 'spirit', I call it, in the timber. Out in it, I feel it touching me—and I think of how it travels all over the world—masts for sailing ships, lumber for homes here and overseas, comes back up in maybe its own kind—pine, hemlock—or some other kind—poplar—and never really disappears, just changes looks. This paper napkin" he held it up "came from a tree. Trees move into classrooms and libraries in the form of paper to educate readers, be company for them just as they are for me in the timber. Trees carry words all over the world."

He shrugged his shoulders. "That just came out by itself. But see—the trees are talking in my voice!"

Without pause August, the former student in the Palatinate, responded, giving each word time to sink in over the growing hub-bub of talk and laughter:

'By blowing realms of woodland
With sunstruck vanes afield
And cloud-led shadows sailing
About the windy weald

By valley-guarded granges
And silver waters wide,

Content at heart I followed
With my delightful guide.'

Sherman stared. "You just made that up?"

August shook his head. "No, those words I saw on a piece of paper—you reminded me of it with what you said, and trees then spoke through me."

Sherman's eyes widened.

August added, with a shrug of his meaty shoulders: "Sometimes I recall words I've seen. Makes sure that people must think I'm weird."

Sherman regained speech. "Then that makes two of us. Is that all you remember?"

"It's just a couple of stanzas of a poem called 'The Merry Guide' by Housman. He's been dead for a long time, but I guess somebody might have a book called *A Shropshire Lad*—or the high school library might have it, probably does. There's a lot more in the book, few more poems not about timber only, about outside, Nature, but you might find some company in it while you're out on Pendock Road in your place. Make up for lack of living persons visiting, maybe."

Pendock slid his paper napkin over. "Here, write the name and title on this once-upon-a-time tree. I'll see what I can find."

August lifted his glass. "Here's to good luck and good company!"

"Good luck and good company!"

And they drank to that, both of them.

Anna checked the clock over the entry door. Rising from a discussion of rye bread baking with Ada Brismaster, she clanged a spoon on her empty glass.

Gradually, then accelerating, the room quieted, she saw all eyes turned to her.

"As all of you have realized, this bell is here to be rung at midnight, ringing out 1932 and ringing in 1933! It is now five minutes to midnight!"

She paused. "BUT nobody here is going to sit where you are or stand where you are while somebody else rings this bell! NO, SIREE! Everybody here is going to team up with the other two or three at your table, or who started out at your table, on one side or the other of the bell, with a piece of the rope in your sweaty hands, and make the old year go and the new year come in."

She pointed at the table where the town board, old Ed Erikson still there and awake, sat.

"This table will begin—some on each side, hook up the rope to the bell, give it a yank or two, hand the two ropes, still hooked up to the bell, to the next table, until everybody has done his or her part!"

Anna stepped up, seized a rope from under the bell, handed it to old Ed. "That's my part; you four figure out the rest for your table, the next is the rest of the board."

Anna began to laugh at what confusion might follow, decided 'It's a party, let it go' and cried out, "The clock says that's the end. GO!"

Ed hooked up his end, Nick Anderson the other side; Nick, about twice the weight of Ed, gave his end a pull; the other two were to help old Ed pull it back, but they both pulled and nothing happened.

"That's our town board, all right," somebody yelled, to universal laughter.

Then Nick waited, in turn pulled and the bell rang the second peal, quivering the liquids in all the glasses; the other board table rushed to keep the bell ringing. After confused and interrupted peals and silence, other tables got the message, began lining up on both sides of the bell, the rope transfer smoothed out.

Jim paired with August. "Only one car from some odds and ends from Weidmann's out on Thirty-Six. All hemlock."

Someone started a chant "Out with the old, in with the new"; it grew in volume, someone else started a handclapping, which more and more rose in competition with the 'Out…In' chant; the foot stomping soon joined in, until the dining room began actually vibrating.

"This place is beginnin'to rock," Lillian screamed in Cynara's ear—but Cynara could not make out the words.

Some of the more vigorous went up for a second go-around on the bell rope.

Gradually, in response to the slackening of the handclapping, the foot stomping, the 'Out with the old, in with the new' became intelligible though hoarse, and had anyone looked at the clock over the door they would have seen that the New Year was past a half hour old.

The departure of old Ed Erikson, the other board members, and Ed's son Peter was the signal for those who were replete with joy but whose exuberance was used up to begin trailing out the door for home and sleep.

Some stayed for some final words of recovery and pursuit of interrupted conversation. Kooker and Brown, with Ahonen and Latvala, finished smoothing out details of that coming spring wheat crop and lambing, with Ahonen reminding Aslak to be ready to help choose and outfit a team.

Sherman Pendock, since Aslak was in no hurry to leave, and since August would get a ride home with Aslak, decided to stay in the Hotel until daylight for a walk home to Pendock Road.

He asked August, whose tie was still neatly knotted, if he remembered anymore of the verses by this fellow Housman.

"There's one came back—I think when all the noise and merriment—the commotion—was going on. It's about a storm in a forest called Wenlock Edge on a hillside called the Wrekin, beside the Severn River—the Britishers have a name for every little place—I guess because they've been there so long, hundreds and hundreds of years, not like us here, yet. I can start it and maybe it will all—or some more of it—come back."

On Wenlock Edge the wood's in trouble;
His forest fleece the Wrekin heaves;
The gale, it plies the saplings double,
And thick on Severn snow the leaves.

'Twould blow like this through holt and hanger
When Uricon the city stood:
'Tis the old wind in the old anger,
But then it threshed another wood.

Then, 'twas before my time, the Roman
At yonder heaving hill would stare:
The blood that warms an English yeoman
The thoughts that hurt him, they were there.

There, like the wind through woods in riot,
Through him the gale of life blew high;
The tree of man was never quiet:
Then,'twas the Roman, now 'tis I.

Suddenly August's mind was blank. Nothing more on the page. He turned to Sherman to shrug off his failure of memory, was stilled by the intensity of Sherman's stare of concentration, the whiteness of his clenched knuckles, his entirety of focus on August.

"I just can't see …"August began …

"'The tree of man'" Sherman interrupted, his eyes shifting, staring into a void.

"I wish I could…"

Sherman, still not hearing, demanded,

"Will school be open today?"

August shook his head. "Today is Sunday, January first, 1933, Sherm. School is out for a week or so yet."

"August, I need to get that book, Housman's. Is there somebody who could let me in, see if the book's in the school library?"

August considered.

"I need to see that book, read all of it!"

August caught Aslak's wave of 'C'mon!'

"Ask Anna now or in the morning—you are staying to sleep here, right?"

Sherman nodded distractedly.

It took a while before all of the movement noises generated by the New Year hysterical joy, ending as in Anna's Hotel all human movement ended, were replaced in Sherman Pendock's wide-awake listening attention by the here-and-there-creaks of a wooden building in January 1933 weather in the northwestern town of Bergland, Ontonagon County, Upper Michigan.

None of which registered over the bar raised in consciousness once he repeated the phrase:

The tree of man…

Too apt, too great a reward, for belief.

Hoping for a contact with a person, any person, not for a hugely meaningful contact, just any relief from the overwhelming isolation...

But the tree of man...

In all of Bergland the remainder of the last night of the old year was lighted only by the dim glimmer of the bulb over 'Hotel'; inside the unconscious sleeping old man in his bed was the tiny but intense light of hope.

A New Year. A new life.

While the thousands of acres of pine and hemlock timber, timeless, eternal, north of town, north of the Mile Road, north of Pendock's house, standing in hip-deep snow, reached up to and over the Porcupine Mountains to stand sentinel over the sandy beach verge of Lake Superior, whose waves ran their yellow-white caps of foam up the heavily-iced light brown sand, deposited the foam, ran back.

In the broad brightness of daylight, January first, 1933, Sherman Pendock strode from the Bergland High School library out the front door of Bergland High School, down its steps to M28, turned west from the point at the bottom of the steps where all who rode the school bus entered their ride home to enter what promise might be his from the book of *A Shropshire Lad.*

A small book, hard cover, warming inside the front of his jacket, the fingers of his right hand, inside the front pocket, cupped around the book's bottom edge, his left arm swinging high front and back, past Piper's Garage, where the hangers-on, inside in winter on the round seats fronting his counter, witnessed the vigor of the stride, the erect spine, the head up and straight ahead, until the corner shoulder bulge of Lakeview Cemetery high ground blocked their view.

Somethin' t'see," said Bill Piper. The hangers-on turned back. To their coffee cups.

The usual New Year's resolutions were created, with varying resolve, most of them the usual 'not to' sort: Not to eat so much, not to gossip so much, not to complain about (fill in the blank).

No tally was made, but the number of 'Not to drink so much' resolutions might have been surprising.

Restraint

The word was a new one for some people. But it had a chance.

As Cynara had asserted to Sherman: If an ideal seems realistic, it isn't an ideal!

Chapter Seven

On Tuesday the 14th of February, 1933, now aware a year had changed, their birthdays that much further behind them, Cynara and Aslak put their heads together to plan their wedding.

At noon the 24th of February, 1933 on Pine Street, Bergland's 'Main' street, the thermometer at the DSS&A depot was at 32 degrees Fahrenheit. At 7 pm, a full moon hung in the evening sky, already clearly visible. The temperature was on its way to a low of 21 degrees.

And a crowd the likes of which Bergland had never seen was gathering at the Cedar Street Theatre to witness the wedding.

The snow on Center Street, crossing Pine from the west end of town, was white and crispy-crunchy underfoot, packed hard by the huge roller, pulled by a team of horses. At that end of Center Street in the heat of July a special week of evenings would host at the grandstanded baseball field a travelling 'medicine' show, where all the kids in the stand would keep a wary eye peeled for the 'medicine' man who was reputed to jab some unsuspecting watcher with a big needle to bring on some kind of 'knockout', followed immediately by another 'medicine' man who would jab in another needle, bringing the victim back to life, proving the miraculous property of the medicine—for just one dollar a bottle!

But tonight a different season, a different show, the other end of the street.

At eight o'clock, in the theatre, The Right Reverend Seeliger, of the Lutheran Trinity Church pulpit, would unite in holy matrimony Cynara Keller, the Post Mistress of Bergland, and Aslak Bergland, nephew of the town founder Gunlek Bergland, masterful teamster of the famous blue-black team of mares, peripatetic news-distributor of Bergland Township and its outlying farms, operator of the iconic Black Model A Sedan seen everywhere at any given daylight hour throughout the township, the for-sure leader of the Luna Light Gang, the makers and distributors of the best corn moonshine and applejack brandy; tall, ruggedly handsome jack of all trades and master of the same, Cynara's cynosure paramour to the delight of every citizen in Bergland and not a few of those mere visitors from Topaz, Matchwood, Trout Creek and points east; Merriweather, Wakefield, Bessemer, Ironwood and even Hurley west across the bordering Iron River into Wisconsin; AND from Ontonagon north of Bergland on the south shore of Lake Superior to Silver City thence through White Pine.

Bergland residents from side streets bordering Center Street were out heading east to the Cedar Street theatre at moonrise. They were the Baileys, led by Mrs., a staunch member of the WCTU before, when, and after it became the WARS, the Brismasters, the Douslins, the Dershnas, the Demarays, the Pedersens, the Petersons, the Barthels, the Scotts, the Andersons, the Fruiks, the Fergusons, the Johnsons, the Dishnaus, the Borseths, the Cutlers, the Becks, the Blonshines, the Buzzas, the Barthels, Hills, Westricks...

Center Street, on both sides from the Ball Park to the Theatre, was lined tightly with cars whose license plates read Gogebic County or Ontonagon County.

One parking space was kept open in the middle front space at the Theatre. At ten minutes to eight Aslak's black Model A sedan pulled up to to decant Haywire Johnson, August Schmidt; its driver, Aslak Bergland.

The cynosure of all the eyes of those lined up at the front hoping SRO signs would be posted at the last moment:

Cynara Keller.

In a taffeta evening gown, conforming to her graceful body, the exact same blond as her golden hair, now done up in a knot atop the rear of her skull, and a pair of sensible shoes of the same blond shade ...... all of which formed a dull background for the glowing, shiny-eyed, red-lipped, smiling beauty of their post mistress's face, Who joined Aslak, in a subdued light gray suit as, he came around the radiator of his black Model A, to slip her left arm through his bent-elbowed right arm and match his somewhat shortened but if anything MORE strutting stride through all the cheering, shouting crowd of hopefuls to enter the theatre, its rows rising rippling to a well-dressed stand in which the only lights were on a pair of cords on the floor, framing the center aisle, leaving the cavernous ceiling masked in darkness, And which lights, soft to begin with, went OUT as the couple, unescorted, at a much slower, majestic pace, passed each pair, so that when they stopped in front of a low table close to the stage, only one light on each side of the aisle, next to the couple, was on, *and as they stood there, those two lights turned their yellow glow to pale rose!*

A soft roar of amaze filled the theatre. In this shade the distance between the bride/groom pair and the watchers diminished until all seemed one. Many reached out toward the pair, thinking they could be touched. Though the attempt at a physical contact failed, it seemed to all—even to the rearmost row—that at this rite of joining the pair to each other, to become one—the watchers themselves came closer to the pair.

And to each other.

Not only had they come closer by leaving their separate homes to come to the Theatre. At the Theatre, witness to the marriage vows of this pair of present loners, their incipient expression of unity, the unexpressed sensing conjoined the watchers to each other.

This pair in marriage joined Bergland's citizens into a whole community, repaired the disjunction experienced by Prohibtion, by the economic, mental, psychic strains of the Great Depression.

All the wrongs, real or imagined, unavoidable or self-initiated, deserved or undeserved, faded out of sight and mind as they witnessed what seemed so *RIGHT.*

Into the light rose glow seemingly generated by the pair stepped the Right Reverend Seeliger, facing the pair across the low table. On it he placed a spidery lectern, on that the marriage manual he and the pair had joined in editing.

"Dearly beloved, we have come together to witness the joining together of this man and this woman in Holy Matrimony. Our Lord Jesus Christ adorned this rite by his presence and first miracle at the wedding in Cana of Galilee."

"Into this union Cynara Keller and Aslak Bergland now come to be joined. If any of you can show just cause why they may not be lawfully wed, speak now, or forever hold your peace."

Near silence, a rustle of clothing and shoe movement, a muffled cough.

"Cynara Keller, will you have this man to be your husband as long as you both shall live?"

Softly, "I will!"

"Aslak Bergland, will you have this woman to be your wife as long as you both shall live?"

"I will!" ringing clearly to the last row.

"Will all of you witnessing these promises do all in your power to uphold these two persons in their marriage?"

Momentary silence for a hiss of intake, then a joyous roar:

"WE WILL!!!"

Facing each other, both hands joined, as the echoes faded, Aslak declared,

"I, Aslak, take you, Cynara, to be my wife, to have and to hold from this day forward, for better, for worse; for richer, for poorer; in sickness and in health, to love and to cherish, until we are parted by death."

Cynara responded: "I, Cynara, take you, Aslak, to be my husband, to have and to hold from this day forward, for better, for worse; for richer, for poorer; in sickness and in health, to love and to cherish, until we are parted by death."

The witnesses regained their composure as the two exchanged rings.

But as they kissed, applause rippled front to back, then all hands noised their approval with a rhythmic beat of hands sending waves of sound ricocheting from the walls.

Lillian shouted to August, standing to her right in the first row,

"This place is beginnin' to rock!"

As if on signal, the stage curtains parted to the tune of the Beer Barrel Polka by the Bergland Orchestra, Old Man Vincent leader and on trumpet.

The Right Reverend Seeliger tugged his wife to her feet; the temporary additional chairs were shoved aside by witnesses coming forward to congratulate the husband and wife they'd seen created, then swinging their partners.

The low table was spread wide with leaves inserted; on it appeared as if by magic a variety of potables, glasses, and napkins...... and in the community celebration quite a few second drinks disappeared from the glass but it was in joy, not despair, and while some began their ways home, none who left had to be helped walk, and none of the dancers lost their rhythm.

But as the last square dance ended, and the musicians stored their instruments in their cases, as August and Lillian separated for the rest rooms, Frank Cutler hissed to Lillian, "Enjoy this one, you skinny hag, you'll never see your own! I guarantee!"

August walked a silent head-down Lillian to the door of Anna's Hotel. Walking slowly back to the car, he wondered at the decorous behavior of Lillian all during the celebration, and her silence with him. So far, she's on the straight and narrow. But odd, the silence.

Lillian had plainly enjoyed the wedding.

She'd gasped, hands to her face, when the lights bracketed the pair fronting the altar in the rosy glow. She'd been a strong voice August had heard above the thunderous 'WE WILL!'

At the dancing, she and August had dosey-doed and swung as the caller directed.

She'd had a good time.

Then suddenly dispirited as he escorted her home.

Somehow, because of him, a washed-out version of the groom?

The last to leave were Cynara and Aslak, now Mr. and Mrs. Bergland; when out of the black Model A stepped August Schmidt, the two were alone up over the hill marking the last of the Mile Road proper, alone together entering the completed re-fashioning of the old Bergland house to mark appropriately the beginning year with the hope of many to follow in a way we can all understand was proper as well.

The number of Mile Road bachelors was diminished by one.

In her tiny neat room upstairs in Anna's Hotel Bergland Lillian lay awake. Should a miracle happen, how disappointing after Cynara would be a plain stick like me.

The timber kept its vigil over the Superior Lake's south shore; the waves slid their yellowish-white foam up the sandy beach, to leave behind their froth, slid back into the waters whence they came; repeated their surge, slid back.

The timber unmoving.

Chapter Eight

The explosion of relief occasioned by and at the wedding generated a change not only in the attitude of Bergland residents, but an explosive change on the Mile Road itself.

On the 16th of March, 1933, August Schmidt's entire rusty tin shack went high in the air to come down spread out as far as the Mile Road in small twisted pieces. While the shiny clean kerosene stove was littered with pieces of tin, some shreds of the wall-length sofa, and a few nails, its position on the far bank of the Mile Road away from what was an 'instant' cellar excavation kept it safe from the force of Aslak's FOUR sticks of dynamite heaving the house and cubic yards of dirt and sneaky under-the-house tree roots high in the air under the cloud of dust and smoke.

"There," Aslak shouted into the covered-but-still-deafened ears of Cynara, Jonas Amundsen, Haywire Johnson, and August, "now all you have to do is square away the corners, pour the footers, and up goes a house for an interstate business man's new home!"

But the plan was not for the usual box-like wood-framed wooden-siding two-story single-ridge-lined domicile, with a dirt-floored cellar relieved only by a couple walls of shelving and one end taken up by a huge potato bin.

The plan's inception took place weeks before at Anna Stindt's Hotel Restaurant, a dinner to welcome the Aslak Bergland couple back from a two-week vacation *in Norway to show off his new first bride* to all of Aslak's kin in Morgedal('morning vale') in Telemark County, on the farm 'Bergland'. Depression 'hard times', yes, but not for the leader/founder of the Luna Light Gang, provider of moonshine and applejack brandy to outlets as far away as Milwaukee, WI., and nephew of Gunlek Aslaksen Bergland.

When at that dinner August Schmidt began describing the mansion of Captain Pabst he'd visited in Milwaukee last Thanksgiving weekend, Cynara, never without a pad and pencil, began sketching what the floor plan sounded like. When the first floor was penciled in, she did the second floor—*the second floor?*—right next to the first, added a swirl to suggest the stairway—slid it over in front of her new husband, with a raised eyebrow and a smile.

A quick scan; he nodded at Cynara, slid the sketch over in front of August, sitting across the table beside Lillian Eunice Ryan, who was once again, as at the New Year's Eve party, a guest rather than a waitress. Anna's daughter Margaret was substituting that day.

August, still praising the Pabst mansions outward appearance of stone sheathing, the crenellated 'widow's walk' roof, with the conical tower dominating the front view, gave a start when Lillian prodded his stout waist below tabletop level.

"… of solid stone the entire outside," he finished, looked down where Lillian pointed with a strong but feminine finger.

While August scanned in some puzzlement Cynara's work, she explained:

"I drew what you were saying about the inside. Is it about like that? It's not to any scale—that's just the arrangement of rooms as I saw what you were saying."

"And I didn't catch where the front door was… "

August ran a forefinger here and there on the sketch.

"Can't be sure on a sketch without seeing…"

Aslak leaned across to cut through the table's conversation buzz: "Come home with us after this is over and take a look at ours. We think that ours is a lot like what you were talking about, smaller, of course. Anyway, take a look at ours."

As Aslak resumed his seat, Anna took the chance, rapped her spoon on her empty glass.

"We're all happy to see you two back safely and happy. But we're more than a little envious, Cynara, that we haven't heard about the trip, what you saw and did in Norway—a place none of us have seen, and heard only a little. Won't you please speak to us all here about the part of your honeymoon that isn't private?!"

A muted but general 'yes, do!' filled in the silence. Cynara rose.

"I cherish all of the moments I spend with this man"—she laid a hand on Aslak's shoulder—"but there was a special tone to our trip and his native land—at least, in what we saw and experienced of it—that I'd like to share with you!"

"Not in its entirety! But a few spots. From what August has been telling us about his trip to Milwaukee, he shows he feels he has grown in some ways, especially in one way—his estimate of his own worth. Enough to announce that he thinks of himself now as not Dutchy but August."

She paused to smile at August, who rose to his feet, bowed in all directions. A smattering of applause, which his unspoken appreciation generated rather than to which he was responding, initiated some smiles and a few laughs, which he echoed, then sat.

"See," remarked Cynara, "August would never have had the aplomb, the chutzpah, to do that as old 'Dutchy.'"

August nodded, smiled at all dutifully.

"I realized," Cynara went on, "some feeling a lot like that. Everywhere we went, even where we were not among family or former friends of Aslak, I felt and saw glances at us that were complimentary, even some envious admiration."

She paused, looked a circular gaze around at all eyes. "I know that's what most of the glances, the stares, the turned heads, were about, because I was admiring those people, their clothes, their air, their buildings, statues, and I was getting the same looks from the people."

She looked down at Aslak, who gave her a broad wink that all could see.

"Okay, they were looking like that at both of us!"

He shook his head as if in denial, pointing plainly at Cynara.

"Then while we were in Morgedal, and on Bergland—his family farm—it was the same thing only ten times more so. His kinfolk adored him, especially his uncle Olaf, who'd come to America like our Gunlek did, but went back. They positively shone when he was around, he talked to them–in Norwegian, naturally—and I picked up some words myself."

She grinned at the table raptly drinking in her words.

"Han er stor kar, ikke sant?", she rattled off, to gaping wonder of all non-Norwegians there. "And I don't mean just 'He's a big man, isn't that true?'. I saw in all of his kinfolks' eyes that they looked up to him not only physically, which everybody except those huge Stindt men do"—looking playfully at Anna, who reddened a bit in pride, yet smiled—

"but with admiration for his accomplishments, his bearing, his confident walk, speech, quiet politeness."

The silence around the table was intense. This woman was strong enough to lay her inner self bare without reticence.

"After a few days of it I was humbled, then it struck me that as wonderful as he really is, as all of them realized and showed, he had picked me to share the rest of his life with him.

"So I must be worth more than I'd thought up to then."

She spoke directly to August. "I realized I belonged on this higher plane. And I've changed my name. All my friends can and still will call me Cynara. But my new identity, and I'm happy and proud that it is, is Mrs. Aslak Bergland. That was the best thing I saw in Norway."

Warden Limpert was on his feet, his glass raised: "A toast to a woman we've all admired from a certain distance, who, we find, is even more admirable up close and personal! To Mrs. Aslak Bergland!"

"To Mrs. Aslak Bergland!"—"Our friend Cynara!" added Anna Stindt.

All sat, except the warden. "Shouldn't we hear a few words from her other half?"—and led the polite applause as Aslak stood.

"Of the many qualities of my wife Cynara I admire, one is her ability to speak a few words but say a lot."

He favored the table's audience with his usual half-grin. "Now don't you ladies take that as a dig meaning ladies talk a lot but don't say much!"

A general laugh; he's up to his usual speed!

"So I'll be brief." He cleared his throat.

"The last time I spoke, standing, to a group, was out in Haywire's house on the top of his one and only table, with a jug of moonshine in front of me along with a whole bunch of one-ounce glasses full of moonshine!"

Haywire's chuckle led the rest.

"Believe me, my reason for that contrived load on that table was to demonstrate the policy of yet unfounded Luna Light and now the policy of WARS!"

At this Peter Erikson, the flourishing barely-aged-thirty Ontonagon County attorney led the applause.

"But what did I, we, see or find in Norway. Of course, I was nine when I came here, so mine was more a rediscovery. My heart was warmed by the respect shown me; I made it plain to them that I got my direction right before I left, and I got it from them. I was pleased to see that things were going well back where I was born—though I hoped it wasn't just because I had gone—and I was most pleased that they took to my wife Cynara so well."

He winked broadly at Cynara, so that all could see. "If I'd had any doubts, it was good to see everybody approved. Or maybe it was their relief that somebody with such apparent good sense was now in charge of me."

Laughter at the table was general and continuous.

"Because it is undeniable that the package is well-wrapped; I was glad to see that the contents were approved, no, admired, by more than myself."

Aslak paused.

"I realize I haven't said much about Norway, but, well, it was our honeymoon!"

And sat.

Anna rose during the applause and giggling.

"Since I'm ipso facto the hostess, it's up to me to declare that before the honeyed words get so deep we can't move we should say good-byes and go home—where I and Lillian are already! But to you, Cynara, and you, Aslak, we preface our good-byes with a great big sort of HELLO and glad you're back!"

At which all dozen or so stood in approval, lined up for personal handshakes of acceptance of the pair as Mr. and Mrs Aslak Bergland, then proceeded out into the brisk mid-March afternoon sunshine.

The last one was Sherman Pendock.

He gripped Aslak's huge right paw, laid his own considerable left hand over both.

"Before I aided and abetted your own outlawry with my equipment, and for a while afterwards, I considered myself an empty, spent husk, with nothing, no human company, to share with me whatever I had left. If I had anything left."

He turned to Cynara. "I found some shoring up with the Lord as my new partner, but I wept inside—and sometimes not inside—for lack of a human link, someone…a friend."

Aslak's grip remained firm. On it Cynara, eyes large, laid both her soft smooth hands.

"Your demand I attend your New Year's Eve party turned me up a new path. Being here helps, partly because it broadens the sharing with my new friend Housman, the English poet."

"What special appeal, for you, in his poetry?" asked Cynara

"He's in a strange land, London, far from his west England near Wales, where I'm from, and he misses his friends, feels good remembering people there, often treats this life as just a brief something, something he can bear."

"How did you find out about him?" asked Aslak.

"August told me, and I got a copy of *A Shropshire Lad*—it's just a small book, some sixty-odd short poems—but there's one about meeting a Greek statue of a man, who chides Housman for feeling down when compared to the 'man of stone' who for ages was and for ages will still be here with a parade of people going by him, much more fortunate than he, while he, the statue, has to stay there. It makes it easier for me to feel someone else felt as I do, and when he ends the poem with

> 'Courage, lad, 'tis not for long
> Stand, quit you like stone, be strong'
> So I thought his look would say;
>
> And light on me my trouble lay,
> And I stept out in flesh and bone
> Manful like the man of stone.

I can go out in the timber any time and feel I'm in good company."

He saw a touch of glassy eyes in their expressions. "And the river Severn is very close to my old home—I'm from Wales, so he's a natural companion to start with."

Cynara advised him: "Ask the librarian to order you a copy for you to have, of your own!"

"I have already, and thanks for including me in your gatherings!"

"It's a pleasure," rejoined Aslak, "Remember, I made you a silent partner when I picked up the stills!"

The three made their good-byes to Anna, who stood in the doorway with Lillian Eunice watching the couple who embodied, who reflected, all that citizens of Bergland Township held dear.

"They look just like the 'happy ever after' ending we used to read in our favorite books," mused Anna. "They are both achievers in their own right. She suffered such a huge, tragic loss when Frank was killed out in Topaz. She may become what she deeply desires—a mother—and they both support a way out of the Prohibition curse souring the attitude of the whole country."

No answer from Lillian. The sight of her tears running their slow path down her cheeks choked off any comment from Anna.

They turned inward to their home and their own lives, Anna pulling the door shut.

For August, his own life was now one of admiration for Aslak's ability with words. The once and even still current newsmonger in Bergland Township had held the listeners in his casual, humorous grip, with side glances and remarks, and though the thrust of some remarks was belittling to himself, had plainly elevated his stature by so doing.

"It's easy to see why Cynara looks at him the way she does; he always makes the men admire his facility and Cynara so proud of the envious looks given her by the ladies present!"

Zwei stared at his master. Mirroring his master's gloom, he was silent.

Lillian was 'one of the envious ladies'. Sitting on the edge of her cold bed, one stocking still on, dangling down over her toes.

"Where would I find another like him—and if I did, would he marry me—and if he did, would ...."

"Damn (none to hear)! This bed's cold!!"

When August came to Pikey's place over the hill, now its remodeling was ended, he was surprised.

Left of the door, waist high, was an electricity flip switch; over head, a light.

He turned to Pikey, standing beside him, that half-smile evident.

"You expect somebody to bring electric power out along the Mile Road?"

"Eventually."

But upon entry to the kitchen, his surprise increased to amaze: It would be entirely alight from a ceiling globe, and at his left was a huge white sort of box with a queer object on top twice the size of a human head, horizontal slots ...

Cynara interjected. "Welcome to our new-from-old house and home, August! I see you must be making some apples work for you—you're in overalls!"

"Yah, once they start to ferment I don't need to watch!" He turned, taking in all of the newly-finished huge open space on the first floor. "You don't try to hide the kitchen work from the dining room, and the sitting room is open to all as well!"

Cynara nodded. "We left a few posts in place, covered to look like rounded pillars, since they are load-bearing.

The guided tour of the wide-open downstairs, the only partitions those around the bathroom, up stairs wound around a central pillar to a gated fence around the stairwell top, several bedrooms, one a nursery, views out immense windows, upstairs bath over its mate below, water tank in attic from well just outside, ... a blur of space, conveniences, gracious living... Back on the ground floor the proud new residents and the dazed visitor, here in part to get ideas for his own new house existent so far only hazily in his own mind, sat with coffee cups steaming in the kitchen breakfast booth.

A broad beam of sunlight from the windowed front door lay a golden ramp beside them.

"We hope to have a family of one, maybe two children, if possible at our ages," Cynara began; "Maybe you'd want to scale down, maybe to all on one floor, ground level."

Both men eyeing her, eyebrows slightly higher, she waved two fingers, crossed. "We can always hope!" she smiled widely.

August, his mind once again sharp after the boggling at what he'd just seen, offered a maxim: "If you don't succeed at first, try again!"

Cynara redirected the conversation: "What are your plans?—new house, new life…?"

Aslak emptied his cup. "Ja, what about you?"

August emptied his as well, tipped it on its side on the saucer, handle toward him.

Cynara, as August began hesitantly, searching for meaningful direction, stared at his tipped-over cup. Meant he didn't want more, likely. But what Lillian Eunice had told her in great detail at the New Year's Eve trade of confidences of her 'talk' with Yaga Lulich, with the emphasis of the cup's position between her and Yaga, held Cynara rapt …

"… maybe only one floor, but I liked the tower corner Captain Pabst had on his mansion in Milwauikee, and as for the stone, it may not be that easy to gather—this is good dirt just about everywhere," August finished.

He rose. "Sun's going toward its home, and I need to do the same." He grasped their hands in his as they stood just inside the door, shouldered his pack of food for the week.

"Come back any time," the wedded pair insisted.

"Probably with a sketch pad and tape measure," he replied.

August had some daylight left, pack of food heavy over his shoulder, for the trip up over, down the Spur to Kallaak's Corner, then down and down some more to the still shack on Section Thirty, his home as it had been Aslak's while the new home was created.

"'A hole in the ground, no extra charge'", he muttered. "And no one to bounce ideas off, or offer some help, right from the start."—saying which, he realized how fully Cynara had helped Aslak.

"I've got a bigger cup to fill than Lil had."

Zwei whined, looking up at his master's sagging shoulders, turned down mouth.

Next morning, August sat on one of the few rocks of any size scattered from the blast. Zwei looked down in the hole, yipped, looked up expectantly.

"Nothing but a round hole, empty, Zwei."

Zwei trotted the few steps to the edge, looked down, barked, looked back over his tail.

August rose slowly, hands on knees for a start up. "Ach, Jaa, I look."

A round hole, sides circular, bottom a big round dent in a mix of dirt and yellow clay.

August shrank from estimating how many shovels of dirt he'd—or somebodies—would have to measure for squaring, for leveling the cellar fl ...

Zwei barked, stood on his hind legs, stared up at August's face; when August's eyes met his, Zwei barked his name, and, still leaning his front paws on August's kneecaps, looked over his tail, down into the hole.

"Something down in there?"

Zwei's answer was to drop on all fours, move to where he'd stood, looked down, looked back

"So weiter." August looked down.

"Noth ..." what was that fuzzy little spot of white on the very bottom, center?

Riding his applewood walking stick like a witch's broom down the near side, Zwei tracking, August recognized when he stood still ... A small endtwig of apple branch, two white blossoms, intact, as unfazed as they'd looked before the blast.

When he held it up, facing east toward M64, he saw over the east edge of the hole the nearest edge of his orchard, the twisted, broken edges of branch ends the blast had sheared, cut, blown along that nearest row.

By the end of summer, all of that damage would have been healed, each tree, branch, twig end, back to normal, for its expected, demanded, contribution.

But this fall, his normal harvest, for August's Applejack Brandy, for fifty-dollar bills, for the footing of his new self, would be less...part of the cost for his new house.

The new words floated into his awed awareness.,

On Orchard Edge the trees are troubled;
Some blasted blooms to earth are cast.

How fitting that the sinking sun, cutting a sharpedged shadow across the hole, himself, Zwei—reminding him that he had not much daylight to get to the shack on Section Thirty—should match his despondency!

Zwei shook his entire body as if just emerging from the lake on the empty third forty on the Mile Road.

"Ja, you show me, jawohl! Alles ist in ordnung!" and they both scrambled up out of the hole. August picked up his bag of flour, cans of beans, the rest of what he'd saved for the weeks down in the Luna Light Gang's still shack, and they made their way up out of the only momentary mental depression made real by the actual cellar hole and began their way back to staying alive.

With a tiny kernel of unease still lodged far back, by the cerebellum?

At the top of the hill separating his forty from Aslak's eighty, August stopped to let his breath catch up. Where he stood marked the end of the Mile Road proper, the beginning of the extension straight west, and the beginning of the Mile Road spur running a half mile north, then bisecting Section Thirty downhill westward past Jorginus' homestead shack, now the distillery hidden in a wrap of woodpile, and still more downhill westward paralleling the Mile Road extension down to the edge of the timber and Amundsen's Creek.

To his left in the late twilight was the reworked home of Ole Bergland, Gunlek's brother, now the 'dream' home of Aslak and Cynara, in which he'd spent most of the afternoon in a state of awed admiration.

Now, in envy. To his right and below was his own orchard, damaged—though only slightly—and a hole in the ground, an emptiness in which he was to begin his new home, to suit his lately realized worth.

How much Aslak owed his new home to the impetus provided by Cynara! Not that she did it all, or maybe even not that much, directly, but if not for Cynara, Aslak's home would be unchanged; his time and affection likely to remain focused on his team, his township wanderings.

Faintly, a bare wisp he couldn't bring out for examination, a stirring way down deep in his subconscious. But it vanished.

Zwei was waiting halfway down the slope. The sun was no longer visible, though its light still showed the way.

August got under way. Passing the mares, heads down, cropping what new grass had begin *its new life*, ja, their home was as it always was, given the seasons.

At Kallaak's Corner, he stopped, looked back the way he'd come, turned his head to look west at the spur road, the still shack invisible on the other side of the rise where, if the new well wasn't sucking up all the water, the spring still bubbled over the rock cleft.

His life was already begun in different directions, just as his recent travels. The train trip to Milwaukee, a repeat of his train trip from New York's Ellis Island clearing house; the erasure of his banishment by Skantz, the welcome success of his brandy, product in part due to Gunlek Bergland's generosity, part to his luck, part then to his own persistence.

Now the die cast once more, locking him into a new house, a Grand Avenue sort of place for just himself?

Was he really worth that? Would it overwhelm him, or would he float on top? Would he, as Odysseus had considered, fall off the edge of some new world?

Aslak and Cynara have fashioned a house befitting their stature, their innate quality.

Am I going at it backwards? About to sit in the Siege Perilous? What can I say is my Holy Grail?

Ironically, Pendock, another solitary on *his* edge of the timber, had asked him, August, for some sort of solace. Some of Housman, the sardonic Professor of Latin, hung in the twilight air as August, trying to be glad, clomped after Zwei past Kallaak's Corner:

> Try I will, no harm in trying:
> Wonder 'tis how little mirth
> Keeps the bones of man from lying
> On the bed of earth.

Nothing more from Jim about scale on flat cars. No news good news?

The potbelly stove in the still shack cooling to warm, his and Zwei's stomachs satisfied, the two stills in the addition bubbling away, August slid off his shoes, was nearly asleep, the thought he'd nearly grasped at the top of the hill still in hiding. The first snore he cut off to a snort, turned on his right side.

Outside, the thousands of acres of virgin timber rolled their extent up to and over the creeks, around Lake of the Clouds, over the heights of the Porcupine Mountains to maintain their vigil over the sandy shore of Lake Superior, its waves sliding up over the sand to place the creamy white crests of foam in a narrow, crooked, ribbon, rollllll back.

Chapter Nine

By the end of the first week, April third, he'd squared the surface corners of his cellar hole out to the stakes of a twenty-four-foot-on-a-side square held twine-cord straight. On the first morning, he'd been about to heave up the third shovelful of dirt when he realized the obvious place to dump the dirt: Into the round-bottomed center. Instead of heaving each shovel-full of dirt up over the eight-foot high sides, it became a process of grub-hoeing the dirt out and down to form the corners, then shoving/shoveling it to fill that center depth up to level out at eight feet.

"Not all bend this middle-aged back and heave up until I heave up," reflected the pudgy scholar of Genesis and Housman, looking with less disgust at the dirt-and-sweat streaks on the sleeves of his light blue cotton work shirt. "Mind can still triumph over matter!"

Mind also informed him to get people who built houses to pour the footers, et cetera, et cetera. Then he could get his mini-replica of Captain Pabst's mansion drawn on paper and let that bounce around in his and (maybe Aslak's?) mind.

And water! Got to find water!

In the morning, he cranked the next batch of raw apples through the peeler-slicer-corer, put yesterday's batch in the mix for ferment....

Restful.

Aslak's first act was to run a length of twine, a big loop in its end, diagonally across the cellar square from inside to inside, he holding the looped end in place, August the other.

"With your other hand," he directed August, "tie a loop about the same size as mine."

They transferred both loops to the other two corners, crossing the first diagonal's passage with twine, keeping it taut once in place.

"You're lucky today, August! Both of these identical in length means your cellar hole is perfectly square!"

August darted into his 'factory', came back with a jug of his Applejack Brandy.

"My decision is to stop while I'm ahead. Here, let's each celebrate my success with a glass!"

Arms crossed in the European fashion, they raised their glasses. August downed his; Aslak took his empty glass, put his own, still full, in that now empty fist.

"I don't drink any, you know that. But what comes next, if you stop now.?"

August grinned. "You tell me of a good builder, I'll pay him well to put up the home I have in mind!"

"Don't start him out with this brandy—you'll never get him to start work!"

Aslak lapsed into serious mien. "In the meantime, take your wheelbarrow, the one you wheel in the apples with, collect all the rocks down to gravel size around here, dump them down into the bottom of the hole, get 'em fairly level down there. I'll bring out Floyd Marsh, he'll get his crew, your house will get going."

Floyd Marsh looked again at the rock-strewn bottom of the hole, at the sketch in his hand, back at August.

"What's this in front? A chimney?"

"No, it's a circular staircase—goes up to a viewing deck with a roof on it."

Floyd turned the sketch this way, that way.

"Looks a lot like a low barn with a silo."

Struck by the words, August answered with what he saw in his mind.

"Make it a hip-roofed barn, to fit the cellar hole, with a silo on the right front with a door inside, circular staircase up inside the silo, cap roof over a viewing deck on top."

"What about the floor plan? The partitions inside? Insulation? Wallboard?"

"No partitions, but insulation and wallboard, yes—but wired for electricity, buried from across the Mile Road, 200-amp board in the cellar."

Floyd thought about it, but thought it best not to say what he thought. This would be his biggest job so far, and the Depression wasn't gone yet.

He turned to go. No use talking—August was staring at the air above the cellar hole.

He reached for the gate latch, looked down and back to make sure that mean little dog wasn't about to speed him on his way with a nip on his ankle.

"One thing more," August called. "Brick the outside, stone for the silo!"

Floyd stared in surprise, Zwei, reader supreme of body language, took it wrong this time, sank his sharp little teeth in just above the shoe top, right ankle, leaped back from the sure attempt to kick him.

But there was no response, nor "Sorry!" from August still wrapped in his vision of what was to be above the cellar hole.

Shaking his head, Floyd Marsh felt a bit of a squush in his right shoe as he slammed his truck door, gunned on down the Mile Road.

Knew, though, that he'd be back with some cinder blocks, a few bags of cement.

He was a builder. That's what builders did.

What August did, when the vision faded, was pick up the wheelbarrow handles, add some of the pieces of house lying around to the load of rocks, tip it all down into to level out the cellar floor base.

Every little bit helps.

Zwei, his job done for the day, lay down to watch, lick a bit of blood off his chops.

Aslak was waiting when Zwei and August traipsed into the still shack on Section Thirty.

"Cynara is having a WARS meeting this evening, so I thought I'd come down and socialize with the tired-out laborer," he greeted August, his hand about to tap August's shoulder. He dropped it back to his belt buckle at the sight of weariness in his gang member's face and demeanor.

"Have a seat. I've brought all the mash and stills up to date, checked the oil burners; the stove is ready for whatever you plan for your supper."

Zwei curled up at August's feet as his master sank down on the side of the cot.

"In fact," Aslak continued, "I'll heat up whatever you tell me you want from the shelf over there. How about some Campbell's soup with a nice crust of graham bread?"

August waved a hand weakly, croaked, "That'll be fine."

When the soup had worked its nourishing magic, Zwei lay nosing around where his hamburger patty had lain, and August inhaled appreciatively at the brandy snifter (yes, the shack now knew a few of the crystal-and-linen sort of amenities!), Aslak, still in the grip of his perpetual news-gathering mode, asked,

"So what did Floyd have to say when you told him what you wanted?" August flexed his arms, stretched with a twist of his torso, sat up straighter.

"He thinks I'm a bit off, like most of the township folks have thought all these years," smiled August, the usual gleam back in his yellowish eyes. "When he saw the sketch, he said, 'What's this, a chimney?' and when I told him it was to be a viewing tower—you know how this Mile Road slopes down out to M64—with a circular staircase inside, and a door inside so I could go up without going outside—he looked at me, back at the sketch, I could see he was trying not to say what he thought!"

"Then he let it out: 'Looks like a low barn with a silo!'"

He reached down to pat Zwei's predator's head, pointed ears, pointy muzzle. "But even though Zwei bit Floyd's ankle as he reached for the gate, I guess Floyd'll be back with some cinder blocks and cement. And higher boots!"

August reached around behind himself, pulled the canvas back support up tight, leaned back, stockinged feet off the floor.

Sipped at his brandy, rolled it around, inhaled carefully, swallowed. "Aaah."

Aslak tipped up one of the empty barrels they'd boiled the mash in at the beginning of the venture, eased his weight down.

"What about the inside?

"I told him to make it a hiproofed barn square on the cellar limits and a silo on the right front, sheetrock over insulation on the inside, no partitions, wire in a 200-amp board."

August chuckled, his belly wiggling. "I guess that was when Zwei saw his chance. Floyd was distracted on his way to his truck, so Zwei showed him he needed to keep an eye on the palace guard dog!"

Aslak echoed the chuckle. A fine story this would make on his round tomorrow, though he was now, a married man, cut back to a mere two-three days a week on his visits; on a given Sunday it was he and Cynara, dropping in, always welcomed, those farm or town homes they visited eager to share the news next day with their neighbors.

"But you know, Pikey, there was more to it for me. If you are ready to go, I'll save it for some other time…"

"Not in any hurry. Cynara's meeting won't be over until around 9; I'll pick her up then."

The first words didn't come easily. Where to begin?

"You remember I was a student in Germany, read a lot then, still have my best books in the stove oven down in your barn. One of the men I read with my teachers and some of my fellow students was Immanuel Kant, who wrote a lot about what can we know and how we should make laws to follow, guide our lives."

Not the best opening; he could see mere polite interest in Aslak's eyes. Get to it.

"Another man, a Scot named Thomas Carlyle, picked up the same sort of thinking, wrote a book called *Sartor Resartus*, Latin for 'the tailor re-tailored' about how we put on ideas and behavior and civilization as we do clothes, dress up the naked ape we were born as, as if to cover up our base selves, forget working the ground for food, wear special clothes for sleeping, build ourselves all sorts of creature comforts in a house, and all of that. You follow that?"

"I follow that."

"What I saw when Floyd seemed doubtful about the kind of house I wanted, I looked over the cellar hole and saw shelter, but with as little fancy decoration, trinkets, fooforaw, cover me for why? Just to show—like the suit, shirt, tie, gold stuff I wear now in town to show others I'm making money with brandy!"

"But it is good—just the smell gives me a tiny lift," Aslak declared.

"My point exactly: See how far we've come from just eating an apple! Now instead of reading the *Farmer's Almanac,* coming in today from getting a show house started instead of from planting potatoes, I'm putting on clothes a long way from how people used to live."

Aslak crossed his legs the other way. "You think maybe we should be more like Zwei—grow hair, lick our paw pads clean, bite, fight, and so forth?"

August sat up, put his now dry-socked feet on the cold floor. "I know that is not possible, even if it were desirable. I just see we think and busy ourselves with a lot of stuff that isn't really life sustaining, and make a living, make money, doing it!"

"Not much we can do about it, August. We're caught up in it like everybody else."

"Look at Sherm Pendock! Worked his way up to taking it easy by wringing whisky out of corn—something planted to eat, not boil, ferment, boil some more, condense the steam, drink moonshine to alter the mind—then got so lonesome for friends he found companionship in the written angst—ja, *angst*—of a fellow near-Welshman, and goes out in the timber to talk to trees!"

Zwei lay still, apparently asleep, no inkling of such self-induced problems.

Aslak checked his watch, snapped it closed, slid it back into its shirtpocket.

"It'll be nine soon. Get a good night's sleep." His 'tap' on August's shoulder was gentle, kind. August fell back, eyelids fluttered, closed.

Pikey flipped the blanket over August's clothed body, adjusted the draft and damper on the wood-burning potbelly stove, closed the door quietly on two tired sleepers.

To avoid the many sharp stubs in the wood path, he rocked his strides up the Spur, around Kallaak's Corner, up past his softly nickering team of blue-black mares, got his Model A black sedan moving up and over the hill on the Mile Road.

Passing the now invisible new hole where August's home had been, he mused, half to himself,

"His brain is sure full, though."

Almost by itself, his black Model A sedan turned right on M64, taking Aslak to town and his Cynara.

"She fills both mind and heart."

Poor rich man August. Was there such a thing as being *too well educated?*

Carlyle, Kant—first name *Imannuel!* Had either of them ever planted a potato? There

She

IS!

Cynara plumped herself into the seat, gorgeous figure, gorgeous face, all lit up with joy to be with her man, wonderful perfume!

"Now this car has the right number of passengers," Aslak asserted, "even if it's still sitting motionless.!"

"But not *e*-motionless!" answered Cynara, tilting to smooch his cheek. "Now take us to that wonderful new home we have all to ourselves until tomorrow morning!"

This time, going past August's hole in the ground, Aslak's gaze, split between Cynara's self and the road, didn't reach that far.

This was what living was all about!

Next morning, topping the hill, they joined August, coming up from the Section Thirty shack, and Haywire, coming from his house near M64 to take the day shift at that shack. So it was a fivesome—six, counting Zwei—stopping to greet, trade a few words back and forth.

Just a few; Cynara looked at her wristwatch, tapped her husband's arm, pointed at the time. Aslak dipped his head. The black Model A sedan spat back a few pieces of gravel. The couple in their chariot sped down the hill for Bergland and the post office.

Haywire's chuckle lacked its usual volume and merry overtone.

"Somet'ing I never..."

August matched his eye-lock on the black Model A, both seeing what was inside, not the car.

"But you, still young, not old camp cook like me!" he jabbed his elbow into August's well-padded side, "What 'bout you?"

"I like riding in a car, but as for getting my own—huh-uh!" August claimed.

Now Haywire's chuckle was back to itself, the twinkle in the eyes, too.

"You t'ink I mean car—oh, no—you jus' foolin'!"

The tease by Haywire, the image of those two, though the car was now out of sight, snapped the wayward thought he'd been unable to call full forth before: Lillian's eyes, faded blue, locked onto his, pulling him into her, that night at Marko's, she holding the sandwich tray. Her eyes seeking help?

Ur-woman, offering. The language: Ur-sprache. That primitive aspect, before what came from the much later culture, Latin, *civilis*, civilization.

What he'd protested to Aslak in the shack last evening, brought on by what kind of a house he wanted, his dressing up in a suit in Milwaukee to fit his self-image, what he showed to others he thought of himself.

Fortunately, so he could get on with life in the present culture, what Aslak had claimed we are all caught up in, no escape, the next image he saw of himself in Milwaukee, bare naked, his chest hairy, his fists pounding his chest, daring all men to attack him, showing women he could protect them….

He laughed out loud at the ridiculous self image. His sight in the present, standing in the early morning in spring atop Aslak's Hill on the Mile Road. That was real!

Haywire was halfway down the Spur toward Kallaak's Corner.

"He gave up on me, saw me in a world apart, I guess!"

Zwei, looking back up the hill from August's tattered gate, barked his name: Yip yip!

He's adjusted, the little beast; even a primitive accepts the need to get on with what you must do! Entering, postponing the check on his apple ferment of yesterday to make sure the cellar surface was close to level, August took the garden rake with him down into the hole.

Show Floyd Marsh a half-batty 'Cher-man' could be sensible to the demands of house building!

Floyd, never mind the ankle nip from Zwei, brought not only cinder blocks and cement, but clean sand and two strong-backs for the heavy manual foundation work needed to base a house soundly, through dry and wet, hot and cold. Also, he had enough scrap lumber, 2x4s mostly, for framing the footers—basically a flat-bottomed ditch about six inches deep around the bottom rim of the cellar hole. On this, when bone-hard, with half-inch steel reinforcing rods throughout its length, would rest the beams on which the 2x4 frame of the house would rise; on these the house would be unaffected by the changes in temperature; the UP was known for extremes of July heat and January freeze.

It was plain he wasn't needed at the building site. Floyd and his two helpers went about framing and mixing the cement for the footers, built a ramp down which the wheel-barrows could move up and down into and out of the cellar, pour the cement into the framing, go back up empty for more. The cement was liquid enough to seek its own level, so insuring that the house foundation was not only square, but level.

So August felt free to work on his applejack production. All of those apples from last fall, kept cool underground in the apple cellar, had to begin the pomace/juice process, make room for the surge of apples coming in the fall. He closed the door behind him, though moonshining was much less an operation to be done in secret since most expected to see the last of Prohibition. Zwei found all of that peeling, fermenting, proofing just too boring, so he busied himself with periodic rounds of the property, reading all of the scent bulletin boards on his way, then setting up to supervise the building activities of two Hill brothers and Floyd Marsh.

In fact, spring was the wrong season for making applejack brandy; distillation to make brandy was beyond August's capability. That's why 'jacking' up the 'proof' or alcoholic strength of hard cider by skimming off the successive frozen water skins atop the cider was called apple 'jack'; it was simple to do, but required nights of freezing cold.

But August could prepare for the freezing cold nights of fall and winter in the UP by making as much cider as he could find containers for. The longer it fermented under its own power, the higher the alcoholic kick; if not of the required thirty-eight percent by fall, skimming off the ice would 'jack up' the cider to brandy strength.

As always, upon entry to his factory, August would enjoy observing the efficiency of its layout, insuring that equipment and work space for each successive step in the process was next in line, beginning with the door nearest the Mile Road, the south side, which would keep his fall supply of apples, reaching in bins nearly to the ten-foot high ceiling, from freezing before being peeled, then ground into the pomace (mush), squeezed to juice, with the finished cider on the north side, for necessary 'jacking' to the desired strength, proof, each morning by skimming off the water frozen on top in each container.

The shorter south side west of the door and the west end itself was completely shelved, for storing the casks, when ready for market, near the Mile Road.

Thus none of the steps from storage, peeling, grinding to pomace, storing the squeezed juice fermenting into cider, then, still on the north or cold side, for jacking, would necessitate criss-crossing, extra steps; nor would the proper sequence of steps be passed over. The next step was there waiting the completion of the step just prior. Those bushels of apples left over when each step of above ground was filling all of his barrels for fermenting, 'jacking', would go down into the cellar under the east end for their retrieval later when there was room for their processing.

Just what he was doing now.

And a soft-tired wheeled dolly joined its several mates in front of the bins. August had not only been impressed by the work ethic he'd witnessed at the breweries in Milwaukee. He'd noted as well the same sort of work sequence layout.

Work didn't mean the same thing as *labor!*

How orderly it all was! August was aware of the focus on system, on orderliness, imputed to Germans—in fact, the proper response, when asked by a superior about whatever the situation was, was 'Alles ist in ordnung, Herr so-and-so!'

"I wonder if that is what we are supremely confident about, or if we are so fearful lest things not be 'in order'? In all this change from solitary brandy maker through new clothes and traveling and identifying my new stature with the new house, I'd guess the word 'fearful' suits!

With the next batch peeled, mashed, squeezed, the juice fermenting, August tilted his chair back, balancing on the rear legs, teetered a bit. The saws, hammers, scrapes of lumber in spurts of noise, the pauses and then floods of words—'the other way!'—'get the thing level' barely understandable behind him sagged beneath his awareness.

He forced his thoughts into order.

What had caused the shift—don't call it progress—from hairy dwellers going hungry, then feasting when food was found or killed, freezing during the Ice Age or Ages, traveling when the globe, for whatever reason, turned warm, greenery flourished, small game abounded,

To groups living more or less in harmony, interrupted by periods of fighting others of their own ilk for safety when attacked, for sole rights of hunting, fishing, root gathering, from following clement weather, to staying in one place, modifying their shelter, their dress, their diets to the seasons? From focus on self, survival, taking, to the present of providing for others whose support, either in goods or money, fostered that same survival?

From the focus on body needs, demands for food, comfort the primal concern, procreation, bristling when challenged by others driven by the same concerns?

What culture allowed men such as Kant, Carlyle, to make their primary concern one's relationship with other persons?

Specifically, why was he intent on having the home he'd directed Floyd to build for him?

"To thine own self be true"

Polonius's words to his son Laertes.

Until I saw what Captain Pabst lived in, that towered mansion on Grand Avenue, I gave no thought to what I lived in. It suited me fine—didn't bother me, hardly noticed it, that the house I lived in was the worst-looking on the Mile Road.

An answer in disconnected parts floated in the air about him, then coalesced into a sentence he allowed in order to 'be true':

Your own success, garnering the esteem of others, drives you to live in a house that will garner you more esteem of others because it supports your own image of self.

Self gratification.

An adult version, modified by culture, which began by sucking your mother's teat. In a culture which, at least for a time, focused on discussing such questions as "What can we know? What is real?" Kant and Carlyle built themselves houses—of renown, not brick.

Kant: Act as if the maxim of your action were to become by your will a universal law of nature.

Carlyle: Do the duty which lies nearest thee.

In both of these, reflected August, there is an ambiguity that bears questioning: 'by your will' is ambiguous in that having done the act, you then may or may not by an act of will make your maxim a universal law which all must obey OR, that by your will to do the act you have already made it a universal law of nature. If that is the meaning, then hesitance to do the act can be expected, so that the act may never be done. Macbeth, when his wife hands him the knife with which he is to kill the king, asks "But what if I should fail?"

And Hamlet weighs the virtue of 'To be' against 'not to be'.

In Carlyle's maxim, one has first to determine which duty lies nearest. The suggested import of the maxim could be that, while striving to determine which duty lies nearest, taken to mean in time? Or to what other concept of responsibility? As a man, or as a police man, or ??

OR, just as with Kant's dictum, hesitance ensues, and nothing is done because what is 'nearest' may be indeterminable, so the time or chance to do the 'nearest' duty may pass, with no recall. In Chaucer's time Fortune was given the 'figure' of a woman whose hair was all gone from the back of her head; once past you, there was nothing by which to hold her from disappearing.

The sounds of busy building kept up their hum behind August. How common here in this adopted country was the assumption that the job in progress was to be done with as little delay as possible; sitting down to discuss a question not directly related to pouring the footers would not occur, much less happen, to Floyd and his two helpers!

So how much of an outsider was he, August Schmidt, then?

If what lay nearest to him was to ponder his reason for wanting, thinking he *needed*, a house reflecting his own sense of his own personal worth, then was he out of place here, should be back in the Palatinate, in the European culture of viewing Kant's and Carlyle's pronouncements while the unpoured cement hardened, the footers something that could wait?

What kept him from rising, from confronting Floyd, stopping his building, was the sight of the barrel he'd just filled with peeled apples' juice preparing for the next applejack supply. Fermentation was already underway.

He'd accepted, had acted upon, that same American idea of keeping the wheels turning. In so doing he was following another dictum of Kant's: '…rational beings must determine for themselves a set of laws by which they will act'.

It was Kant's so-called Categorical Imperative that suggested one must consider other humans as ends, not means. Not like a cave man, whose focus was entirely upon self, make use of other humans as means to an end.

'So act as to treat humanity, whether in your own person or in that of any other, in every case as an end in itself, never as means only.'

Which one of August's teachers had been quick to cite as a re-wording of the well-known dictum in the Christian Bible: 'Love thy neighbor as thyself.'(Lev. 19.18) Which, August mused as the hammering and sawing continued behind him, also had its own provoking ambiguity: One must love oneself in order to love a neighbor. And could the phrase 'love oneself' be construed as 'a good self-image'? Or was that the sin of pride? In my own culture, my own experience, ministers seemed intent upon not only preaching that this world is far inferior to Heaven (even though Heaven's streets may be described as paved with gold in the song 'O, dem golden slippers'!), but that mortal man must believe in God and do his work in order to be worthy of God's saving grace—i.e., we are of little worth else?

Be that as it may, that man's focus must shift from self gratification to respect for others seems plain.

Once again, in a world of his own thought into which the noises of building could not penetrate, August said to himself:

"Another way of saying this about my house-to-be: It will serve as not only a monument to my success, but as an example, an urge—even a universal law?—that, work as I have, and you may live as I live, in a house like mine."

Just so might one consider the Luna Light Gang endeavor: Yes, it was begun as a means for members to earn cash in the Depression, also in order to preserve the great timber riches—yes, for lumber = money, but also as a way of observing God's greatness in its creation, if that was in conformance with one's Christianity, but even for pagans the presence of that great expanse of majestic conifers or hardwood initiated a feeling of reverence, worthwhile in itself, valuable, as it was to Sherman Pendock, for spiritual uplift.

So thinking well of myself, deserving a marvelous house, *is* self-gratification, *and* it allows me to love viewers of it, inspiring perhaps the work to earn one like it. Just as the Luna Light Gang, of which I am a member, conditions drinkers to restrain self-abuse by enjoying the first drink, eschewing the second.

And somewhere, likely, is another maxim: The laborer is worthy of his hire!

Thesis: House beneficial—to me, to an 'us' (if!), to community harmony/goal.

Anthesis: House detrimental—to me, to an 'us', to community vexation/insult

Synthesis: House neutral? Create discussion of value to me, us, community?

Assuming rational approach—OR emotional violence, antipathy at best?

Silence outside. A glance at his watch: noon. I'll go out and sit down with them, see what they have to say about my house.

Herman Hill, his younger brother Harold, sat with Floyd Marsh, each on an upended small keg of nails, an opened lunch pail beside them, a pot of coffee suspended over a small trash fire in front of them, on the far, north side of the cellar hole. August brought his cake of corn bread still in its square tin and a bottle of Miller's Lager over to join them, used a stack of two-by-fours for seat and table, facing the cellar hole as they did.

Floyd spoke to answer a question he thought might arise.

"I know the footer frame seems to be diving down a bit into the rise of your land into the hill. But that's because the lay of the land goes up toward the top of the big hill, just like the Mile Road going uphill, and our eyes are pulled the opposite way by the footer frames."

"I hadn't seen that until you mention it," replied August, the Hill brothers remaining silent—Floyd was the boss, what he said they wouldn't gainsay.

Floyd popped the last part of a pork sandwich into his mouth, without asking seized the tin of corn bread, dumped the cake which August had made in it on the still shack stove top last evening out on the two-by-four table-top in front of August, from the pail of drinking water dipped a dipperful of water into the empty tin, strode down the ramp, placed the tin of near-brimful water across the nearest corner of the footer frame in plain sight ten feet away.

"Keep your eye on that tin for a minute," Floyd claimed. "You'll see that the water stays level."

August made no reply.

"We went to the highest point, the highest corner, made the footer frames level with that corner," Floyd went on, intent on making the man paying him for the work have no doubts about its quality.

"How did you make certain of that?"

Floyd reached for his tool array, came up with a sort of stick about half as tall as himself.

"See that little bubble under the glass right here?"

August nodded at the sight of the bubble slipping around as Floyd moved the piece of wood.

"This is called a 'level', because if you lay it like this," Floyd laid the level on the stack of two-by-fours next to

August's bottle of Miller's Lager, "where the bubble is tells you how to move the board to move the bubble to the inside of the two lines on the glass, see?"

Floyd lifted the end of the top two-by-four, his other hand holding the bottle of Miller's. August saw the bubble slide between the two lines graven in the middle of the glass.

"We leveled the footer frames from the high corner; now we're pouring the cement, wet nearly as water, into the frames. Like water, it slides to the lowest part, rises from there to the top of the frames, then keeps moving. When it's all full, the top of the cement is level with what was the highest corner of the hole's bottom; when it's hardened by tomorrow morning, the base, the foundation, of your house will be level, and since we square with this"—he held up the square—"as we go up, and check the plumb also with the level held vertical along the studs, your house will be level, square, and plumb. Not leaning in any direction," he finished.

August nodded. "Both the cake tin and the level do the same thing."

"But the level is a lot handier, and we can't use the cake tin for plumb."

August saw something more. "And you use the law of gravity, water always seeking its own level, to move the cement to where you want it." Floyd eyed the plump brandy maker with new respect. "I'd heard you were a smart man!"

"Like you and building, I make the best use I can of what I've got." Floyd fished the folded, wrinkled sketch out of the zippered chest pocket of his overalls.

"Tell me why you want the tower on the corner…what will you see from the top, here?"

August put the last piece of his cornbread down on the stack of two-by-fours, his table.

The three house builders sat, waiting. What he said they'd likely spread around, enjoy having their own audience.

August cleared his throat with a double-glug from the Miller's Lager bottle, was careful to set it down, wouldn't tip while his eye was off it.

"You have a rough idea of how many roofs you've been up on, finishing off to keep a house, a building, dry inside?"

Herman, Harold, Floyd all looked at each other, eyes widening, self-conscious grins starting.

"Okay, I'll put it this way: Can you remember any single roof you came down from without having stopped, put your hammer down, just looked around from a high place?"

Their eyes emptied while their minds searched as best they could.

While their minds fluttered over the two-part question—'How many?' 'Any one?'

August emptied his Miller's, leaned it against the side of his table, on the ground.

"What I'm going to see from there what's from here out east away the hell-and-gone past M64 to maybe the Norwich Mine or partway to the Little Nonesuch or just a lot of land, some bare, some timbered, and enjoy the chance."

Their eyes, alive again, came back to him.

"And I'll have a ladder, an inside ladder, up to *above* my rooftop to do it!"

Their heads bobbed in acknowledgment. They'd been there. They understood.

Floyd looked into August's eyes, then rose, gestured away from the hole.

"Take a few steps with me, get something straight you might not know."

What can this be? August thought. Will he refuse to build such a crazy house?

Out of the boys' hearing, Floyd said softly,

"You have a bad enemy in Bergland. Frank Cutler tells me, 'Don't build any house for that damn German. We just got done killin' a bunch of them Krauts and now this fat one is trying to lord it over the rest of us'."

August stood stone-faced. Floyd glanced back the Hill brothers. "I told him I'm a builder, your money is just as good as anybody's, and I got a family t'feed."

Floyd crinkled up the waxed paper from his meal.

"Sort these two-bys by length, men. So we don't have to handle 'em over and over looking for what we need."

He turned back.

"He cussed at me, then. He says, 'Build it so it falls, or leans over bad. We gotta drive them Krauts outa here.'"

August looked away; Floyd laid a hand on his shoulder.

"I'll make your house exactly the way you want it and it's s'posed to be. But you keep an eye out for Frank. He can be a mean bastard, talks good to get folks on his side."

August studied Floyd's expression.

"I want you to go ahead what you've begun."

Floyd turned, returned to the job.

"Good, keep 'em sorted that way."

There it is, August thought, simple as that. Get the lumber arranged to assist in orderly material selection. While I am the ridiculously analytical academic, continually reflecting on symbols like the way we can be sure my house is square, level and plumb to prolong its existence while doing what it is supposed to, but our own values, our own certainties, our own actions are impossible to prepare, test, maintain for permanence. And all of my thoughts of such significance (?) change the house not one whit!

August picked up his empty Miller's Lager bottle, tossed it in the trash barrel, an empty 55-gallon steel drum up on end. Zwei stopped, marked it for a bulletin-board for any passing stranger four-foot to read and beware not even a foot above ground. What was to be seen from a rooftop, a viewing tower, was none of his concern. Tending to what went on where he walked, that was his job.

His maxim: Right makes might.

Chapter Ten

Next morning, Wednesday, April 12th, August left off apple peeling when Floyd Marsh and the Hill brothers pulled through his gate.

Do this before they get started.

"You start earlier'n we do," noted Floyd. At August's sober face, he halted. "What's on your mind, Dut—August?"

August pointed at his factory door. "Come in, we talk more about house."

"Sure thing. Wow! This is how you make it, huh?"

August pulled out a couple of old milking stools, there when he took over, set them side by side just inside the door, sat, waved Floyd to the other.

"I hear yesterday many banks are closing, I need to have your estimate of how much you need from me to build this house"

Floyd leaned toward August, elbows on his knees.

"I was surprised when we didn't talk this over before we started. Are you planning on taking a mortgage on your land to pay for the house?"

"That word is Germanic in origin. 'Gage' is German for 'pledge', 'mort' is Latin for 'death'—like 'kill me if I don't keep my promise'! I don't think I will, but we need to agree on your pay, I think?"

"Absolutely, August! My usual rate is $5 per square foot. Let's see, 24X24 equals—576 square feet, one floor, right?"–August nodded—"times five equals just under three thousand. I have to guess at the tower—maybe five hundred dollars-I say, estimate, around $3,500. Depending what wiring, water, so forth, maybe another couple hundred."

He looked up from his figuring, his eyes asking the question.

August smiled, now at ease. "No mortgage. I pay you a thousand cash today, more when you say. Is deal?

Floyd stood, offered his hand, August stood, they shook. "Deal!"

Halfway out the door, Floyd turned back. "I'll get Aslak to haul out some loads of two x sixes, more two by fours, boards,–we'll finish the cinder block cellar today and go up higher, couple more weeks and we can puzzle out the tower. Still a deal?"

"Ja, ja, still a deal!"

August sat on his work bench, picked up another apple for the peeler. He heard Floyd's directions to Herman and Harold, then his truck start, pull up the hill toward Aslak and Cynara's. Might catch them before the daily trip into the Post Office.

A day begun early is well begun!

An hour later, his barrel of apple pomace pressed to juice, August sat to light up his meerschaum, realized he hadn't heard Floyd's truck coming back, nor Aslak's black Model A go by. No sooner had that thought surfaced when he heard some wheels—a wagon!—coming down the hill, the measured hoofbeats of–must be Aslak's team!—

What he'd never seen: Aslak's team of blue-black mares, the wagon, Aslak's huge freight wagon, behind them *and on the seat Aslak and Floyd with Cynara squeezed between them* Cynara's shining face, white gleaming teeth smiling, both hands waving HELLO to August's stunned face, the meerschaum forgotten in his hand!

"Can't stop!" Aslak asserted. "Got to get the wife to work, pick up your lumber!"

Zwei opened his jaws, but no snarl came out. Dog and master watched the team of mares, the rumbling wagon, seat jammed with merry riders, disappear down the Mile Road.

August turned to resume with the apples, realized the juice would ferment just as fast if he weren't watching, saw Harold following Herman around the top row of cinder blocks marking the top of the cellar walls, Herman laying the solid four-inch cap blocks on which the two-by-six planks, on edge, forming the channel for wiring and water pipes, and the foundation for the upper story, would rest.

Like most immigrants, not familiar with banking, and twice shy of the risk of banking, what with the apparent weakness of banks, August had kept his money first under the couch on which he slept, then down at the still shack lent them on Section Thirty.

So off he went, up to the top of the hill from which the Mile Road Spur went north, then west to the still shack, with Zwei eyeing the Mile Road ditches for targets alongside. August trudged down around Kallaak's Corner, past the rocky cedar clump knoll where the spring water rose to flow through the pipe Stanko Bositch had laid into the woodpile façade behind the still shack to the stills.

Inside the one-room shack, at the bottom of the barrel filled with loose corn kernels, lay August's treasure of fifty-dollar bills. With his hands elbow-deep in corn, counting by what he felt with his fingers, he came up with twenty bills, some yellowish dust to blow off.

Probably the only bills of any denomination in America with the pleasant slight odor of ripe corn. August, ever attentive to details, had planned to store his money up where he did the work of earning them, pleased with the idea of money with the odor of apples, from being stored in an apple barrel; but when Aslak promised to blow up his house, it seemed wiser to keep his wealth where he slept; hardly ever did anyone go by Section Thirty, while a bit more traffic went by on the Mile Road proper.

Storing the bills in the corn barrel reflected August's efficiency (he earned the money), the decision to hide it where he slept his caution, and the idea of spending money which would astonish its recipients with its unique aroma his penchant for individuality.

Though August recognized that modern man clothed himself, body *and mind*, in ways that tended to deny his animal self, he fearlessly created his visible self to his own satisfaction. It has been said that people tend to keep pets which resemble the owner. Like Zwei, August had no doubts of his role, though he greeted even strangers with a smile, Zwei with a snarl. The little cloud that followed August was still shadowing him: What might Skantz be working up to? No news is bad news?

As August proceeded to a lonely site to engage in secrecy, gathering money, the wagon-load which had passed him at his gate made no bones about their entry into Bergland to spend money. In fact, word of the coming once again of Aslak's team had preceded them by a few minutes by word of mouth—beginning as they rolled by the bench warmers on a fine early spring morning outside of Piper's Garage at the intersection of M64 and M28.

Nick Anderson burst inside Piper's to call Earl Brismaster at the Trading Post, on Bergland's main(Pine) Street.

And as always, everyone in any building on East-West Center Street, and from the inter-section of Center with Pine, be it residence or business, was standing on the sidewalks of those streets to observe and admire Aslak's wonder team.

And to keep optimistic about somebody building something in the Depression

Aslak, reins in hand, wore his usual half-grin; Floyd, well aware of the accolade this team had enjoyed in the past, waved in acknowledgment to his town neighbors, plainly delighted to be a part of this mini-parade; Cynara, delighted to be seen in her husband's company almost as much as being in his company, smiled and waved with abandon, with a small dipping of those golden curls to the few whistles of male appreciation.

And the two beautiful behemoths making the parade possible pretended to be unaware!

As the team moved past the tag end of spectators, the people kept pace, stepping onto the road behind the wagon as the sidewalk proved too narrow for more followers. By the time the team turned the corner for the last block of Pine Street before crossing the railroad tracks to enter the lumber yard, the would-be watchers from both stores, both saloons, and various buildings from as far away as Anna Stindt's Hotel and, believe it or not, the ball park at the western end of Center Street, the crowd was too tightly packed for any movement.

So they stood and awaited the in-yard movements of Aslak's miracle team of blue-black mares, the furthest away craning to find a view not blocked by the heads in front.

When the front wheels of the wagon were even with the Post Office door, the team, with no audible command, nor any minuscule tightening of the reins in Aslak's hands, stopped to allow Cynara off into her Post Office.

Her debark was not simple nor swift. Aslak shifted left to the very edge of the seat,

Cynara then stepped cautiously down to stand on the single thill or drawbar going from wagon front axle to the team's collar loops.

There Cynara stopped, left hand supported in Aslak's left paw.

Two problems:

The only open ground to which she might hop was directly in front of the wagon wheel.

And her door, opening outward, was blocked by that same press of people.

"I guess I'll have to go into the yard with you," she trilled up at her husband.

But Earl Brismaster, Trading Post owner-manager, after years of hopeful waiting, watching this avatar of Venus walk past the store window, saw his chance.

Elbowing standees roughly aside, he plowed his portly bulk to stand in front of the wagon wheel, hold up his arms:

"Just lean over into my arms; I'll clear a path for us, get your door open, the wagon can proceed," Earl trumpeted over the clamoring crowd.

Earl's fantasy was realized when Cynara, seeing her husband's expression of 'Go ahead!' stepped, leaned, was caught, and in that embrace, carried to her miraculously opened door. The actual embrace, though utilitarian, fulfilled the fantasy of years!

And the team, with no audible nor visual command, stepped out as one, to a huge exhale of wonderment from the witnesses.

Across the railroad tracks into the yard went team and wagon with all deliberate speed.

The yard boss ordered the huge swinging gate shut behind the wagon.

"Can't do any loading work with all you people cluttering up the aisles," he roared atthose relatively few onlookers who, allowed entry behind the wagon, informed the crowds who filled Big Marko's Tavern, Archie Lackie's Saloon, Anna's Hotel Bar when the team, wagon loaded with lumber, had disappeared west on M-28, turned up north on M-64.

Nick Anderson, constable, head of the DSS&A section crew, Bergland VIP in size and mien, held forth in Big Marko's Tavern while Yaga plied the drinkers with roasted pork sandwiches, seized by voracious eaters, listened to the deeds of the wondrous team.

"I saw it, so I'll have to tell it straight, though I know it's hard to believe. Aslak sat talking to Floyd Marsh, not even looking where the team was headed. They went straight ahead down the main aisle between piles to the T. Had to go left or right."

Nick paused, stuffed half of his sandwich in under his bristly white thick mustache, went on with the chewing, swallowing, enjoying the suspense.

"The team made as wide a swinging turn as they could, blowing sawdust off the courses of lumber even with their nostrils, and the front wheels of the wagon scraped the same piles, only lower down, near the end of the turn. The rear end of the wagon cleared the pile on the other side by a yard, at least, finishing the turn to the left."

Nick swallowed the last of his mouthful. "I wasn't watching Aslak's hands on the reins. Bill here was doing that: Tell 'em, Bill."

Piper filled in: "One finger on Aslak's left hand moved like this"—Bill held out his left hand, palm up, imaginary reins in the cup of fingers—"the first finger moved like this, a quarter of an inch toward his thumb, the mares began the turn!"

The listeners, the foam in their draft beers near the bottom, voiced their delight.

"Show us that again, Bill," called Bill Barnaby.

Which Bill Piper, hands cupping as if holding team reins, did for the breathless fans, who traded "Did you see that finger move?" with their mates at the bar and in the booths.

"Of course, the wagon needed to go left because that's the direction to get the siding for the house loaded first, the two by fours next, the two by sixes last, so they'd come off first at August's cellar," Nick instructed, needlessly, his knowledgeable hearers.

"Now the mares needed to keep the turns wide, so the siding boards sticking out the back end of the wagon wouldn't catch on any piles—you know how narrow the yard aisles are, just enough for the dollies to go down the narrow gauge tracks from mill to the next pile"—Nick marking time here for the empty steins to get refilled, the foam leveled with a swipe of the ruler across the stein top—"so that first turn with the wagon empty was just for practice, or maybe for show, for who knows—those mares knew they were being watched, y'betcha"—to nods and "Rights!" from the hearers—"and of course they stopped exactly where the wagon should be at the right pile of siding, one less than full," Piper taking over smoothly, "And here the mares did it all on their own, Aslak not even looking at that pile, just talking to Floyd!"

The drinkers banged their steins in appreciation. "Those mares! They either know what's wanted or they read Aslak's mind!"

"If he wasn't looking at the pile they couldn't have been reading his mind, you dopes!" barely rose above the racket.

"Well, you saw the load going back up out of the yard and up Main Street," Nick ended, knowing that his version, embroidered, would be echoed over Bergland for days after.

On Sunday the 31st of May Floyd Marsh lay on the rumpled bed in the full-bellied drowse of after dinner. Even in the UP there can be unusually warm spring days, especially in late spring days. This afternoon, though, the heat, the belly full after roast pork, yams with gravy, green beans, cole slaw and apple pie, Floyd got only about halfway to sleep.

In his mind, behind those closed eyes, he gazed at the paired stacks of $50 bills secured by a big band of rubber, supine in the top drawer of the bureau along with his clean socks.

The bills were in two stacks. Otherwise, in one stack—and how he wanted them to be in as high a stack as they would make—he couldn't get the drawer closed: The last few on the top of the single stack would bump up against the bureau drawer frame, no matter how hard he pressed down on its top.

The inside edge of the stack would dip just far enough, his right knuckles pressing down with all his weight and force, but about an inch in, when he had to move his knuckles back a bit, the stack would reassert its height, the middle would bulge back up, and the drawer would stick hard enough so that he feared he'd rip the top bill just getting the drawer open again!

So two stacks: $3,750 in $50 dollar bills. His for building—no, creating—an original masterpiece of a home to August Schmidt's specifications, outside and in. With water piped in under pressure, a 200-amp board for when Rural Electrification came out to run power from Aslak's transformer, keeping Aslak's water pump sucking water out of his well, the Frigidaire in Cynara's kitchen humming, up the hill then down the hill east from Aslak's to August's new home.

Well, a bit more than half would go to the sawmill for the lumber, and to Shankey, for the bricks, but just about $1800 was his, Floyd Marsh the builder, with a new different-looking house to his credit out on the Mile Road.

"I wish it was in or closer to town," he came out of his trance to mutter. "Nobody but Aslak and a few others will ever see it."

But it *was* nice to dwell on the stack of bills—$50 each!—that would still be left. What if he took it to Ewen, put it in the bank, earn some interest? Or for checking? Use some for a sign right by M28, front of his house,

>Floyd Marsh Construction
>Free Estimates!
>Custom-built Homes!

Another nice picture that let him drop off to the Sunday afternoon nap.

On their week-day trips into the Post Office and back, morning and late afternoon, the newly-weds had remarked the slow but steady progress on August's unique house.

"I wonder how many of the few passers-by will call that a small barn with attached silo," Cynara remarked to Aslak more than once. "Not many will know, as we did, that it's really a house," Aslak would respond. "It just looks so much like all the barns, in Matchwood, especially."

What gave it away was the ocher bricks. The word that an unusual something was going up on the Mile Road, and observance that Floyd Marsh's work gang was busy someplace, drew more than usual trekkers from town out along the Mile Road, mostly on foot, but a few outsiders, from as far away as Ontonagon, and even Ironwood, came out to stare.

The notice in the *Ironwood Daily Globe*, a short story by Grace Hill, still the *Globe's* stringer in Bergland, was what triggered the visitors from far away. Her brothers Herman and Harold, of course, were the entirety of Floyd's 'gang', so her story was from the horses' mouths, so to speak, accurate in fact, and dressed up in tone by Grace's genuine liking for what many women envied, was assigned a good spot on page three.

Nor was the *Globe* story a one-time shot. The first story, by Grace, caught the eye of the Ironwood paper's women's page editor, who, when the time was right, motored out to get a first-hand look at what was going on and what was planned for the finished product, down to what kind of wallpaper August had in mind.

In fact, even the *Detroit Free Press* picked up the story, and…

But that's rushing things.

When the *Globe's* reporter/editor of the women's page asked August about the wallpaper he had no ready answer.

"I haven't seen that far ahead in my mind's eye," he began.

"But it would have to be in some earth tone," the lady persisted.

August stared at her. "Earth tone? But the inside walls will be lath and plaster, that's gray, like cement. Why would I cover it with wallpaper—just paint is what they do, isn't that so?"

"But you should liven it up, with maybe tan wallpaper with yellow flowers on it or something, don't you think?"

August scratched his head, gave Zwei, who was starting to lift his lip in a snarl at the woman's combative tone, a bit of a push aside.

"What with the bricks and mortar going up for the outside, I think I'll stick with the plaster on lath," August decided.

"Well, tell us (there was a photographer along) about the one-room idea. Most houses get some privacy with partitions—bedrooms, kitchen, bath—as a rule."

August felt a faint glimmer of a desire to emulate Zwei's wish to snarl. Best not!

"Well, I saw what Aslak and Cynara did with their house, all the first floor open"

The lady reporter was scandalized: "Not the bathroom, I hope!?"

"No, that's upstairs."

"Oh. And where is their house?"

So after a hasty promise to photograph the brick exterior—

"That tower with the stairs at the viewing deck, covered, on top, is like no other in Gogebic County!"—the lady, with a promise over her retreating shoulder to come back when the interior was finished, was off up the Mile Road hill to 'do' Aslak and Cynara's interior.

This being a week-day, the reporter found the house empty, the mares returning her long stare as she waited in vain by the front door. Back at August's, she had to be content with the photo, a dramatic shot with the late afternoon sun casting a long shadow of the tower pointing north east, directly at the pristine blue of Aslak's lake, with the white birches as a backdrop, on the way back out the Mile Road.

She did run the photo with a brief summary of the intended inside of August's house, which, plus Grace's story, is what the *Detroit Free Press* ran to generate a flood of the curious, many of whom became the envious, some of whom became the mimics, if not of the tower, to the point of tearing out at least a partition here and there in their own homes.

One who became none of the above slammed both fists down on his table in the Merrill Building Cafeteria, jumping his coffee cup out of the saucer to slop the hot black liquid on his own lap, triggering an agonized leap up and back and a shouted growl of enraged pain.

Skantz.

His swift survey of the others at his table assured him his history of rude scorn, of a hair-trigger temper, kept them feigning ignorance of his present blow-up.

Good! Any sympathy tendered him was unwelcome. Had always been. It implied he was weak enough to value it.

He used the already perused section of sports news to wipe up most of the coffee on the table, dumped the cup and saucer in the common sink, stormed back to the deserted huge office space where, as did the clerks for other companies, he handled the payments based on the lading bills issued to various railroads, including those to the DSS&A.

In this noontime solitude, all the other clerks who worked at the dozens of desks in the large office space avoided him until the last minute when they too had to resume their work. Here Skantz re-read the story, with pictures of August's new house, its vistas west and north of the wilderness and cut-over thousands of acres visible from the Mile Road.

His eyes bulging, his teeth clenched, his face flushed above his black beard, Skantz once more pored over the details.

That miserable fat punk! I'll see that I get some of the rich dumkopf's money yet! He thinks he's got me by the short hairs, but he's not that safe, even not that on the ball to know what I can cook up for myself down here and plus what I can cook up for him up there, that smug little German know-it-all!"

He sensed the closed door behind him opening, air pressure moving. He pretended to turn the pages, spend some time looking through the issue of the Detroit *Free Press.*

Nobody asked about the rage in the cafeteria.

For most of May and June daylight, Aslak's and Cynara's house was locked, she at the Post Office, Aslak doing most of the day work at the stills, with Haywire and August sharing the night shifts.

None the less, aging the brandy in the red oak barrels must be observed. Coloring for the eye, smooth to palate, *kick* to belly—that was August's Applejack Brandy!

At Anna's for dinner in May, with Cynara's Post Office door shut, Cynara asked if Anna was satisfied with her new waitress.

"Better, really, than I'd hoped."

"No doubts even at the beginning?" Aslak wondered. "She was a hell-raiser for years!" "I was watchful, even trusting Yaga's word as I always have. It *was* a relief to have somebody else doing the legwork at meal times, though. I was pleased to see how she kept herself practically invisible, but pleasant to the customers, quick to spot a need and to be Sally-on-the-spot, polite, but becoming quite sure of herself."

Cynara eased her seat, leaned her elbows on the table. "There weren't any men who had known her as her lumberjack self who created problems?"

"I saw a couple, but she handled them well—no punches thrown! Mostly attempts at the usual kind of earthy talk, but she turned them aside and after a few arrows falling short the men took her at her new personality and a couple were even glad, I thought, they didn't have to keep up the old behavior."

Cynara nodded. "I saw that she had character, 'sand', at the New Year's party."

Aslak added, "She does things whole heartedly, we know that."

Careless that Lillian might overhear, Ann went on. "In fact, lately I've been telling her that she ought to relax, not be here working from get-up to bed time every day. I said to her,

"All work and no play was making 'Jill" a dull girl.'"

"Now, when the last customer has gone, and we close up, I always sit down with either a last cup of coffee, or mostly, a small snifter of brandy, before I head for my bed. Join me, let's let our hair down. You're getting too wrapped up in work, work, work!"

What altered their relationship from boss and employee to co-workers:

An observer of the two after hours would first find some amusement in the difference not only in size but in demeanor. Anna was right in urging Lillian to relax; she plainly was always under some slight strain, as if playing a role she didn't quite like, or trust herself to act properly—a far stretch from her former loud, obstreperous gaiety, that screeching laugh.

Anna as always was frank, direct, exuded confidence, elbows on the round table in the bar.

"I'm happy with my new helper, Lil—okay if I shorten it to one syllable?"

Lillian, both hands around the warm cup in front of her, met Anna's gaze, head up, but shoulders dropping into relaxation..

"You've been awfully good to me, Anna," she began slowly, raising her voice and speeding up to a normal pace, "and I can't begin to tell you how important this chance has been and still is for me."

With both hands still around the cup, she lifted it, sipped with a bit of air. It was hot! She put the cup back in its saucer deftly, still Lillian; looked back at Anna.

"It's easier to do what I want to do if I think of myself as Eunice, my middle name I never used. Even an echo like 'Lil' reminds me of…"

She looked away. "I hope you don't mind. My new life line still feels flimsy…"

Anna reached across, enfolded Lillian's hands in her large warm grip.

"You bet I don't mind. Eunice is a good name. I'm fine with calling you Eunice!"

Anna rose, stepped around behind the bar, the glass clinked, something glugged vigorously, she returned, plonked down two small snifters of brandy.

"We should celebrate your new name, it fits your new self: *you nice!*"

Anna raised her glass, extended it across. "Here's to your new life and name!"

Eunice hesitated, then brightened, tapped her own snifter to the proffered one.

"You drink to that; I salute Anna Stindt!"

Being alone, they sipped the brandy, unspurred by a crowd emptying their glasses to follow suit.

"You know, doing toasts at this round table reminds me of what I've been reading about King Arthur and his knights.

It must have been a lot bigger than this one, because it had thirteen seats, chairs with solid wooden backs, like thrones, maybe,..."

"Jack had a book by somebody with a bird sort of name about the Round Table, and ..."

"Bulfinch, I bet, that's the author of the one I got from the school library. August told me about it, said I might like it"—

Eunice, heated a bit by the brandy, broke in: "August knows a lot, doesn't he!"

"Funny, you wouldn't think it to look at him, and sometimes his English sounds a bit different, but he must have been a real student. And it's as he said, there is a bunch of stories with magic places, and spells on people, and most of them have some beautiful maiden in distress who falls in love with a handsome knight who fights and wins and it must have been an exciting life, kneeling before a King or a Queen who taps you on the shoulder and says, "Rise, sir whatever!" and off you go, in armor on a horse, on some errand that's called a 'quest'!"

Before Eunice could respond, Anna, also heated by the brandy at the end of her always busy days, blurted:

"Say, maybe I should have tapped you on the shoulder with a–what, a bread knife?—and said—No, wait, first, 'Kneel, Lillian,' then tapped you with the bread knife, and then said 'Rise, Maid Eunice!'"

Their hearts full; their snifters drained, they headed up the stairs for a good night's rest.

Chapter Eleven

At that Sunday's breakfast, a July 2nd thunderstorm denying Aslak and Cynara the woods hike, Anna was quick to correct Cynara's mention of a new air of confidence in Lillian's mien:

"She's a real treasure, as good if not better than Grace was, bless her ambitious soul down there in Marquette college, but she's not even Lillian anymore. She's taken her middle name Eunice to be called now."

Anna nodded, with a smile at their surprise, "Yep, nice woman is now Eunice! Say it a bit differently, describes her well: You nice!"

Aslak nodded approvingly, Cynara gushed, elated, "I knew she had grit, that little dynamo! She's a woman to admire, after my own heart."

She turned, searching, waved to Eunice, "Come on over!" and stood to give Eunice a fierce, joyful hug. "Now we both have new names! Welcome to the group!"

When she was free to speak, Eunice volunteered, dropping her glance to Cynara's waist,

"But you're one step ahead of me—maybe two!"

Cynara turned back to Anna. "Can you spare her for an hour or two to visit our new place?"

Anna nodded. "I can, I told her to relax once in a while, she's been a regular slave around here, she needs a break! Give me that apron, and that tablet, you go with them!"

Thunder rumbled, but the rain god let them get into the black Model A, Eunice in back with the pile of blankets and the rope which kept the glass jugs safe during delivery.

Once they made the turn up M64 past Piper's Garage the rain pounded the top and hood to make conversation impossible, the wipers on the windshield trying but the downpour forcing the Ford to slow down to about twenty miles per hour.

Aslak swung the wheel hard left to enter the Mile Road. The wipers still swam back and forth in a frenzy that allowed only sporadic sight of the graveled pair of tracks.

"Haven't seen the likes of this in my lifetime," Aslak wondered.

"Maybe the rain is the christening for the new woman in the back seat," supplied Cynara, her bouncy good humor even in pregnancy undiminished. Her predilection for seeing events in terms of the Bible was still her mantle, though no longer her mentor.

"This is spooky enough as it is," Eunice protested. "I can't see out my window!"

Then they were out in bright sunshine halfway up the hill.

At the top of the hill Eunice, with a quick gasp, leaned forward to grasp the backs of the two front seats.

"I've not been up here, though a few times at Haywire's. You are right on the edge of the wilderness, I'd say!"

"Hardly any one goes by, we like the privacy. I see everybody in Bergland at least once a week—that's okay, but I like the solitude to even things out," Cynara declared.

"We've got a good share of the modern world inside to make life pleasant even when the weather frowns."

While Aslak rounded the hood to make Cynara's descent easier, Eunice hopped out of the near back door, and took in the house, the orchard with apples of several kinds:– crab, delicious, Wolf River monsters, striped Ben Davis—, the glossy white paint of the house a strong demarcation for the weathered gray of the woodshed and barn.

Over the short white picket fence linking woodshed to house appeared the mares' heads.

Both Aslak and Cynara went over to give each mare its daily ears and nose caresses, which the mares, more like appreciative dogs than stolid horses, closed their eyes and nickered softly, moving their heads in small nods, shifting their hind feet, stretching out their necks as the two moved away toward the waiting Eunice, who smiled uncertainly, still hesitant to move freely, her shift from brusque vigorous assertiveness as Gallopin' Lil still close to the opposite extreme.

Which Cynara, as had Anna, saw, and linked her left arm around Eunice's shoulders.

"Come on in, honey, *we'll* give *you* a cup of coffee for a change!"

Aslak moved toward the woodshed, the storehouse for his wood-cutting saws and axes.

"I'll be back in a couple of hours. I need to cut some more wood down at the shack. You have a good visit, roam around with this woman who lives here!"

He was careful to make his 'tap' on Cynara's shoulder a playful one. She and Eunice, at the front door, turned their heads to see him disappear, crosscut saw and axes, newly filed and oiled, bouncing, dangling, from his zig-zagging shoulders as he practiced that strut which identified him all over Bergland township.

Eunice, her reserve shattering, blurted "That man! You've got it all, and goin' to have a baby on top of everythin'!"

Cynara hesitated, then decided to show Eunice their house inside first. Time for response to that last comment after. Aslak wouldn't be back for at least an hour.

"Come in so I can show you how we've improved our home!"

The door closed behind Eunice, but she didn't hear it.

SPACE

Eunice gulped, choked, coughed—as her face reddened Cynara clapped her on the back, then nearly dragged her to the sink faucet for a glass of water.

On the fifth try Eunice exhaled, took a real breath and the handkerchief to wipe her eyes, blow her nose, try a weak smile.

"It's just so big, so surprisin'!" then her eye was caught by the circular staircase in the middle of the wide-open first floor.

"Let's go partway up, we can see it best from there," Cynara urged; Eunice took hesitant small steps, then walked to the base of the staircase, placed her right hand on the newel post.

"It's so smooth and shiny!"

Midpoint of the first of the two curves Cynara halted her. "Now take a look at our first floor."

Looking north, the long axis of the house, Eunice saw the living room on her right; on the opposite north wall a window framing the long gentle slope down toward Kallaak's Corner, a cushioned seat inviting a spectator, the team of mares now grazing side by side in the lush meadow, the long silk of their tails whipping leisurely from side to side.

At the west wall, a huge fieldstone fireplace, empty now in July; to her right, and going all the way to the front, east wall, that half of the first floor a gigantic parlor with several nooks of seats, casually arranged around a rectangular coffee table, and two round, low tables; standing lamps here and there as in the sitting room by each room's sofa.

Gracing the middle of the parlor east wall, another fire place, of green mossy-looking brick, its mantle a stone to take away one's breath: At least ten feet long, a foot thick, glazed smooth on top, rough chipped underside. Throw rugs, with deep reds and blacks in broad weaves, in both rooms.

Cynara watched Eunice's eyes feast on the grand splendor.

"We can't decide yet on what to do with the parlor walls," Cynara explained. "There's only the orchard out there, so the windows are just normal size. We'll probably just keep our eyes open for some paintings or whatever—maybe some antique tools, shelves of things people used back in the old days."

"I'm just speechless," Eunice protested.

On the top floor, four bedrooms: Two smaller ones above the parlor; a master bedroom over the living room with two windows looking down over the slope to Kallaak's Corner, the doored bath with the electric water heater in its tall closet over the kitchen sink.

The two women, Cynara the apogee of fruitfulness, Eunice the epitome of barrenness, stood side by side back down at the living room window gazing at the mares, heads down, cropping the newly-wetted grass, the mares glistening blue-black in the July sunlit noontime.

"You belong here, Cynara. I am outside, lookin' in."

Silence. What can I say, Cynara thought, other than agree?

"What makes you think so?"

"You goin' to birth a child by a man who loves you, you love him; you now live in a lovely home. Your wish is about to come true."

Eunice looked down at her fingers resting on the window sill. "What we're lookin' at is like a mirror of you—the lush grass, the mares who serve your husband in work and in producin' colts. In the clearin' past that clump of woods you know your husband, your lover, your baby's father, is workin' at his dream of providin' what most men want, and by teachin' restraint t'everybody, givin' hope, just like you, the mares, the grass, everythin'"—she raised her eyes to Kallaak's Corner—"'n I'm just a shell."

Cynara's throat locked.

"Off my old path of self-destruction but not growin' into anythin' beyond better than a shell, while you are what I can honestly say I wish I could be. I just can't DO what you do, so I can't BECOME what you ARE."

Eunice faced Cynara. "That's what makes me think I am on the outside, lookin' in."

"Let's sit down—I'll put the coffee on—while we think and talk more about this. Sit over here where we'll be looking toward the mares as before."

In a few minutes, the electric coffee pot set to perk on the stove, Cynara sat next to Eunice on the sofa.

"I have a hope that what you now feel may not be exactly true, and I'll tell you why. You remember at the New Year party I told you that I also despaired both for my future as a mother and even as a Christian; Anna and Hattie sat down with me just as we now are and I found that things were not just as I'd thought—and I was feeling a lot as you do now."

Eunice shook her head. "But I know that to have a child, get pregnant, I have to have in me somethin' for the man to get started. But I've never had any monthly bleedin'."

Cynara's eyes widened. "But the story you told about breakfast in jail...?"

"That was just a story—to tell in Marko's."

Cynara grasped Eunice's hand.

"I'm sure you know that the opposite—not to get pregnant—is the wish of many if not most women: Not to get pregnant, even when married; and that a common term among women for menstruation is…"

"The curse," Eunice nodded. "And most women I know who've had a child, or more than one, don't look forward to the pain of labor, or mornin' throw-up.. That's what I heard from my mother, and all our acquaintances, growin' up."

On the stove, the little bulb atop the percolator showed a pulsing light brown geyser of water, a noisy clatter of pressure.

Cynara returned with the tray, two cups, spoons, cream, sugar.

Eunice smiled at the tableau. "If this is an omen, it's a good one—Yaga and I had a good session over some coffee a while back!"

After a few sips Cynara resumed.

"So how do you feel about the usual morning sickness, the labor of childbirth?"

Defensively, which Cynara took to be favorable for where she hoped to go with Eunice in the discussion, Eunice sparred at first.

"You're the pregnant one here; how do *you* feel about them?"

"Like you, I've heard a lot about them. I've been so wanting my own child—selfish reasons—and to quiet that little gnawing about being fruitful as addicted Christian, as I confessed to you before, that I am ready for the labor pains as part of the price for the child. Anyway, I'm past the nausea, which was only for the first month. Labor pains don't last forever, either."

Cynara centered her cup in the saucer. "Now you!"

Eunice made a moue, her lips down at the corners.

"To be honest—and this I won't forget I have to be—I've heaved my guts up a lot of times. But the labor pains—aagh!—I used to look at my narrow hips and shuddered more'n once at how I might have a lot of pain, maybe even die, even with help, tryin' t' push a fully developed baby out of me."

She spread out her hands. "But even so, how would I raise my baby"—her voice caught—"I've never said those two words together out loud before—; I don't have a home for one, if I don't have a job, I don't have the money to feed it and clothe it nor the time to spend with it."

She folded her hands in her lap. "Anna gives me a room, my meals, a good percentage what she takes in—this Depression, it's goin' down all the time. All the things I've been sayin'—you have them all. I don't. Don't see I ever will."

Cynara marshaled her thoughts. This was different, being the counselor, not the counselee!

"If you were still what you were a year ago, would you be less or more able to have and raise a child?"

Eunice stared at her. "Less, of course! What kind of a question is that!"

"The kind to make sure we start on the same page. Now, today, you are more able than a year ago.?"

"Y-e-s."

"Have you thought of how you might improve in those last areas—having some money, a home, time at home?"

In a low voice: "Jack won't have me; even if he did, he never wanted any children."

"So that's as far as you went?"

In an even lower, softer voice: "No place to go."

Now ready with her direction, Cynara asked:

"If you could—sounds foolish, but if you could choose only one or the other: Would you choose to be pregnant, or to have a child? That is, do you want to be pregnant, prove to yourself and everyone else you really are a woman, or do you simply want a child? Think about it while I take a look to see if Aslak is on his way back."

Wanting to free Eunice of *all* pressure of her own presence, Cynara went out the door. She glanced quickly toward Section Thirty, heard the ring of Aslak's axe.

Eunice was returning from the sink. The little table was clear.

"No difference, either way. I couldn't afford to raise one."

"But?"

"I think I'm worth more, doing for the customers and so for Anna, who needs someone. I think she's pleased with my help. So I have made myself a somebody, even if I can't ever get pregnant, thanks to Yaga and then Anna."

"Would you divorce Jack, or he divorce you, to get that settled, open a path of some sort? Just in your own mind, get that block gone?"

Eunice rose, walked to the window seat, stood for a moment. Cynara saw her hands clenched, knuckles white.

She turned back, chin up.

"Jack and I were not married. His folks knew it. We just pretended to be married for up here."

She exhaled, drew in a long breath.

Cynara smiled, rose, tugged Eunice down beside her on the window seat.

"If you knew of a man who had a home, could afford to keep you and a child, was satisfied with you, and the child, in every way, would you see that as a new path? Would be enough, just the one child? For both of you?"

"I don't know of any such man." She walked over to the chair, sat, crossed her ankles, her arms.

Cynara read the defensive signs.

They heard Aslak at the woodshed, the ring of the crosscut saw, that ribbon of prime steel, as, swinging on its peg, it banged the woodshed wall.

Cynara, her hand on the door knob to greet her husband, her love, her enabler, looked back at Eunice, also standing, arms straight, ankles open in a normal stance.

"So whatever the reason for calling Jack an obstacle, he's no longer an excuse, is he?"

Aslak saw he was in at the tag end of something, but he made no comment, except "I'm going to pick up a load of shine at the shack, then some brandy at August's, and if you'll volunteer to give me a hand with the loading I might be persuaded to give you a ride back to Anna's. Is it a deal?"

Cynara gave him the usual welcome welcome; the kiss pleased both and sharpened Eunice's envy. When they came up for air, she gave Cynara a pat, smiled up at Aslak:

Glad for some action,

"And I won't break a jug of either!"

Cynara held the door open; as Eunice passed through, she gave the following Aslak a conspiratorial wink and closed the door.

That's a bee in her bonnet!!

In the black Model A sedan, up the hill, turn left on the Mile Road Spur, down around Kallaak's corner, up over the knob, back the car up to the door of the still shack, stop.

Aslak looked over at Eunice, fumbling for the door inside handle.

"What did you think of our new home?"

Eunice gave up on the door handle. "Now I know what the inside of a castle must look like! That central staircase is awesome, but standin' halfway up and seeing the whole first floor just by turnin'...!"

Wearing the ever-present half grin, Aslak leaned toward her, reached across to flip the door handle down. A whiff of fresh sawdust, the rest just vigorous *man* swept over Eunice.

Aslak opened his door, stepped out and down, walked around the radiator when he saw she hadn't moved.

"Not that high," he held out his left hand.

Her head clearing, Eunice was glad of the help down. Kept her from falling against him.

Aslak was moving toward the door. "I'll start stacking the jugs on the door step, then I'll show you how to wrap the blanket, and go back to bringing the jugs out."

He stopped at the bottom step, looked back with some concern.

"Are you all right?"

Visibly back to normal in appearance, Eunice nodded. "I'm okay."

During his absence, inside, picking up the first jugs, Eunice tried to grasp her sensations.

I know he's supposed to be a real he-man. But I felt like a *woman* must feel when we stopped. He just *oozes that* ... Am I ... waking up?

"Open the back door," Aslak directed, coming down the steps with two jugs in each hand, the thick fingers through the loop handles.

The door opened toward the rear of the Model A; she stepped back as he veered around the opened door, put the jugs on the floor in front of the back seat. Taking the old gray horse blanket, folding it once lengthwise, he wound it on a sort of snake path between the jugs, so that no glass was touching glass. The opened half of the blanket lay on the seat.

"Get the idea?" He loomed over her; she hung on to the front door handle, nodded.

"I'll start stacking them on the door step; you set 'em up like this, both sides, then on top of the seat, see, it slants down and back, so they won't tip over when we stop. Open the other side door when this side is full."

She hung on to the front door handle until he disappeared into the still shack.

Breathe! He's Cynara's husband! What *is* this feeling!

I'm wet!

"Okay! Here you go! Get with it!" and Aslak disappeared back into the still shack.

The weight of the jugs full of moonshine, the effort to get them on the back seat, the care needed to wrap the blanket as Aslak had, the stretch to get the doubled half of the blanket to reach the length of the second pair of jugs, brought Eunice back to her senses, her head to clear, her heart steady.

A dozen all told, six on the floor, six on the back seat, leaning against the seat back, no glass touching glass.

The shack door closed, Aslak leaned in, inspected the arrangement.

"Couldn't do better myself. You're a comer, Eunice! Hop in and we'll get over to August's for the brandy!"

Back in form, Eunice did make the hop, the door closed firmly, and off they chugged, the jugs rumbling but no clangs as the Model A growled up the Spur, left on the top of the hill, down to stop just past August's gate, then back in.

Just a brief glance as they passed the gate—what is that? Then gone as Aslak backed in through the gate. No problem with the door this time, step down, a little jump, really, and this time it was August standing close, his face sober, yellow eyes wide in surprise.

But he could speak. "I was going to put this cask on the floor. Now I …"

Neither heard Aslak's door bang shut, but now he was making it a threesome.

"I brought along a new temporary helper today, August! Lot prettier than you, too!"

"That I can see!" from August: A twin to his fascination with this woman and the one in Marko's.

For Eunice, a mixture of apple aroma and pipe tobacco, shorter and heavier than Aslak, she made some sort of reply, the *same feeling as with Aslak at the still shack* I think I like whatever is going on with a radiant smile that dazzled August.

"Biggest smile I've seen on you!" from Aslak. "Now that you two have met, let's get on with those casks of brandy—back seat, they'll have to go."

While they arranged several jugs in front of the jugs on the back seat, Eunice let the big house draw her close.

A barn with silo attached!? No, light brown brick siding, stone tower with a roofed deck on top; hip roof on a high wall, small windows this side, heavy-looking wood front door, shiny brass latch handle …

A man's hand on it thumbed down the latch.

"Go inside see how you like," August muttered in her ear. "Is new, ja?" Ach, his English lost!

Smaller, wide, open just like the one over the hill, ceiling open to the rafters, heavy beams for ceiling joists. Kitchen stove, kerosene? to her right, sink and cutting shelf on the wall, water heater?, dining room; to her left, enclosed bath, sofa facing a stone fireplace, closet with cot against far wall.

Zwei, unseen outside, pushed past her, trotted over to rug by the cot, circled, dropped with a grunt, head on paws, staring into her eyes.

Parquet flooring.

August edged by Eunice, touched her elbow. "Come, I show you the basement." English coming back, *gut!* He stopped beside the bathroom door, bent, lifted a ring from the glossy yellow-brown parquet, pulled up a door opening on a stair *circling down* into a dark cavern.

"No electricity yet, but soon will come, I'm told!" Ah, English back! "Wait here."

August picked up a lantern, levered up the glass, from his front pocket came a match to rip into light with his thumb nail (just like a 'jack! Eunice marveled); when the glass came down on the lighted wick, August started down the staircase, cleared the floor joist without dipping his head, waved Eunice to start while he held the lantern, standing on the floor.

Potbelly wood stove at front wall, large enclosed bath next to the stove. Double bed in a room taking up the *entire rest of the cellar!*

Eunice could only stare.

"…subflooring up on two by fours over the cold cement, then the parquetry on top of that for looks and for insulation—dead air between cement and subflooring is one of the best insulations. Well, now you've seen it all," August moved Eunice toward the stairs.

At the top, he levered up the lantern glass, blew out the flame, set the lantern down by the bath wall.

Aslak held open the door. "Not many houses like ours, do you think?"

Eunice said something like "I should say not!" moved alongside the Model A, remembered to say "Thanks" to August.

Eunice wasn't very responsive on the way to Jim's house on Center Street. Aslak didn't push. He thought it odd, since before the two name changes she'd been a compulsive talker. And he thought he knew why—her monotonous every-day-a-working-day at Anna's must be a strain which a momentous pair of visits to see how other people lived only made her usual day all the more like being in jail.

Maybe his own heaven with Cynara had blunted Aslak's powers of observation and perception

Eunice herself couldn't begin to define what she'd experienced. She'd not felt that shiver, that *dampness*, before.

That Sunday night, just before falling asleep, she hoped August would ask her to take in the view from that tower.

His new home, still awaiting electricity from Aslak's transformer, whenever money might show up in Ontonagon County's annual or special dollop from the RFC, hadn't changed August's living style. He still carried water into the house in a pair of buckets from the pump out by his 'factory', cooked his meals on the shiny almost-like-new kerosene stove undamaged in the dynamite blast, still visited his outhouse on demand.

But this Sunday evening his volume Bulfinch's recounting of the Arthurian myth, the German version he'd taken with him in the steamer trunk from the Palatine, lay open on his lap in the kerosene lamplight.

Nothing unusual in his vacant gaze at the door to keep Zwei from his sound sleep on the rag rug at August's feet.

However, what August 'saw' going out the door was a vision of the same kind as in the Arthurian tales—a fair damsel (more or less).

A first for this long-time, never married bachelor.

Eunice.

As was his own, a name given at birth, now resumed to fit a new person, new self-image.

No more Dutchy, no more Gallopin'/Tiger Lil. A discarded soubriquet.

From the spelling, 'sou-', and 'quet', French.

Another first: August eschewed opening his dictionary to peruse for the word but sank back in his chair to resume the imagined door closing behind

Eunice. And the way their eyes had fused that evening in Marko's over her tray of sandwiches.

Chapter Twelve

Late afternoon, Sunday, October first, 1933, they stood with August on the tower deck over-looking that same vista, from a different angle, that had been their Eden last winter.

Green patches of cedar, spruce, balsam, pine. Bright yellows of poplar; dull yellows of soft maple, bright reds of hard maple, light and dark browns of a few oak from horizon to horizon. All second growth.

Behind the lake called Aslak's, north of them, the white of the birch colony formed the contrast point for the whole kaleidoscopic palette of autumn.

"We've walked everywhere we are now looking," Cynara mused. "Last winter it was so white, so cold-looking. Now it's just as near and as far, but it's alive in color patterns and known to me from walking through, camping underneath, waking up to them,…"

All three were silent, absorbing the sight, her words.

Cynara turned to August.

"Has anybody—Pendock, maybe—been up here?"

"No, just myself and Zwei—and you two, many times."

At their surprised stare, he added, "And the newspaper people, of course!"

"August, ask Sherman to come up here, he can come through the woods the same way we did for Christmas dinner, see this broad, deep view of the second growth spirit, a change from nothing but his big timber!"

"And no other friends, people you know?" Cynara persisted. "Or do you want no one else?"

August searched for an acceptable answer. Who would walk the three miles out and back from town?

"Listen," she went on, "Eunice comes by here with us, when Anna can spare her, all right with you if she comes up here, enjoys the view?"

Through the bright spots and mental buzz August saw and heard, he managed, "Of course; any friends of yours are welcome. Don't be formal! My house is your house!"

The sun to their right rear sank behind the hill. They stepped down a circular staircase a match to the one centering their own first floor.

"Come have supper with us," Cynara urged. "We've got partridges tonight!"

August nodded gratefully; Zwei's ears perked up; he recognized the word.

The next morning, a clear sky, a bit of frost making all the sun touched a-glitter, August saw his duty: His own orchard, mostly Delicious, but with a few Striped Ben Davis, Rome Beauty, and Duchess here and there, would be raided by deer unless he got them in, began the apples-to-brandy process.

The time for visions is over; get busy for the promise you made to the people in Milwaukee to give them all you can.

All of the gear—the peeler, which as it peeled, also cored each apple—he'd put away shiny clean in the spring, the table for chopping, the press, the fermenting barrels, were all ready for use.

So, out with the wheelbarrow, the ladder, the pocket apron allowing him the use of both hands—made him almost a prime mover of a huge apple bag with pockets in front and on both sides leaving only a narrow gap along his spine.

And quickly twist and pull each apple, all the Delicious first, the earliest to ripen, careful to leave the spur on which next spring's blossom would grow, all of them pollinated by the hordes of insects warm, wet weather spawned; careful too to knock as few apples to the ground as possible lest, bruised, they'd be unfit for the brandy process.

Under each Delicious tree already there were, on the few apples fallen in the week prior, hordes of various kinds of insects, some of them able stingers, for August to disturb only slowly and gently as, once the apples within reach of one standing on the ground were in the apron pockets, the ladder came into play. Careful with the ladder, also: Any bruise of the bark into and through the greenish under layer into the white of the wood makes an entry for disease, fungus, insect borers.

And as each wheelbarrow was heaped full of the amazingly heavy golden fruit with a slight greenish cast at the top and at the blossom end—the bottom—up with the handle bars and, again *gently,* move the heap of potential delight and wealth inside his 'factory' to store, again *gently*, each apple in the bushels next to the peeler/corer for late afternoon's first step toward the gallons of August's Applejack Brandy, whose ultimate wealth his new clothes, his new home, declared to all who saw, visited, understood the work, the skill, the persistent effort, waved the wand for the magic.

With Zwei in constant attendance, snapping at a wasp who buzzed his ears, moving into the shade or warm sun, tail a-wag at each notice of his presence by glance or word.

By Thursday, October 5th, all the Delicious were at work inside the factory; August hauled all the hardier red apples inside, their processing to wait while the few Delicious down in Jonas Amundsen's huge orchard, at the end of the Mile Road extension, were gathered.

Hard, demanding labor. No minutes to waste—ripe apples require immediate attention.

But August could draw on members of the Luna Light Gang, those who were jobless, and though they were volunteering without pay, willingly walked out to the Mile Road, joined August for the ride down to Amundsen's cornucopia on Aslak's sledge, a chance to not only observe the team of mares but to be a part of those fabulous creatures who in the presence of Aslak, though seemingly requiring little actual guidance, were there at the noon time and evening end of picking to haul a sledge packed with bushels of first, Delicious, then, when they ripened, the Rome, the MacIntosh, even a few Granny Smith apples, those deep green emeralds, up the half-mile of steep slope, around Kallaak's Corner, a half mile uphill to the Mile Road proper, then left downhill and through August's gate to halt for the sledge unloading at the door of the factory.

Whose help would be remembered with a gift of brandy at Christmas.

Eunice, when the slack of Sunday afternoons at Anna's left her free to visit, came out with Aslak and Cynara after their habitual Sunday noon dinner, coming back to work on Mondays as Aslak brought Cynara back to her Post Office.

But no slack time for the tower vista viewers could August spare except for greetings and farewells to August as, on Sundays he was immersed as on all days with batch after batch of apples moved from storage on the far side down that side and then across to the final stage of fermentation of the cider, and 'jacking' that cider, until, enough water taken off as ice, the liquid floated the hydrometer at the 'proof' level for August's Applejack Brandy. On the following Mondays Aslak with his team of mares took a wagon loaded to make the axle hubs groan to the Bergland DSS&A depot, there loaded for delivery to Milwaukee.

By return mail to the Ewen bank August's account swelled into the thousands in those days when gas at the pump at Piper's Garage was a dollar for five gallons and a coke or an ice cream cone was a nickel.

By mid-October the trees were bare; the vistas of leaf color gave way to bare branches tossing in the winter winds.

Snow fell; the as-yet unfrozen ground beneath refused to accept those first attempts to smother it, and the rillets ran in the ditches along M64, long years away from being more than gravel. Would-be deer hunters crossed their fingers for tracking snow.

In the evenings of October August and Zwei were thankful to fall asleep, at times awakening after the evening meal by the guttering of the lantern, only to blow it out and sleep the night through, tired not only by the physical work at the brandy-making but by the pressure to use to that end every available apple lest some ripen, rot, and be lost to them.

Not so on the other, the western, side of the hill. In the evenings, and on the afternoons as well when not enjoying the tower as an outdoor pavilion for a drink and conversations as the weather was inclement, the threesome of Aslak, Cynara, and Eunice had time and the desire for conversations sometimes on serious subjects, but serious or with laughter, essential to Eunice in her growing ability to feel communal in her daily life.

While Aslak was down at the still shack in daylight, or with the team, while the apples lasted, at Amundsen's orchard, the ladies could talk freely.

At first it was about clothes.

"Gosh, you're so tiny I think you must be around an 8!" Cynara guessed. They sat side by side on the sofa in the parlor, leaning forward, heads bent over the Montgomery, Ward catalog section on women's dresses; Sears, Roebuck catalog, like the other, an inch and a half thick, 8×11 at least, to one side for later comparison.

"In my forties I don't need any of these frilly lowcut things," Eunice claimed.

"But it doesn't hurt to look at," Cynara replied. "Look, there's one just about the same as the one I've got in the closet!"

Heavier now, less than two months to go, she nevertheless with a bit of the old spring came back holding in front of herself a brown and yellow light wool weave, knee length, dress, zipper top with a white roll collar, 2" wide belt of the same material, dull silver buckle.

"This can be worn at work, or socially during the day. Here, step out of that green working cotton thing you wear in the restaurant, try this one!"

Eunice draped her gray cardigan sweater over the sofa arm, pulled her dress off over her head, to stand, reaching for the dress, in her underwear: bloomers, dickey-like top.

No need for a second look in the long oval mirror: Eunice was entirely covered from neck to her ankles, with enough width left over for her twin to be in the dress with her!

'That's enough for the try-ons!" laughed Cynara, which encouraged Eunice to giggle as well. "What do you weigh, anyway?"

"I don't have any idea," Eunice returned, her voice echoing out of the voluminous folds as she pulled and wiggled her way free of it. "I do feel stronger since I've been gettin' enough sleep and to eat in Anna's, and the few clothes I have are tighter than before."

As she raised her arms to let her 'green thing' drop back over her, Cynara drew in a quick breath.

Eunice's body looked like nothing so much as that of a boy just out of a sick bed with a miraculous tuberculosis recovery. No swell above the waist, a barely noticeable flare below.

Her face must have showed her dismay; Eunice reddened, busied herself with the small arrangements with her dress, turned away to rescue and slip back into her cardigan.

For one of the few times in her gregarious life, Cynara was at a loss for words. The fun of looking at new clothes for Eunice could not continue until some bridge had been fashioned from her obvious recent angularity—or had it begun much earlier? remembering what Eunice had said was her reason for assuming the guise of a tough lumberjack: She'd never reached womanhood.

Delay won't help, it'll just be a curtain between us.

Coming closer, not touching; don't invite a collapse, keep it matter-of-fact:

"Honey, for as long as I've known you, you've always been thin—but I always thought a better word was 'wiry', like a metal spring."

Calm, standing up straight, Eunice met Cynara's gaze. She's picking that up from me, she's got resolve.

"Were you always, even in your teens, that thin?"

Hands clasped loosely together, fingers interlaced, Eunice let a trace of a smile appear.

"I'm feelin' better since I've been at Anna's, as I've said, but in my early teens I'd get intense pains, achy like a toothache, part way up my back, and not much appetite. Since then I've not changed much, though out in the woods with the 'jack's I worked hard, ate all I could. You could say, though, that I've always looked the way I look now."

She turned her head, moved back to sit back on the sofa.

"Have you seen a doctor about it?"

"No, when I wasn't out in the woods I was in some saloon drinkin' or passed out at home."

Yaga Lulich would have been proud to see her self-control, brave enough to view her past without shrinking.

"Once some people I knew came out to Jack's and my house. They said to Jack that they wanted to see me. He told me this later."

"Sure, come on in," Jack said, "There she is, mostly under the bed. You can see her there, she's passed out."

Cynara moved back beside Eunice on the sofa.

"Wednesday the 1st of November, I go for a check-up to Dr. Blake in Ewen at one p.m.; the Post Office will be closed. Will you come with me and see what he thinks?"

For a moment, Cynara's question loosened Eunice's control. Her eyes misted, but she brushed away any tears before they could form.

"If it's all right with Anna, I will."

Cynara seized her hand. "Good girl!"

"I've got money to pay the doctor—I'm on a percentage with Anna!"

Aslak's shoes, being scraped off outside the door, brought them back to the present.

"You two got any sort of leftovers for a starvin' moonshiner?" he roared, startling them into movement until they saw the old half-grin on his face.

While Cynara and her husband embraced, kissed lovingly, Eunice felt the same thrill, a bit of the same damp as of late. Maybe some day, with a husband who was like that, she herself might live that instead of just watch.

That evening, Sunday the 15th of October, after a venison roast with onions, baked potato with sour cream, corn from the Section Thirty patch, apple pie from just two apples of the Wolf River tree in their own yard, Aslak opened what was a subject on the minds of most of the Bergland Township who, despite the lack of money from the sawmill, had not pulled up stakes for jobs elsewhere.

"I see the relief truck out on M64 just about every time I go to town."

Cynara took it up. "Yes, Mrs. Thompson said, last Wednesday, when we stopped by there, that they've been getting a big sack of cornmeal every week. The store bill, she said, at Rosberg's, was big enough without buying Kellog's corn flakes or the other dry cereals, so they each have a bowl of corn meal mush with some of their own milk, maybe a teaspoon of sugar, for breakfast. It's a change, she said, from the potato dumplings they call …"

She turned to Aslak.

"Klepp maat." Aslak supplied, an emigrant from southern Norway, here at age nine.

Cynara nodded her thanks, with a bit of a smile. "And she makes enough, mornings, on that big wood cookstove, so that their supper is fried inch-thick slices of cornmeal mush, solid by that time, with a few dabs of corn syrup they *do* charge at the store."

"How come you two were over there?", Eunice asked.

"We try to visit once a week with some of the other people we know out here, and in town, too."

She tapped her husband's chest. "He always has been a walking newspaper, for the farms out here—Bositch's, Simondsen,'s, Harju's—especially, and of course Haywire, Jonas, and August (he used to be 'Dutchy', just as 'Haywire' was really Herman Johnson). Lately, we go in the Model A; at first we walked, but now, and with the cold and snow of winter, we ride."

Eunice looked the question.

"They all seem to enjoy it—some of them have a little something to have with the coffee when we visit; they look pleased to see us at their door. And we like it, too. Life out here, at the end of nowhere, unless, like Pendock, you have the timber as a friend of some sort, can be awfully monotonous. August is the only reader of his kind of books, Olga Thompson gets a Norwegian newspaper with a sort of story section. The rest don't read, are not—the farm people out around here, I mean—much for English, so they like somebody like Aslak, who can get along with anybody, to visit."

"I get—we get—some men in Anna's who get just coffee or a sandwich. They like to come in for a visit with the other bachelors, talk to Anna, and sometimes even me. But even there there's been fewer customers."

"This program—the Federal Emergency Relief Act—has worked two ways," Aslak went on. "The farmers had food like corn not selling, and people with families, like the Thompsons—actually two families, the Nilsens, Olga and five kids, too—didn't have enough food, enough cash after taxes and clothes to buy it, so the Federal government bought what the farmers had a lot of, so the farmers could have some cash, then turned the food, like cornmeal, over to people like the Thompsons."

His face flushed with enthusiasm, Aslak grinned at his rapt listeners. "Guess I can still toss out a few words, huh? And lately, with the WPA paying money for men to fix some of the roads, like that huge bank on the south side where our Mile Road starts, it's much better than a handout, like the relief truck, men get paid for work."

Slowly, putting into words as they came to her, Eunice took what Aslak had mentioned a bit further.

"I say that making money by earning it, having the money to buy what's needed, is only just half. It's important not just to have the money, but to feel you are worth something—in your own mind, maybe in other people's mind—how you think of yourself."

The two were silent: Aslak, as was his habit when others spoke; Cynara, knowing from her own breakout with Anna and Hattie how important it was to hear yourself say your belief.

Eunice too was silent, her vacant gaze at the opposite wall, visibly 'seeing' her thought.

To Aslak, if she'd been a machine, he could have seen the parts moving.

"Yaga Lulich got me to say what was on my mind, sort of talk to myself, hear what I was thinking, make it plain, and ... in some sort of order."

Life came back into Eunice's eyes. "She said, '*Do* what who you want to *be* does, to *become* who you want to be."

Aslak quickly assented. "Early on, a few jokes about the work program, but it will do what it was intended to do. That will build on the new life."

To lighten the mood, Cynara, rising, added to her husband, "As you have helped me become what I wanted to be by giving me this!"

Both of her hearers, Aslak humorously, Eunice wistfully, responded with genuine smiles.

"Now let's do the dishes, clean up the kitchen!" Cynara picked up the plates.

The only argument August ever had with Aslak was about buying his own car. August felt he might be asking too much of Aslak, what with all the hauling of apples up from Amundsen's and then the multiple loads of brandy down to the depot.

The second time he had voiced his concern, on a Tuesday afternoon, October 17th, Aslak grew a bit brusque.

"August, I go to town and come back twice a day in a four-cylinder Model A anyway, nicht wahr? When I get back now, with Cynara, six miles, gas five gallons a dollar."

August grinned at the amateurish German, but "Well, but..."

"But my butt! All it takes is a bit of loading the night before, I drop Cynara off at the Post Office, rattle over to the loading platform on the tracks, shove the brandy off with Ed Borseth giving me a receipt. I bring the lading bill back here, you give me the check, the same routine the next morning, I pay Ed for the yesterday's transport to Milwaukee, we do this until it's all done, sometime maybe in November, or however long until everybody's satisfied."

"Yes, but..."

"Wait, I'm not done! Whatever brandy is sold around the township gets figured in just like the shine: You, and I, and Haywire, the producers, split half the profit three ways!

I haul the shine, I haul the brandy to Jim's house. You don't have the time to share in the shine work, especially now in apple harvest time, but you share one-third of one-half of the shine sales, just as I share the same in your brandy sales, though I do damn-all in its production here in your place."

He reached out to 'tap' August's near shoulder, rocking him on his stool perch to bump the side wall with his off shoulder.

"I agree," August, with a chuckle learned from Haywire. "You've knocked some sense into me!"

Aslak turned to head down to town to pick up Cynara.

August grabbed him by the loose green twill blousing out the back.

"Wait!" He spun around on his stool, his back now to the apple pomace press

"I notice lately in the bank statement the deposits from our gang, my one-third of one-half, are going up at a surprising rate, even in this hard time. How come the sales are going up?"

The old half-smile was there on Aslak's craggy face.

"In Jim's opinion, and he says that's what he's hearing from our gang, the Hill brothers, Pete Kalamber, and his own customers, that the other producers can't match our price or our quality shine—we're taking over a lot of their customers! I guess if money's scarce they want the most and best they can get for less money!"

Now the chuckle came from Aslak. "And Jim says two of his customers came over to thank him and our policy for convincing him to take it easy drinking. He feels better, his kids come to him now with school homework now that they see he's awake after supper, not snoring in his chair with the jug on the table. And get this: His wife serves him his after supper shot for dessert with a kiss!"

August and Aslak laughed, slapped each other's back. "Just what I needed, something to cheer me up in this quicksand of apples, peelings, cores, pomace, day in day out!"

Yet as he swung back around on his stool, a protesting but willing slave to his trademark product, a pair of thoughts struck home:

"Tell that to Cynara for her next WARS meeting, AND, let's think of a kind of label for the shine and brandy jugs, good idea right?" —shifting just enough to evade the next 'tap'!

Quickened by the free give-and-take, Aslak swaggered to the black Model A at the gate.

"Here comes your man, Cynara!"

Next Sunday afternoon, October 22nd, truly a sun day with little wind, August was glad to join the couple and Eunice for dinner, all feasting on Lake Superior white fish on Aslak's side of the hill, then helping with cleanup.

August, a heavy dinner plate peeking out of the drying towel in his hands, surveyed the electric stove, the humming heat transfer case atop the Frigidaire, the sinking coals of hard maple in the north fireplace.

"It's a nice change for an afternoon, out away from apples for the first time this month," he asserted. "But I hope it won't be too long before the county gets enough from the RFC to bring power out north along M64; maybe they'll hook me up and transfer up to you, do you think?"

"There's more to it than just the RFC," Aslak said. He stuck his head out of the door to judge the weather.

"We haven't been up on your tower deck for awhile; let's try it up there, and I'll bring you up to date."

"I'm taking a sweater for me and one for you, Eunice; and a blanket for a kind of lap robe in case it gets chilly for the three of us"—she winked at Eunice—"while the men can show just how tough they are, we won't have to shiver!"

Once outside—first, the detour over to the barn fence to stroke the mares' velvet noses, pat their cheeks and scratch around their moving ears—it seemed warm enough, no snow except for last night's dusting among the bushes and second growth, the road itself bare and dry, to walk up the hill and down the other side to August's new splendor.

In spite of having to stop for a breather on top, Cynara proclaimed that

"This kind of exercise is what Dr Blake recommended last visit. I'm on my feet a lot at the Post Office, but my heart rate doesn't go up much. The more oxygen I take in the better our little what's its name will grow!"

On the way down walking on remnant ice glitter seemed risky enough for Cynara to hang on to Aslak's offered arm.

Which suggested to August that he offer his; with a brief hesitation, Eunice accepted. To her no help seemed necessary, but when her nearness, and the feel of strength in his arm, took her once again into that vague glow of excitement, she was glad she'd accepted.

Not on the way up, but when they turned into August's gate arm in arm, *her* heart beat had speeded up. Good for her health, and not just physical body health, either.

But she had to let go so August could unlock and open the tower door. And up the twin to the circular staircase on the other side of the hill, the hand rail had to suffice.

At the top, the view was grey with a dusting of white under a few small clouds dotting the windless sky, but the sheer expanse, the sensation of miles and miles of second growth in all directions, leafless hardwoods with scatterings of lost sheep evergreens kept them silent while they drew in deep breaths along with the sight.

"Do you ever think you might get bored, looking at all this?" Cynara asked August.

"Not so far, and even in winter I think there will be little changes now and then, even if just more or less snow, so I just admire what there is, stay here a while, then get back to work."

When were all seated, with sweaters and blanket within reach, on one of the long benches, it turned out that the men were on the ends, the ladies in the middle, next to each other, and Cynara warmly touching Aslak, while Eunice enjoyed a different and better contact with August.

Whose question about electricity coming up M64 to branch up the Mile Road was gone, replaced by a different kind. And while it buzzed in his brain he felt a hand slide under his forearm to clasp his hand in hers.

He turned, hoping his awareness of the touch would not end it, mixed with the warning to self: At your age don't get excited, to meet her faded blue eyes and her try at a smile, as if to say, 'Okay?'

His own fingers, tightening on hers, was the answer.

"Now, to get back to the power and the county crew," Aslak resumed, "I hear there's some kind of argument in the town board about favoritism bringing the line to our place, money that could have been spent coming out as far at least to the corner north of town to get power along M64 past the Mile Road north to Simondsen's and Bositch's, come up here as a branch instead of straight north from Gogebic Station through the woods."

He cleared his throat.

"Anyway, that's what Peter Erikson says his dad told him. I wouldn't be surprised if word about that has got up to Ontonagon, and tossed a monkey wrench somehow into powercoming up M64. That's as far as I got; maybe Peter can get some more on it up in Ontonagon."

Silence for a while. Aslak gave the blanket a better covering of Cynara's ankles for which his reward was yet another dazzling smile. His mitt squeezed her near hand. They communed by the touch of their bodies and hands declaring their mutual satisfaction, in the literal sense of 'making full'.

August and Eunice had overflowed: He in terms of the same whirlwind of conception that, on the train returning from Milwaukee, had erupted into the word 'MARRIAGE'—the possibility that, in his new identity, new capability, he might be capable of providing for a wife and even family.

An overflow of thought.

Much less, for Eunice, of a future possibility: A return in stronger force of that thrill, the new feeling of—what *was it?*—a sensation of heat, as if her whole body was blushing? From August's touch, her hand in his, no aroma in this cold/warm sun blend.

Sitting on the bench of a viewing deck owned by a unmarried man as if….

"Ja," Aslak began, "and I hate to disturb our appreciation of this unusual and beautiful view we're enjoying, but I had some other word from Peter—about this road and titles to the land on it, including mine and yours, August."

Aslak, from his far end of the foursome, looked past the women's suddenly focused faces.

"There's been a fair amount of muttering going on in Bergland about it,and other things, too, Jim tells me, being talked about at the pickup point on Center Street. It's beginning to sound as if the good will we built up, maybe not just by us, is beginning to break into some different pieces."

Cynara remarked, "You know, in the Post Office some people, some men, don't meet my eyes as they used to. They seem embarrassed about something, but they don't say anything about what it might be."

"Not to keep you guessing—but what I started out with, the land along the Mile Road, Peter tells me that the other day Frank Cutler came in, wanted to look at some deeds on Section Thirty, this section and down into Amundsen's woods, he might want to get some wood cut, see who to ask about it."

"Á'course, he didn't see him, Myrtle just happened to mention it, 'cause when he left he didn't close the book, and when she picked it up to put it back, she noticed he had left it open to the page with the deeds for the Mile Road. My father's from his brother, and such."

Aslak cleared his throat, saw the concerned, questioning faces.

"Normally, he wouldn't have mentioned it to me, and first of all Myrtle may not have ever thought to mention it to Peter."

Aslak looked away, the half-grin absent.

"But the word all over the township is that Frank Cutler has been getting to be a real yahoo about things in general and some things in particular. And one of them is people havin' enough cash to build new houses or redo them up pretty fancy, when this here Great Depression has most everybody scrapin' the bottom of the barrel."

"Well, now the cat's out of the bag I might as well close the bag. If he's looking for cordwood to cut, for his stove, he and everybody else in the township knows I own from my father all or most all of Section Thirty, so if he wants to cut some stove wood all he has to do is catch me coming into or going back out of town to ask me."

He brought the half-grin back in place.

"August, I'll see you later for the particulars you might want to hear. For now let's put it out of our minds, we can take care of it if it doesn't take care of itself! Say, who's that out there?" and he pointed at the lake to their left front.

For awhile they forgot any concerns about Frank Cutler, or at least on the surface, watching a young man wandering apparently aimlessly around the blueberry tussocks on the far side of the lake, just inside the hillock covered with head-high white birch.

Eunice, who as a lumberjack had driven a team in the area to the north, supposed it was one of the Thompson boys on the farm next to Haywire's on M64.

"You're right; she was in the Post Office the other day asking how he could get muskrat fur to Sears," Cynara added, smiling at Eunice right next to her.

In bringing her glance back from nodding at Eunice to corroborate her observation re who now lived at the Thompson farm, she didn't miss the absence of Eunice's right hand, though her forearm next to August's was in view.

But Cynara didn't betray her notice by looking back and up into Eunice's eyes.

Nor did Eunice betray her awareness of Cynara's observation by yanking her hand back out of August's.

Self-possession on the part of both—but August's firm grip had her hand trapped, too!

After a while of chat about how nice Bergland looked with the amazing amount of trash gone from yard, street, and roadsides, Cynara declared herself in need of some rest, maybe even a later afternoon nap, so the foursome moved down the circular ladder, marveling once more at its solid feeling, no tremors with four people simultaneously stepping down its covered tread, and its clear wood luster, enhanced by shellac.

"I can hardly wait to get home," Cynara claimed, giving Aslak a sly pinch inside his forearm as they stepped toward August's gate.

August in a tone declaring the politeness of his offer, asked of Eunice,

"Have you ever seen brandy being made from apples?"

To which, evidence of her move away from the extreme of insecurity since her dialog with Yaga, and an ever so slight recovery of the since-dormant if not destroyed self assured manner of Gallopin'Lil, Eunice slipped her right hand openly into his left, and replied,

"No, but I'd love to!"

With a smile up into August's hopeful face.

In they went.

Aslak didn't resist Cynara's tug toward the Mile Road as she tossed over his shoulder,

"Thanks for the visit on the tower deck!"

Inside his apple factory, August apologized for the appearance.

"Usually I have everything picked up, but in the fall rush to get most of the apples in the chain of brandy making I let some things pile up, like those peelings here just inside the door."

"It gives a nice aroma to this first time visitor, though," Eunice demurred. She gave his left hand a little squeeze for emphasis.

"I have things set up to keep waste motion to a minimum. Down the left side I have the shelves for storage in bushel baskets, next is the peeler, then the pomace in the press, then at the end the barrels for the apple juice out of the press to ferment into cider. In front of the barrels, the trap door to the cellar. Then, coming back up the right side, several spaces for cider barrels coloring from red oak, approaching the proof level of brandy as I take off each night's layer of ice on top of each barrel until just inside the door, close to the Mile Road, are the jugs ready for either town at Jim's house on Center Street or to the depot for the DSS&A to take to Milwaukee."

Eunice followed his discourse intently, not letting go of August's hand. The sensation of belonging she first felt, sitting next to August, touching, on the tower deck, grew stronger as she stood in his place of business, learning the process of making brandy, being invited to comment on how he ...

"And doing this you made enough money for the house?"

"I paid Floyd Marsh cash on the barrel head, half to begin, the rest when we both agreed it was all done—water found and pipes laid, house wired with 200amp board for when the power comes out here. I kept the kerosene stove so I can cook until the power comes, then I'll get a stove like Cynara's and Aslak's."

"You do what brandy-makers do, so you are a brandy maker." Eunice stated.

August, no less fearful than Eunice that he might be mistaken, be rebuffed, hesitated. Should he, never married, a bachelor at forty, invite a new role?

Always solitary, once and still somewhat of a scholar, make such a huge change?

Speak, share, the truth. See what happens.

"I do more. I see you when you are not here."

Eunice shook in a fit of trembling. Overcome, she turned, still holding his left hand in her right, hugged his arm fiercely with her left, pressed his arm tightly against her suddenly hot, subtly contoured front.

August had never held a woman in his arms. In all of his reading, none had informed him of what was pressing against his left arm.

He could turn neither toward her nor away.

Eunice gasped, tightened her body pressure against his arm and hand for a long moment.

She turned her face forward, leaned back away, dropped her left arm, held his hand, looked up at August's wondering face.

"I've never heard those words before. From anyone."

August murmured, "I spoke the truth."

"I'm glad. In my new life I wonder before I speak if I am sayin' what I should. In my old life I never did that. And ..." she stopped, stared deep into his eyes to weigh what next.

"I don't want to fall back into what I was. I want to do *for, not to* people."

August, without words, said nothing.

"What you just said did somethin' for me. It told me what I wanted to be for you I really am."

Her words unlocked August's.

"You are for me what I want you to be. Never before has a woman appeared to me, though only in my mind. Now I know what I have missed. It makes these moments with you so much more valuable."

Touching only hand to hand, both stood silent, eyes locked.

His life-time habit of caution slowly reasserted itself.

"Come," he said, turning to his right, gently moving her around also, "I will walk you up and down the hill to Cynara's. I think we should consider where we will go in this new way of being."

Eunice, awash in a repeat of that new feeling, aware of the dampness, nodded, pressing down any urge to continue, to build toward more, now.

"We have plenty of time to grow into what we feel now," Eunice agreed. "If I wanted to act in a hurry I *would be* fallin' back to my old ways! See, you are even now doin' *for me*!"

When night fell, August, his factory back to its accustomed neatness, fell asleep not with a vision but a recollection of her touch, her words; Eunice, relating only the factory sequential relationships from apples to brandy to her hosts, to dream of his words, his touch.

And what more might ensue.

While in the dark of that late October night, the carpet of timber to their north, to the north of Bergland Township, reached as before to and over the Porcupine Mountains, stood sentinel over the waves of Lake Superior thrusting their yellow-white tops up the sandy south beaches, leaving their froth on the sand, rolling back into that great lake.

Chapter Thirteen

On Wednesday morning, November 1st, August waited, waved as the black Model A sedan went by.

All of the season's apples that he could garner were in the cider-to-brandy stages. His function now was the timely jacking the ice off the cider, testing with the hygrometer to reach the desired proof for August's Applejack Brandy, seeing to the desired deliveries.

A license to return to a life of relative leisure, study, visits …

Remember Skantz' threats!

Later that morning he strode out to M64, ferrule-tipped apple walking stick in hand, in coat and tie—and rubber-footed boots! Snow and/or slush could be expected any day!

Intent: To enjoy a good dinner at noon at Anna's. First, visit Jim Ferguson for the latest on scale log shipping on the DSS&A.

At Piper's, the garage repair door was down; inside, Bill told him why.

"No cars in there to be worked on; if somebody does come in, I call Jim at his home."

A rueful grin at August. "Depression's not over yet!"

He turned the corner off Ash onto Center, waving his apple walking stick casually at Mrs Shankey's face in the window—without acknowledgment—passed by Archie Lackie's saloon on the corner of Center and Pine, ended up with a knock on Jim Ferguson's house halfway down the gentle slope of Center.

He was about to repeat the knock when Jim opened the door.

"Come on in, August! I was down below, took me a few minutes to realize what I'd heard was a knock, and then to come up the stairs!"

They moved downstairs to the distribution room.

August saw evidence of much use for fellowship, ease, enjoyment.

"Looks like people hang around in here—read magazines, toss darts—hang a few pictures."

Jim took it further. "Yeah, Grace Hill brought in a few of her watercolors of scenes around Bergland—the quarry alongside the road up past the Huberts' place, the grandstand up in the park, this view of the mill from the dock—to give us something to look at beside the bare walls. I subscribe to the *Open Road for Boys* and the *Grit*, and Talarico brings in a few copies from his barbershop, like these *Saturday Evening Posts.*"

August thumbed through one. "Who reads these?"

Jim grinned. "Pete Kalamber and Kale Borseth have boys who come in here with their dads, they sit for a good while practically memorizing the *Open Road.*"

August's eyes widened. "Boys come down here?"

"Sure. They know what their dads do. It's a family thing. If the kids grow up in a house where their dad, maybe even their mom, takes a drink—ONE DRINK—to loosen up, act up with their kids, pay more attention to them—then they're already seeing how pleasant some restraint, with liquor anyway, can make a family be."

August nodded, saw another value. "And at the same time, some if not all, have some idea of what too much, an abuse, of liquor has, is, or used to be, in some families, or even their own, so they can be proud of their dad for his self-discipline, see their mother doing something helpful for their dad, not criticizing him as some wives, mothers, do."

Jim nodded, his face serious now. "August, you remember telling me that we were doing something we could be proud of?"

"I remember."

"I see it all around town. People are walking around with their heads up, talking in groups not just in Marko's or Archie's. Aslak started something that is going to live, to get this town–*keep* this town–in hope of something better."

He poked August's chest above the gold tie clasp. "And what *you* contributed—that thing with ouisge beatha, the water of life, that Aslak took to Cynara's group that night—was just as important. It got the women started on restraint instead of abstention."

Jim threw up his hands. "Hell, even Reverend Seeliger backed us up in his Easter sermon!"

Both men stood in awed silence, realizing how a simple idea, probably ridiculed initially, had taken hold, proved its worth.

August swung his right hand around the comfortable, inviting arrangement—ironically, enwrapped by walls of shelving holding jugs of moonshine and brandy.

"And what you've made of what could have been a rather grim pick-up point fits right in with the whole picture."

"I thought when I started to fix it up that I liked it better, so the rest of them might, too. Couldn't hurt! Instead, they chip in, add what they can to it."

Silence again, while these two, one a garage mechanic of Irish forefathers, who, when the Irish potato famine brought them to America, did so in hope; the other an educated, intelligent German, whose nation, as had others in a land long civilized, looked abroad for fresh land to provide opportunity, viewed the embodiment, the realization, in its basic meaning, of the hope that brought them here.

Of the material, one, August, a creator; the other, Jim, the purveyor. Of the idea, a symbiosis inoculating willing sharers against despair.

August cleared his throat, turned to leave.

Turned back. "I almost forgot. Any new word from Lederhof about the scale?"

Jim shook his head. "Not one load for Bergland's outfit has come in to DSS&A. As far as I know, nobody is out working for Gunlek in the woods."

Walking toward the steps up, Jim added, "I don't think there will be any from that Milwaukee office, from Skantz, for you to keep a check on."

Back on the first floor, August shook his head. "I know he's too smart to give me something new to hang on him. I know also he must be getting frustrated, and when he runs up against something, he won't quit. He wants his own, his dirty way, or else."

"You aren't afraid he'll try something up here to get even, are you?"

August clenched both fists. "I must be ready for whatever he tries. He knows I have what he is willing to use anything to get: Money."

Jim touched August's elbow.

"There's more than Skantz for you to be concerned about, August. Let's sit here—remember how Anna came knocking at the door for 'shine and brandy"—he sat opposite August, pulled up his chair, leaned toward August, elbows on the green-checkered oilcloth.

"I hear all the time, not just here down below on product night, but up at Piper's though I'm not there that much any more 'til cars get running again."

He stared intensely into August's eyes, his face tight.

"August, Frank Cutler hates your guts and he doesn't care who knows it. Not only do I hear about it from the gang, but when I'm up at Piper's, in working on a car or up front if Bill leaves me in charge. His regular rant is he just got back from 'killin' Krauts', in his own words and here's another 'lordin' it up', again his words, out on the Mile Road. 'Next thing you know', he keeps ranting, 'he'll be drivin' 'round town in some fancy car while all of us are sloggin' about scrapin' the bottom of the barrel.'"

August listened with internal twisting. The vision of Jim's center of good will, of camaraderie, fell in pieces behind his eyes.

"August, if what Waldine his wife has told some of the Ladies' Aid, that Frank brought some disease—no name mentioned—from France, gave it to her, and it's beginning to affect his brain—even if that's true, people in Marko's are listening, a few even buying him a beer."

"And there's been a few not too happy about all the glory about your new house—that turret with the deck on top—in the Detroit Free Press."

Jim's concerned voice faded a bit, as if he were distant, to August's ears.

"August, I'm not expecting a gang out there with torches and a rope. But I'd hate to see you blind-sided some day here in town, or you hear the tramp of feet and see some torches coming up the Mile Road from Marko's some Saturday night."

Jim sat back, left his arms on the table.

"I sound like I'm blowing it up too much, maybe. There's many admire you, could be friendly. But I felt you should know. Forewarned is forearmed."

"Let me know, you need help," Jim held the door open, to August going down the front steps.

By the time he reached Cedar Street, turned right toward Anna's Hotel, his shiver of apprehension slid into a quiver expectation.

Eunice would be working in the restaurant!

The black Model A turned in, parked, as August turned onto Railroad Street at a few minutes after 11:30. He and Aslak climbed the steps, entered the restaurant together.

Cynara waved them over in the nearly full restaurant. "I needed the walk today," she explained. "Some days I just get het up in that office and need some fresh air."

"I saw the CLOSED sign on the door," Aslak replied.

August, his attention on the kitchen door opening, slid into the far seat by feel, was able to see Eunice, both arms laden with full plates, make a speedy beeline to a far table, fan out the plates with the dexterity of a faro dealer, scan all the other tables while hastening toward the Mile Road customers.

With a wide smile for August, her hand on his shoulder, she rattled off the special,

"Meatloaf, hash browns, green beans or corn, slaw, water to drink?"

They answered in kind, she was off after a light tap on August's hands, folded on the table top.

"I see you get the special treatment today, August," Aslak had the half-grin with a strong bit of knowing in the eyes.

"Oh, you and I are just that same old married couple," smiled Cynara. "What *did* bring you into town today, August?"

"I visited Jim, had a good talk. I'm impressed with how he's made the delivery point a gathering point, carries out that idea of one drink restraint operating for more than just sobriety."

Before Cynara could ask for elaboration, Eunice was back with their plates, and off to answer calls from a middle table.

"Now," insisted Cynara, "How does Jim go beyond 'just sobriety'?"

August downed his napkin. "He encourages hanging around, talking over whatever the gang members, there to pick up their customers' jugs, want to talk about; he's got reading material there—*Saturday Evening Posts, Open Road for Boys, Field and Stream*—and if the sons of the men come with their dads for pickup, they have something to read, they can listen to and even join in with the gang members, see how orderly and pleasant the supposed vicious beastly world of moonshiners can be."

"As the twig is bent, so grows the tree," Aslak offered. "The atmosphere there and at home, seeing their dad showing some self-discipline, gives them a role model, and at the same time helps grow respect for their dad. So Jim, I think, takes a shot at influencing the future for the youngsters."

By the time they'd finished, with a slice of apple pie, the restaurant was almost cleared. The clock over the entry way showed close to half-past twelve.

A clatter of silverware from the kitchen, and Eunice came over, sat with the three.

"You got rid of the apron in a hurry," Cynara observed. "Are you ready to go?"

"Go where?" August asked. "I thought I could visit with the waitress for a few minutes!"

"She's going with me to Ewen," stated Cynara, "She hasn't seen a doctor in years; she needs to put on a few pounds—if I could give her some of mine I would!"

"That's why I'm in here," Aslak offered. "They need a ride to Ewen. And we better be on our way."

"If it's all right with you, I can sit down with somebody in the bank, see how I'm set up for some deals," August said. "Is there room in the back seat? Maybe I can have a few words with Eunice there!"

"Of course, partner!" Aslak agreed, rising, brushing off a few crumbs of pie crust.

So out they went, Anna wishing them a pleasant afternoon, waving good-bye at the top of the steps as they swung around the corner of Railroad and Cedar Streets, up to M28 and east toward Ewen.

Since what Eunice wanted to talk about was too personal for the ears of Aslak and Cynara, she had to content herself with holding August's right hand (Aslak's rear view mirrow showed their faces only) while they whizzed through Topaz, making the two square turns to cross the DSS&A by slowing enough so that the Model A, much lower slung than the Model T it replaced, didn't lean outward enough to risk tipping over.

In Ewen Aslak parked by the bank, close to Dr Blake's clinic. Aslak went to see what the general store offered while the ladies headed for the clinic and August entered the bank.

Mr Greenberg, whose wife ran the Ewen Hotel and restaurant, was visible through the open door of his separate office. August nodded hello to the Maki girl who stood behind the grilled window with the overhead sign 'Teller' and the scooped-out basin in the window shelf through which all documents and money were moved in and out.

There was no one else in the bank. The Maki girl nodded permission as she saw that August was headed toward the president's door.

Mr Greenberg rose, welcomed a solid depositor with some spirit.

"You are out and about, I see," he added, reseating himself, pointing to the chair beside his desk. "What can I do for you today?"

"Some general business—I know what my balance is from the statements you send me each month—but I'm thinking of buying a car, so I'd like what advice you can share, about cars and loans and so on."

"Of course we'd be happy to lend you what you think you might need." He rolled his chair back, turned to face August directly, crossed a casual foot over his opposite knee.

"To be perfectly honest, cars don't cost that much compared to the size of your account with us. Of course, what you want to pay for a car depends on the kind of car, and would be between you and the car dealer, but most cars are between five hundred and up, with cars like a Cadillac, the top cars, a thousand or more."

August silent, he went on. "There's only one dealer in Ewen. He has some new Fords, I think a Chevrolet or two, and some used cars I see in view as I come past each day. You might want to go to Wakefield, Bessemer, or Ironwood for more variety."

"While I'm here, and have some time to spare, I'll take a look at what's here, I think. How is the banking business going these days?"

"We do have some loans out, but business is slow—you can see there aren't many folks inside this bank! And it's the same all over, I hear. Hoover has put some safe footing under most American banks, so we think we'll weather the Depression. And the outlook is better though it hasn't shown up much in new accounts. People are pinching what pennies they're earning, but something will come along and as I say, we're hopeful."

August rose, turned away. Mr Greenberg, as he went with him to his door, added, "I see the Weidmann brothers are getting into the logging business around Ontonagon; some pine and hemlock, but mostly hardwood for GM and those car factories—steering wheels, and so forth, I hear—so there'll be some more jobs to fill in for Gunlek Bergland's closing."

Maybe that's why Lederhof sees no more logs down at the depot from Bergland's outfit, August ruminated. I hope that standoff with Skantz stays as it is!

What if he should buy a car, touch off Cutler's rage?

And leave contact with Eunice to chance?

At the car dealer's his suit and tie, along with the applewood walking stick led the owner to lead him over to a nearly-new Lincoln Le Baron convertible Roadster, but August wanted to get a sedan.

"Partly because I need it to haul some merchandise every week or so," he told the eagercar dealer. As in the bank, August was the only customer.

"And I want a new one," August asserted. "Used often means an immediate repair ofsomething or other!"

"Oh, of course!"

One of the sedans was a new Buick with fuller skirting fenders, but all the accentuated curves in the body styling looked too girlish, French, maybe.

With the new Chevrolets and Fords he got down to business.

The Chevrolet Six, a roomy sedan, caught his eye, for $555, four doors, black, a solid, strong look. And six cylinders—it would move a heavy load of brandy!

"Understand, today I'm just looking. I'm going to have to learn how to drive, shift, and all that, first!"

The dealer's best deal, though, seemed to be the 1932 Ford. Model As had given way to the Model B. With a V8 engine, its acceleration and best of all, its power, was what 'sold' August. Sixty-five horsepower!

When he'd seen enough, and heard enough, August went back out on Ewen's main street, leaving the dealer with a promise to be back but no deal.

Still nobody waiting in the car.

Oh, here they come, back from the Dr's place.

Eunice's eyes were bright, her face an excited faint pink. What Dr Blake had told her, when she followed Cynara's private audience with her own, and he'd heard her history of kidney trouble, followed by years of strenuous lumberjack labor with heavy drinking added, with an originally-skinny body to begin with, was that her history seemed an open-and-shut classical history of delayed menstruation.

The good news, when he learned of her forswearing alcohol, and strenuous labor, with an improved diet, was that, in spite of her being near middle age, and with the unusual (to *her*) responses to male nearness a good sign, her chances to begin menstruation and subsequent pregnancy seemed entirely likely!

All of which she kept to herself, giving Cynara only a generalized summary on the order of "Keep on the way you are and your hopes up. Mental attitude can make it happen or keep it from happenin'!'"

But, back in the Model A with Aslak and Cynara sharing her good news that all was in order, apparently, for a safe delivery of a healthy baby in about six weeks, her grip of August's hand was fierce with joy!

And when she debarked at Anna's he had to be content with her "See you next Sunday afternoon!" delivered to all three.

But when, on Thursday morning, he'd finished checking all of the fermenting cider, decanting and corking all that had become August's Applejack Brandy, and the day lacked that pressure of strenuous activity so common up until today, he devised a plan.

Not at the drop of a hat.

First, look in the mirror, that nearly full length one hanging on the wall just inside the front door. What do you see?

All right, go put the meerschaum back in its rest by the easy chair.

Front view: Over five but not quite six feet tall. Little detectable wedge-shaped narrowing from shoulders to hips all the male models seem to have. Best single word: Wide.

Face also wide, normal nose, chin; hair, yes, with eyebrows medium, all three black. Eyes brown to yellow. Expression: one of mild interest, no frown. Smile—huge teeth stained with pipe smoke nicotine.

Profile: Slight forward bulge shoulders to crotch. Normal buttocks. Quite erect, really.

Summary: Average. Overage? Grade: Medium

Accomplishments: Brandy maker acclaimed for quality from here to Milwaukee. Income from brandy evident: Clothing, new home paid for, a healthy account in the Ewen bank, and a goodly stash of fifty-dollar bills under a supply of corn in the Section Thirty shack.

Grade: Excellent, if not unique in Ontonagon County!

Esteem of Peers: Satisfactory. Well, not Cutler—and some more: Many?

Now for a decision: How desirable is it to change bachelor status to married man?

He rose to walk back and forth, his footsteps muted on various area rugs, ringing on the inlaid bare floor. Not because he could think better, but because considering such a change was upsetting. It made him nervous, strangely unsure of where he might go and how to get there as well.

Assuming he was serious about wedding Eunice.

What exactly was marriage? To start, you lived with a woman. You did things with her that were pleasant, delightful, even ecstatic for as long as you lived or she did. You were the provider.

Children. Aha! If Cynara was exemplary, the women wanted them, even with the strain of pregnancy. But they are built to do that! How would pregnancy, birth, a child taking up the attention you'd come to enjoy, change things?

He envisioned a wife who was barren—or what if he himself was sterile? An agnostic, he felt no religious imperative about being fruitful.

Question: How happy would Cynara be if she had proved barren, or lost her child before or … No need to ponder an answer to that one.

So how about shifting the perspective from his own felicity to that of Eunice? If it was of great importance to her to have a baby, how about doing it to please her, never mind how much he would like fatherhood? Would he, did he, want her to live with him just the same?

How about if he wasn't doing it—marrying her—for his own delight but *just for her*?

Let's dig into that: Would he agree, if, let's say, Eunice discovered herself capable of giving birth, of getting pregnant, and chose him as rich enough, in fact the only eligible male she could live with after, especially in need of haste because of her own approach to the end of child-bearing age? When it would endanger her own life?

If Eunice were willing to risk her life for a child of her own, wasn't it cheap to deny her?

Put it this way: If he married Eunice as a means to his own pleasure, wouldn't Kant say he was failing to regard her as an end, but as a means to his own end?

August realized Zwei was following him back and forth and around the house-size room.

He sat back down in his chair. Immediately Zwei hopped up to circle around then lie down, head on his forepaws, on August's lap.

Wasn't it plain that though he'd acquired Zwei as a watch-dog-companion, he was now treating his dog as an end, not just a means to an end?

No matter if he should begin living with Eunice as a means to either his or her end, might it not grow into an end in itself?

If all of his reasons for not marrying and for marrying were cinder blocks, and he put the 'not' and the 'for' on a scale, which way would the scale dip?

"Even you could see that, couldn't you, you hairy little four-footed lion?"

To which Zwei, as usual for answer, barked twice—his name. Good as a pawprint in ink at the bottom of any document!

So, the decision is ...

Wait: If I marry Eunice just for her sake, when she realizes she's not doing anything for me, didn't she say she wanted to change, do *for* others, won't she feel unhappy? And how about what I talked to Aslak about, that concept of the more 'clothes' we put on, the more we deny our primitive nature? Which is desirable: To respond to our basic needs—eat, sleep, fight, mate—or to 'dress up' our life with stylish clothes, live in fancy houses, pretend, say nice things all the time?

But how tenable is stasis, being a 'man of stone'?

Back off, try another approach.

If primitive is Thesis, and civilized is Anti-Thesis, A goal = Synthesis

Trial synthesis: Meet primitive needs in a civilized manner.

In commoner terms, if the 'How' is the negative, change it to positive: Charm, not Club!

In translation: Spend enough time with Eunice developing our relationship to the point where we agree on goals and method; what and how.

Spend more time with Eunice means I need a car. Can't lean on Aslak all the time, and one afternoon/evening a week with Eunice is not enough, and a foursome is not the way to better knowledge for a twosome. We need private time together.

So Thursday morning, November 2nd, 1933, after skimming the ice off fermenting apple cider, testing with hygrometer for the 'proof' desired for August's Applejack Brandy, the business proprietor, in his suit, but with rubber-bottomed boots for a snowy road, with his applewood walking stick, strode out the Mile Road and down M64, to show up at Ed Borseth's depot in Bergland to see about trains for Ewen or, in the other direction, Wakefield, Bessemer, or Ironwood. He had, in his inside coat pocket, an envelope with a significant number of fifty-dollar bills retrieved from the Section Thirty corn barrel in between Haywire's night shift departure and Aslak's arrival for the day shift at the stills.

Get a one-way passage. He'd get back under—well, not exactly his own power. But it would be under his sole control.

How wonderful, decisions made, to be in motion!

In Ewen, the owner was delighted to take a learning spin with August.

Demonstration: Turn key, motor starts, in cold weather use choke, richer mixture.

Clutch in, handbrake off, gear shift up to First, let out clutch smoothly, not too fast, accelerate with pedal, clutch back in, foot brake, Neutral gear. Stop.

Practice: Start, slow, stop. Start, slow, stop.

Start, shift to Second, then to High, slow stop.

Repeat. Go to gas station, check oil, fill tank, back to auto dealership.

For the 1932 Chevvy Sedan, black, four-door, $600. For the 1932 Ford Model B, V-8, 65 hp, four door, $675.

He headed out west on M28 for Bergland in the Ford.

After the last big curve out of Topaz, during the mile-long glide down the hill into Bergland, he turned left on Cedar.

No breakfast. Instead, there'd been the hasty dash on foot, Zwei giving up at Kallaak's Corner, sitting down to wait his return, the dig for the fifties, then a dash mostly uphill, then nearly sliding down to his own gate, Zwei panting in protest, he was hungry.

Being late at Anna's for a noonday meal was not important. He'd have whatever Anna could rustle up.

See Eunice. See what happens next.

When he barged through the front door and checked the clock, a good meal was a strong possibility: Only 1:45.

Both Anna and Eunice came out to greet him, the sole customer. Anna offered a friendly hug, which August accepted and returned; Eunice remained slightly behind Anna, but with a welcome smile—and a wink.

"What can we get for you? We have pork for a sandwich, okay?" Anna offered.

Looking at Eunice, August asked, "If the slave hasn't eaten yet?"

A shake 'No' from Eunice.

"Then how about a couple of sandwiches?"—Anna caught that she wasn't included—"and we share them?"

Anna nodded to Eunice, who darted back into the kitchen, while Anna led August to the far corner table, sat in the chair he held out for her, pushed back in as she settled.

With a glance at the kitchen door, Anna leaned a bit over toward August.

"She seems up on a cloud today, what's going on?"

Up on a cloud?"

"Yes, she keeps humming some kind of song; excited, happy—not that she's been sad, or anything, just more so. Remember I said not so long ago, that she was working too hard, or trying too hard? Now she's just glowing to look at, and singing to herself! Is she breaking up under the strain of being the opposite of Gallopin' Lil?"

"Here you are!" called Eunice, marching out to them, holding high in one hand a tray, the contents covered by a cloth, in the other hand a coffee pot with two cups.

Anna sat back, couldn't hide a smile at August—once again, she correctly read the signs of a woman's response to a man in her presence—then rose.

"Oh, I just remembered ...." She began, about to publish a completely non-existent set of circumstances which demanded she leave the two to themselves.

Then she saw that the two she was leaving hadn't heard a word.

With a sigh taking the place of the smile, she returned to her desk by the front door.

Some women are just lucky!

Until Eunice had draped the cloth, a dish towel, over her shoulder, delivered both plates, poured two cups of coffee, she didn't meet August's eyes.

Then, seated, she did.

August, unable to move, fell into her faded blue eyes, for keeps.

Neither looked down at their sandwiches of good rye bread with a thick slice of pork in between the rye slices attempting an escape to the plate on all four sides of the rye.

August finally managed: "What time are you done here tonight?"

So many of his earlier questions to himself were answered by her failure to respond, to continue his capture in her eyes without, apparently, hearing him.

Not one to give up easily, he repeated it.

"What time are you done here tonight?"

Her gaze flickered for an instant. Her mouth opened, her lips moved.

Not a sound.

"What time shall I come back for you?"

At her desk, Anna grew concerned. Speechless Eunice? Had her apparently wasted body by some indirect path shut down her ability to speak?

Again, Eunice's mouth opened, her lips moved, and she must have answered, for August rose, place his hand on her shoulder, and said, "I'll be here to pick you up."

Then August turned and walked past Anna out the door without giving Anna so much as a glance.

"She can't speak above a whisper and he's gone blind," Anna reckoned, but she knew that wasn't so. A few minutes later the clock struck two. Anna stopped at the table.

Neither sandwiches nor coffee had been touched.

But when Anna picked up the tray leaning against Eunice's chair leg, Eunice gave a tiny shake of her body to return to a living, respondent human creature.

"I'll take those back to the kitchen," she said, in an absent-minded way.

"I've got them," answered Anna. "You take that applewood walking stick to the coat room before somebody else comes in and walks out with it."

"I'll take it up to my room," Eunice replied. "Somebody might take it in the coat room, too."

On the stairs a twinge, then a stab of pain below her navel doubled her over.

Then it vanished. A warm flow oozed down her thighs. She yanked the towel off her shoulder, applied it, held it there, leaning against the railing, her world bright, a glorious entry into her long-denied, hoped-for ascent into womanhood.

Goodbye, Gallopin' Lil.

Chapter Fourteen

The turn off M64 onto the Mile Road was a test for August's neophyte driving skill. Most of that side road entry was blocked by a semi-trailer with a high stack of long, long heavy poles a foot thick at their base. Next to it was a slightly smaller but heavy truck with a posthole digger at its rear revolving a huge auger pulling dirt up into a growing heap.

He watched the auger lift its revolving inclined planes until the huge screw at its tip cleared the hole's edge, the auger swung to one side.

Behind the cab of the semi-tractor a huge clamp seized the top log—a power pole, August realized—swung it erect over the hole, released its grip to let the post thump down to the bottom, nudged the pole erect, held it there while two men with shovels threw stones and dirt into the hole to hold the pole in place.

Didn't take many shovels—the hole was barely wide enough to take the pole. The tamping with inch-thick iron rods firmed the pole's position.

When all the vehicles had been rearranged for the next hole some fifty feet west on the Mile Road August could finish his turn, creep past the trucks, the trailer bed, the men who stood watching the drill handler swing the auger toward the stake marking where the next pole was to stand.

Well out of the way, August set the handbrake, recognized the man standing closest to him as Herman, the older of the two Hill brothers, who'd worked on August's house.

"You don't work for Marsh anymore." Not a question.

Herman kept his foot on the shovel heel. "Yours was his last job—no new houses going up in Bergland Township. He's doing repair work now—doing the work himself."

August shook his head in sympathy. "Depression still not gone, they say."

Herman kept his eyes on the auger already half-buried its length into the spot for the next pole.

"Money came from county—part of that rural electrification program." He turned, his lips in a slow grin. "Something's better than nothing!"

Nothing germane to add, August turned back to his idling Ford. When he pulled to a stop by his factory door, Zwei was peeking around the far corner, his body hidden. But he bounded out as August closed the driver's door, stepped around the radiator.

"Just me, partner! I'm now a car-owning man!"

Zwei padded to the left front wheel, lifted his hind leg, identified the true owner for all who, at his height, read this kind of a bulletin board.

August, suddenly famished, went in to see what he could stir up that would be a lot and a treat.

And what he could whip up for a treat to go with a brandy for his date later this evening.

How about an apple pie in the 13" MACA Dutch oven hanging in the fireplace?

Down in the unheated cellar he decided to use two MacIntosh and one Wolf River from his personal cache. With the apples cranked through the hand-peeler-corer-slicer he wasted no time in mixing and rolling a crust from white flour and lard, draped half over a tin pie plate, dusted his hands.

Next, he laid and lit off a good fire in the fireplace, centered the oven on the swinging bar over the fire. Back at the shelf, he laid the string of the continuous slice from the Wolf River in the center, circled it with the two MacIntosh slices. Before he added anything, he nipped off and ate the core/stem ends to decide how much, if any, sugar to add to the filling.

Hmmm—a tablespoon of … brown sugar sprinkled over the top.

Now the top crust, crinkled all around the edge of the tin, a kitchen knife around the rim to trim off the excess while holding the whole thing at eye level, set it back on the shelf.

Good-sized hump in the center. But kind of blank, bare even with the vents cut in.

There lay the trimmed strips, odd pieces. Not many.

Some kind of design on the top crust? He thought, laid the pieces in a certain way, one on the left, the other on the right. E A.

Took up his clothes-pin with the cotton cloth wad on the split end, ran it sopping with melted butter over the top of the pie. Careful!

Laid a piece of green wood on the fire. Tested the oven-heat with a drop of water; it bounced off with a sizzle.

In with the pie on the middle removable shelf! Now, what to take the place of the pork sandwich I left untouched?

Anna checked the clock over the entrance door to her restaurant. 2:30. Her glance swept over the empty tables, the clean floor. She walked across the wide floor to the picture window fronting on Railroad Street.

Quiet. A shagpoke, what people here called it, a blue heron, lifting on its huge arced wings above the tree line hiding the near edge of Lake Gogebic, beat its slow leisurely way to the southwest, its wing tips measuring the whole of the millions-miles distant faint sun's diameter, then gliding, straight-back legs now hanging, to land on the opposite, the south shore.

Not a living soul in sight.

"I hope the days when this restaurant was hardly ever empty like this, when trains from both directions would spit out passengers wanting a meal, or a drink, or a room for at least the night, was a daily occurrence, come back soon."

It was a faint hope, like the yellow sun through the fall haze. If it weren't for the Luna Light Gang, patrons and suppliers, could she stay open?

I'm not getting any younger. I know, if I close up this place, I can go back to the big farmhouse at our crossing, Stindt's Crossing, where Rudolph has his dairy, make myself useful.

What I did here was make a living in the rush times, when the bachelors who didn't hope to stay, but to follow the lumber, the logs, to make their living and hope they'd last out a year or two, let the last years come/go how they may, needed a bed and a meal.

Economic orphans. A long way from the camaraderie of the Round Table in here. And how about my own adopted orphan? Where will she …

Relax! Remember August?

Again, the clock. Nearly 3!

Haven't heard a sound from Eunice upstairs. Better check.

At the landing, Anna called:
"Are you awake?"
A faint "Yes."
"Come on down, we'll have a brandy."
Silence, then, "I wish you'd come up."

Anna understood at first glance. "I'll be right back."

"Here, I don't need this anymore and the whole box-full is yours!"

Downstairs, at the bar's small round table, Anna patted Eunice's hand.

"I remember what mine was like; I can't begin to imagine how this is for you, but I'm *so* glad *for* you!"

"I can't put it in words, yet. Maybe I never will find the right words for it. I feel, now, as if my whole past life is erased, washed away, and I'm free—but I'm lost at the same time!"

"How do I think now, how do I know…? "

"Well, it's said 'Be careful what you wish for, you might get it!', but I'll help how and when I can. Remember, you've been on a good path now for months, and just plain habit, what you've been doing, will take over most of the time."

Anna looked down, then up.

"I have to say this, because it's such a good sign: You are positively aglow—your eyes gleam, your face is peach and pink—you look eighteen, not thirty-eight!"

Anna paused. "Can I hear what you and August said today, here?"

Eunice's glow deepened in a blush. "He's comin' here, he has a car, at seven to pick me up. We have some things to talk over, from Sunday."

Anna studied her partner's face, a smile slowly forming.

"Let me guess—we need a bit of brandy in our hands first?'"

Eunice's blush paled back to a glow. She nodded.

Armed, Anna raised her glass: "To a woman's future and her own family."

Eunice raised her glass, touched it firmly to Anna's: "Goodbye, Gallopin' Lil!"

After the last supper customer—of the half-dozen in all—was gone, and the tables all set for whatever breakfasts were demanded, Anna saw to it that Eunice was materially prepared for an evening out and given such advice as she saw fit, which could be summed up as "Fools rush in where angels fear to tread."

And at five minutes to seven Eunice opened the door, flitted down the stairs to the passenger door held open.

Off they went, both hearts near to bursting, as new to self and other as Adam and Eve.

West along Railroad, north along Ash, empty house on the corner of Ash and M28. West on M28, north on M64 past Piper's, Ontonagon Fuels tank truck blocking the garage wide doors, past Lakeview Cemetery on their left, Demaray's, opposite Leonard Erickson's(used to be Jorginus Nilsen's) dip down into Cutler's hill, across the culvert for Indian Creek, up the north side of Cutler's hill. Green-eyed reflections, two does and a buck, stock-still.

Past Jackson's farm on the right, next to the new CCC camp, immediate left, west, on the Mile Road.

"Those are the poles for the power line up to Aslak's", August gestured.

Eunice inhaled, sat as erect as possible. "I'll bet you're glad it's finally here!"

"They said they'll be back in the morning to set up the transformer, bring power into the house."

"For you, a whole new way ..." she let it die unfinished.

They went by Haywire's tarpaper shack, Amundsen's white frame one-story.

Zwei was waiting at the gate as August, practiced now, swung the Ford Model B in to stop opposite the door to his factory.

He touched Eunice's forearm. "Let me open your door for you."

Holding it open while Zwei read his eye-level bulletin board on the other side, he reached in to offer his left hand. Eunice, touched, took the offered hand, stepped out showing a touch of regal carriage in her movements.

August held her hand, turned, both now facing his factory.

"I join with you in remembering our meeting of minds, and bodies, Sunday evening. When we turn around, we face a new place, with that evening's understanding behind us a springboard, a starting place for this evening."

Eunice met his gaze. "I will always remember. Just by standin' like this, hearin' what it means to you, I know you better than I did before."

The vision of the two of them, standing there, formed her next words: "My past, before we were here that night, is a great desert."

A double bark from Zwei.

Eunice shivered, stepped around, tugged his hand. "Let's go forward from here."

Zwei plunged past them through the opened door beside the tower. In the glow from the fireplace coals, the warmth of the room, the warmth of their concurrence, they moved hand in hand to that fire, flameless all though burning still.

August gently doffed his coat, picked hers off her shoulders, came back from the hangers to rub his hands together over the Dutch oven, smiling at her visible curiosity.

"I think you can smell what's in there?"

"I smell apples but I've never seen a Dutch oven before!"

He picked up the mitten from the hearth, lifted the lid, held it tilted open enjoying the pleased amazement in Eunice's expression.

"That's for later, with the coffee. First we have a brandy, ja?"

Eunice hesitated.

"I've already had my one brandy earlier with Anna."

"To celebrate—what?"

"We'll probably get around to it a bit later—I'd rather wait."

He nodded, disappointment a fleeting shadow under his eyes, like an owl's flit across the full moon. "Your choice."

She relented. "But about the brandy, this is a new day for me with you. Yes!"

The snifters, small, of crystal, rang in the ceiling rafters like the call of Annunciation.

"I went through my mind about what we should do with this time we have together, only ourselves, to decide where we want to go from here. You should know that at least up to now I began as a serious student, thinking I might want to be someday a German professor in some European university. Then, the more I heard about America I decided I would finish my education here. I was hired as an office worker in Milwaukee—I needed to earn some money for my education here—then I was framed for a crime, had to leave my job and come up far from Milwaukee. I came here, made a living just off this homestead forty, then got going with brandy and was successful as you see."

He got up, put a few logs on the graying coals, came back to sit with Eunice close to the fire.

"Oops, I have to take the pie out now!"

The pie, a honey-brown apparent masterpiece, was set to cool on the kitchen table.

"I hope," he said, "that it's as good inside as it looks on the outside."

"I'd be surprised if it isn't," Eunice smiled. "I think you must know somethin' about me in the time I've been here, before, that is, the time I hit the man who drove me up here from Chicago."

"That's balanced by what you've become in the time since then," August responded. "And I guess that's part of the desert you just said outside. And you should know that what I've heard said about since you started working at Anna's has been both wonder at the change and praise for your persistence."

Eunice turned a bit, facing August. "For almost all of my life since about twelve I was angry because I'd never become a woman in the sense of bein' able to bear a child. I never changed my body's development in all that time, and I will be forty–one in December."

"I'm going on forty-two come January," was his response.

"One of the things I was known for was using crude language,about myself, anybody."

"I'm goin' to be honest with you, about myself, an intimate thing most women wouldn't say."

She inhaled. "This afternoon I learned I could get pregnant. Whether or not I can carry it to term ..."

"You learned this from Dr. Blake?"

"Yes. He said that my history of kidney problems, hard work as a lumberjack, and heavy drinkin' made ova development and bosom and hips expansion out of the question. But, I think, now, I am a normal woman in that way."

She fell back, her gaze locked on his. "There, I got all those words from Dr. Blake!"

August raised her hand to his lips. "No lumberjack, or would-be lumberjack, could remember those words, or would have used them if he could have remembered them. I think they tell me that you have the intelligence to understand my attraction to knowledge and learning. And your willingness to discuss your new capabilities so frankly with me tells me you possess the courage to continue moving away from the desert you mentioned."

He moved to adjust the damper on the fireplace chimney, came back to sit beside her. "I think we are congenial in important ways. You would no more sneer at my addictions to any literature, devotion to learning, than I would sneer at your past, however coarse and crude and aggressive it might have been."

"I hope you will accept me as a student hungry to learn," Eunice answered, "to study past wise persons' writin's, to appreciate poetry, words—those studies you bring to a point, like the 'tree of man' that Sherman liked in the wise way you do. You are a wealthy business man, you earned, not inherited, your wealth; at the same time, your knowledge of such things as ouisque beatha—yes, I heard people in the restaurant talkin' about it—shows you are aware of a lot of ideas. I hope some of that will rub off on me, in our time of friendship."

August took her hands, pulled her to him, held her gently, absorbed by the lilac aroma of her hair, the apparent physical fragility of this woman he had *seen knock down a grown man, drag him across Marko's saloon floor and fire him into the snow of the street.*

"I hope our time will continue. I don't want to consider any break-up of our time as friends, should we go no further, grow no closer."

"For while we have been quite practical and reasoning, don't doubt that I feel toward you as a man does for an attractive woman. I have no reason to doubt that I am able to start a child, though, like you, I have not so far."

"I can feel, this close against you," she murmured, "that you can become a father. And don't you doubt that we can move closer than friends, though be friends as well. Part of the reason I hope my outward appearance, my body, will become more attractive, more promisin' of bringin' delight to you by lookin' at me, is that I want to please you that way."

He kissed her upraised nose, her cheeks, her closed eyes, then parted her lips with their first kiss, firmly but gently. Her arms tightened about his waist.

Then she drew her upper body away. "No further tonight. Can we try the pie now?"

"You might as well learn where things are—I'll make the coffee, you cut two pieces of the pie—just rummage around for the pie cutter, the plates, the cups. In plain English, make yourself at home!"

Which, once he lit the kitchen kerosene in its mirror-back sconce on the wall, she was able to do!

The pie's crust was crisp, the filler tart and sweet.

"I shall remember this pie," August reflected, placing his fork upside down on his empty plate, tines toward the center, handle tip on the table top. "Once we broke through the crust of our uncertainties, I found the substance of our relationship to be what I had hoped."

Eunice responded, sure now that what she said, how she felt at the moment, would be welcome, well received:

"You made this for us, which tells me you wanted to have somethin' special for me—that you wanted me to enjoy somethin' you had made, to please me, to show me your warmth of feelin' for me. And," she turned the pie remaining slightly, "you see that when I cut the pie, the 'A' and the 'E' are still there. I want us to stay joined, close to each other."

"That tells me you are already aware of and enjoy seeing relationships, meanings that reflect personal attitudes, intents."

"One thing more," August went on, "what you just said suggests to me a further symbolism in those letters, something I wasn't aware of when I made them, but what I see now is true: Those letters were formed from pieces of raw crust overhanging the pie tin edges I trimmed before I put the pie in the oven. They lay scattered on the shelf, just as discrete as we were. Now they spell our first letters, making letters, forms that make sense."

Eunice's pale blue eyes shone, seemed to darken: "And, now they are made firm by havin' been baked, having benefited from heat."

August grasped her reaching hands. "So no matter what others may think, say, we are firm in our union from this time on, whatever kind of union we form."

He shook his head ruefully. "Though I think I must be pretty dull, most of the time!"

Eunice slowly freed her hands, pushed the pie out of the way. She stood, stepped around the table corner to meet his rising embrace. "For now, only on the surface."

Both pushed gently to gain space. He opened his mouth; she said the words:

"I need time to make this fit into my present, give me the goal of my future."

"I'll start the car, let it warm up."

Zwei tagged him out.

Eunice turned slowly, taking in her surroundings. The gleaming squares of parquetry, the vaulting underroof spaced by the crossing ceiling joists, the islands of use—kitchen, bath, cot—and the islands of promised conversations, of warmth; the vast cellar underpinning a solid, strong base of what she was now seeing. Imagining the bed, the island of love and blissful rest at the cellar's far wall.

Her breath caught in her throat. To stem the tears of joy, she made for her coat, thrust her arms into the sleeves, wavered toward the opening door.

"We're ready," he said.

"I'm with you," she was able to answer.

"What I'm talking about is coming back with all the money you can get your grubby hands on. And I'll be waiting at my phone so don't get any ideas about taking off, or stashing what you come out with. *Now* do you get it?"

The black-haired hulk across the cafeteria table smirked. "Nuttin' I ain't awready done more'n once," he growled.

"Everything won't be set until Thanksgiving," Skantz repeated. "You got that?"

"I'm ready any day. Jus' give me a few days notice."

Brusque, abrupt, careless of sensibilities, Skantz rose, left the hulk sitting there, sank into his half-crouch walk back to the half-empty office pool. Like those empty seats, his would be so come the New Year.

He wanted all the money, the long green, the moola he could scare out of August Schmidt for his out-of-a-job bonus.

There ought to be plenty of those fifty-dollar bills stashed somewhere in that new house.

Exactly what the hired-but-not-yet-paid goon was thinking!

How the pickup would go, pretty close to what this office creep wanted. How the shake-out of the dough would go—up to himself, wasn't it?

Monday the 6th of November Anna set the brandies down on the little round table by the bar.

"Eunice, the crowd in here for breakfast, and once or twice a week for noon dinner, is about the same it's been for awhile, but the evening meals are a losing proposition."

Eunice nodded. "I've certainly noticed."

Anna went on. "That's the bad news. The good news is that you have the afternoons off starting today, except for Thanksgiving Day, when we'll have a buffet until late afternoon. I think you have something going to fill in your free time!"

Eunice's eyes brightened. "Yes, ma'am! August and I have been talkin' about some short trips around—Ontonagon, Ironwood, mostly—but there's not much to see or do there Sundays. There aren't any movies here anymore, but Ironwood has a theater."

Anna raised her small snifter, waited, they clinked to Anna's "To the future!"

"How are things going with you and August?"

"We're sorry only for startin' so late in our lives—but it's true that neither of us would have been attracted to the other until lately."

"What's happened because of that is the opposite of everybody, about, whose shall we say 'first love' is at the beginning, and at your ages the shine is worn off. Now because of that delay, I would bet it's more enjoyable because of his loneliness and your stress earlier."

Eunice agreed. "Yes, havin' a long and excruciating experience until now makes the now seem, and actually be, most enjoyable."

She laughed. "The other day, Sunday, Aslak told that story about the fellow who carried a light hammer around, every couple hours he'd hit himself—on his head or thumb, like that—and his friend finally asked him why he did that and he said, 'Because it feels so good when I stop!'"

They chuckled, finished their brandies.

The phone b-r-r-red.

Anna answered, handed Eunice the phone.

"Dear, where are you callin' from?"

"From the house; Herman Hill said to let the phone company know if I wanted a phone line. They use the same posts, run the wire under the road in the same tube as the power line but in a separate pipe, so now we have a phone!"

"Gosh, the Mile Road is gettin' modernized in a hurry!"

"I called the theater in Ironwood. Tomorrow afternoon they are showing *Coquette,* with Mary Pickford. Would you like to see it—if Anna can spare you between noon and evening meals?"

"Yes, I would and I know Anna will!"

"What time—one p.m.?"

"I'll be ready! Bye!"

"I've got a suggestion," Anna watched Eunice hang up the phone on the wall box. "After the movie—yes, I can hear the other end on that phone—go with him to the main street and go into a nice dress shop, get a couple of dresses, skirts, blouses, a pair of nice shoes. Have you got any money for that?"

Eunice smiled. "Haven't been anywhere to spend anythin'—you've saved me all it would have cost me to eat and sleep!"

"You're sure? I can help you, if you need it."

"I'll take enough to get started. August always wears a suit; I have to look my best now, don't I!"

"I've noticed," Anna's eyes tightened a bit, she dipped her head, a sly upturn of her lips, "you are not exactly as straight up and down, front, back, and sides—as you were a few months ago. Remember what Doctor Blake told you in Ewen. Buy what you want now, but also what will fit for next year—dress in expectation, my dear!"

"In fact," Anna went on, pointing an index finger like a pistol barrel at Eunice's chest, "those aren't empty Bull Durham sacks any more!"

"You heard about that?"

Anna, still a big, hearty woman, laughed in delight. "Probably everybody in Bergland Township heard what you said to the driver who asked, coming up from Chicago!"

She studied Eunice's expression carefully. "And I mentioned it as a bit of a test! Not too long ago you didn't want to be reminded of those days. I think now you are armed against any fears about Eunice falling back into 'Lil'! Congratulations!"

"I love the aroma in this car," Eunice breathed deeply. "It smells just like apples—of course!" she jabbed his arm with a finger.

"When apple cider gets to a certain point I run some through a cloth to filter out the solids and use it like vinegar.

This morning I took a load of brandy to the depot for my outlets in Milwaukee, then, just now, I wiped the inside, especially the back seat leather, with some of it."

"Next time, can you take a load in, let me help you, bring me out to help with the loadin', unloadin'? In the afternoon, I mean."

"Sure thing. We're in this together!"

In the theater a boy with a flashlight splashing its light on the grimy red aisle carpet, they moved down down to the front row. Hardly anyone else was there to see the newsreel views of men standing in lines for jobs, for soup, in Chicago and New York City.

When the lights came up prior to the Mickey Mouse cartoon, Eunice remarked, "Those men for soup looked better than the men for jobs in those lines in Chicago."

They laughed along with the sparse audience at the antics of Mickey and Pluto, then sat back to enjoy the much ballyhooed film version of the Helen Hayes stage role on Broadway.

Its first scenes developed Mary Besant, a Southern belle heroine, with a long string of beaus. Her father, Dr Besant, a typical family tyrant of the South, banished her final favorite, a basically good young man but hot tempered and a layabout. When he returns the two are caught in a situation compromising his daughter's reputation. The raging father takes tragic revenge on them both.

In the car, he looked at her, the motor idling.

"Let's not look for omens in this—there's no irate father around for either of us! Let's do something pleasant to take our minds off the movie for awhile. There's still daylight, I'm not hungry for any meal yet."

Eunice's face bore a residue of regret.

"Let's drive around, see what's open for business, I want to get some new clothes."

"Good. And I'd like to look at electric stoves, some standing lamps. And I like to look at you, so we'll go into clothing stores first!"

What a disappointment: Ironwood had not one single clothing store for ladies. Nor for electric stoves.

They did find a delicious meal. Ironwood, and Wakefield had, in the mine heydays, when open pit mining for iron ore attracted Welsh immigrants, gained a reputation for meat and vegetable pasties. They were a sort of stew wrapped in what seemed a pie crust.

Nor were Eunice and August strangers to the meal. All over the Upper Peninsula the presence of the miners' 'box lunch' had encouraged entrepreneurs to set up small pastie shops. Even in Bergland, right across M28 from Piper's Garage, a sort of hole-in-the-wall pastie shop flourished.

The shop owner, on the shore of Wakefield Lake, laughed at their expectation of finding clothing stores, or even a single one, in Ironwood.

"Every home with a Monkey Ward or Sears catalog has its own store. All the traveling you need to do is to the Post Office and back home!"

By the time they were back nearing Bergland, dark was closing in.

"I would say Cynara has those catalogs," August volunteered. "We can drop in, visit, come away with one or both catalogs,—or, better still, you and Cynara can see what there is that you like while Aslak and I look over the Model B and so forth."

Cynara was enthusiastic about the latter system.

"Look, it has been six months since I've thought to look at clothes except maternity dresses and I haven't even looked at our new Fall catalogs. So we—you and I, Eunice—are going to put our heads and these two new catalogs together and if our men can't find anything to talk about or do, then it just proves how superior to them women are!"

"That's what it's like to be married," Aslak joked to August as they, a flashlight and a lit lantern in hand, went out into the dark of the moon to give the new car the once over. The initial point of wonder was under the hood: "Holy smoke," Aslak erupted, "*eight cylinders!* That's twice mine! It must burn the gas like a thirsty camel drinks water in the Sahara!"

So of course nothing would do but to take it out for a spin, August sitting in the passenger seat while Aslak, with minimal floundering, found the right levers, pedals, and all to get out the gate, left to M64, turn right, and *accelerate past Jackson's farm gate in* a matter of seconds that left both driver and passenger shoved against the backs of their seats until the car resumed a normal forty miles an hour as they dipped down and over Cutler's Creek and were at Piper's Garage, where Aslak could pull in, back out, and return at a normal smooth pace allowing notice of a dashboard with lit dials, a windshield wiper that ran on the twelve-volt battery, not the compression of the engine, a heater with a fan, an overhead light on and off by a switch, an engine coolant temperature dial on the dash, not out on top of the radiator, and an oil pressure dial right next to that dial.

"The reason for the quick pickup on the highway is only partly because of the eight cylinders," August explained to the horse expert. "But the 'V' means that all the pistons go not up and down but in a 'vee' line—the force of gravity is diminished."

"I noticed that the engine was twice as wide as mine," Aslak admitted, "but the only thing I could picture was that maybe there were two rows of pistons, beside each other, and I couldn't see how the crankshaft could be driving one drive shaft back to the rear wheels so I didn't ask."

"Long as we're out here by ourselves, I'll fill you in on the details I left out up in your tower. It's not pretty, August, but you should be aware of it. To make it simple: The Gang is doing all right, people still go along with our restraint policy and the quality of our 'shine, along with your brandy, is pulling customers in every week."

"It's about the deeds out here?"

"What did my uncle, Gunlek, say to you about your forty? Did he tell you to do anything out at the courthouse?"

August pondered a moment.

"Best I can recall, he said 'No money, you go settle next to my brother on Mile Road, empty farm there. I give land to many, I give land to you. You need help, see min nevo Aslak."

"You never went to the courthouse, paid any taxes on it?"

"Wouldn't I get a tax bill?"

"Not if your name wasn't on the tax roll."

August sagged back against the seat in his new, sweet-smelling Ford V-8.

"So I don't own the land."

"If that land had been sold to anybody, I would know it. My father owned all of that Section 29 as well as Section Thirty, by deed from my Uncle Gunlek, who owned thousands of acres up here—for the lumber. And I inherited it from my father. First born son and all that. I'll be happy to sell it to you tomorrow for a dollar."

"Of course—that land is my work, my home, some day soon maybe my family!"

"There's more to it, August. Frank Cutler doesn't want that land, he wants you off it!"

"Even if we got the deed signed, sealed, and delivered to your hand tomorrow, he could always say you sneaked in to buy it only because he found you didn't own it, and use that to add to all he's been working at, getting some sympathy, for the past year or so. He hates your guts, August, and he can keep hollering about how you were 'squatting' on it—the word he's using all over town. The rest of his pitch—Jim says he gave you the bones of it just the other day."

August, faint of voice, nodded. "Ja, German I am."

"But there's more yet, and now it gets nasty. Frank Cutler is dragging up every bit of Eunice's past he can get his hands on, calling her every name in the book, using words I wouldn't call my mares, and he's seen the two of you coming out of Anna's hand in hand. So now he's got you tied up with this woman, whose history everybody in Bergland Township has heard more than once, saying how rich Krauts are ....well, I still won't say the rest of it."

"So now you have the entire picture. I, Cynara, and when other people are aware of you and Eunice they'll all be glad for you. But there's already bad noises, and there'll be more for you and Eunice to contend with. So, think about buying the farm. Talk it over with her. Be damn sure you both are on the same page. You're not thinking only of August, any more."

Back in the house, the ladies were just closing the catalogs.

"We found some things just right for Eunice—and some things I just might have to get back in shape for in a few months," Cynara declared. "Just look at this" she flipped the Sears catalog back open, "here's an Anne Adams house dress with Raglan sleeves and a Flapper style drop waist and a large-button semi-belt! That's just perfect for Eunice! And we found a flutter-sleeve in robin's egg blue for afternoon hen parties, a flutter-collar pullover with empire waist, with double-hanging ruffles, and...."

She stopped, seeing the men's eyes glazed over.

"Okay," Cynara finished. "I can see I've lost both of you. Eunice will wear them and then you'll see how great she looks!"

When the coffee cups were empty, Cynara sent them home.

"I showed Eunice how to fill an order blank, there's one in the Sears catalog. You two can take it from here."

In the Model B, Eunice said, "I have to be ready for the breakfast servin' at Anna's. Let's fill out the order tomorrow when you come after one, and then I'll open a bank account in Ewen and write the check for the order."

Silence; August cranked his way around the corner on to M64.

The look of tired care on his face stabbed a spear of fear in her heart, then eased as August said, "And we can look at electric stoves and lamps, make it one order. I've changed my account there to a joint account; you can write checks on that."

She leaned over, pecked his cheek. "Thanks, one day, maybe soon, but I like the idea of having an account of my own. Besides, my last name may change—or has it on your account already?"

"No, but I'd like to whenever you want to."

"Give me another month or so? I want to fill out some more of me first!"

At Anna's door they sealed their words with a kiss.

"See you tomorrow!"

So on the 10th of November, the day before Armistice Day, August thought in a twist of irony in Anna's otherwise empty dining room that afternoon, they chose a GE standard four-burner stove, oven below.

"I don't have any confidence in bakin' in a Dutch oven," Eunice admitted. She also listed some other clothing items without his help or close observance, mostly lingerie.

"All set now?" August queried.

"Yes," she smiled. "Oh, I feel so *rich,so—I can't find the right word*—I'm so far away from …"she threw up her hands.

August ventured a guess. "Since this has to do with clothes, how about like a new thread in a new weave? Or a new design in a new material?"

"How about some new coffee in a new cup?" suggested Anna, hovering out of nowhere, coffee pot and two clean cups in hand.

As she whisked away the old cups, clattered the new into the same saucers, began filling the cups, Eunice saw a former scene, with Yaga.

"Anna," she said, her head lifting, her back arching into erect, "please sit down while I share something with both of you."

Anna set the pot on the near corner, leaned forward on her elbows.

"Like the time I tapped you with the breadknife and said, 'Rise, Lady Eunice'"?

"Very much—it's about identity." She turned to August. "I'm beginnin' to see things, their meanin', like you do." Swinging her gaze, back to Anna, then again to August, she began:

"Yaga showed me what I was back then, the mornin' after I slugged the man who drove me up here from Chicago, by askin' me to identify with an empty cup of coffee, tipped over on its side, on the table in her kitchen, the cup between the two of us, Yaga and me. To make that same cup, me, be useful, it had to be tipped back up, not by her, but by me, with no help, to show that I wanted to be useful, just as the cup has to be up to hold coffee."

Anna and August were silent, attentive.

Eunice inhaled, went on, gazing alternately at each of her audience of two.

"I filled that cup, the old me, with fresh coffee; I came here to do what I'd begun to learn was satisfyin'—"

"Filling you up" from August.

"Right!—doin' not *to* others, like hittin' them, but *for* others. I did what women do in order to become a woman, stop tryin' to keep on bein' a lumberjack."

She waved a hand at the two empty, used cups. "I'm not my old self, I'm not the same old cup."

Focusing now on August. "Yaga began this way of lookin' at myself, and at others. You showed me how to do it, that it is a way of thinkin' not new, not silly."

Now she turned her focus on Anna. "And you helped me to fit in, doin' for others, so I am now a new cup. And you just filled it with new coffee. When I receive these things I ordered, I will be outwardly a new cup, to match what I am underneath the clothes."

With a face flushed with joy, eyes sparkling from an inner light, Eunice sat back, still head up, back arched, erect.

"What I said before, I say again: Congratulations! We helped, but you had the kind of steel that kept the knife sharp. We just honed it."

August was silent, his eyes shining his admiration, his love, once more falling into her light blue eyes.

"Well," Anna declared. "I have some work to do with the books."

She rose, turned, left them. Stopped, turned back. "Some of your happiness has rubbed off on me. I envy you and thank you for sharing that happiness with me."

August smiled at Eunice, their hands covering the order blank, no entries as yet.

"Will you allow this order to symbolize our joining by allowing me to contribute to the new ensembles, the new cup containing a lovely woman I love?"

Eunice smiled, returned the squeeze of his hands.

"Your presence, your love, has created a response in my heart and my body. Insistin' on makin' the new cup all by myself would deny that response."

She drew the order blank to her. "I'm with you!"

At the Ewen bank, he said nothing as she created her own account. His check was mailed with the order. Clothes and stove and standing lamps.

After all, the idea of the cup, the new suit, the name change, described him as well.

But still near the surface, '*Wonder 'tis how little mirth, Keeps the bones of man ...*'

By his own table that evening, it seemed a wise idea to see what was available if it became impossible or even unlikely that he and Eunice could stay here, happily.

He dug his credentials from Heidelberg out of the top drawer of his steamer chest, its ironwork bands the work of his father as a parting gift. In the envelope he addressed the faculty dean of Northern Michigan University, in Marquette, asking if any vacancies for a man of his qualifications existed or would exist within a year or so.

Cynara would give him the address at the Post Office.

Best to have more than one string to his bow. And he couldn't make brandy forever!

CHAPTER FIFTEEN

That second Sunday in November, the 12th, while Eunice and Cynara were busy talking as they readied the hearty noon meal in Cynara's house, August, Aslak, Haywire and Jonas were hauling seasoned stove wood, cut in the spring, up to the still shack on the spur road.

The same sledge was the carrier, the blue-black team of mares the motive power. The source of the stove wood was the land Aslak had inherited, on the north side of the last leg of the spur, eighty acres of second-growth maple, birch, a few oaks, poplars, with a thin scattering of white pine.

In the twenty-odd years since the blackberries, those everpresent bearers of huge, black, juicy berries the black bears sought out once the tall timber was down brought life in the form of sunlight to all the seeds years dormant, had replaced the huge pines and hemlocks, to be followed with raspberries, the second-growth was still more of a promise of fuel for stoves than a luxurious mature proliferation.

In plain words, there was a lot more brush than trees worth cutting down, then up, for wood to keep the corn mash bubbling.

So, rather than destroying the next years' worth of fuel by cutting down brush to get the sledge next to the piled, now cured stacks of wood, the four men had to snake their ways from those piles out to the spur, where, slightly downhill from the Section Thirty still shack, the mares stood hip-shot while the men, that race superior to them, managed armloads of split chunks of wood, rough bark on the outside, sharp-edged on the splitline, with the odd splinter jutting into their forearms, stepped high over lopped-off branches, leaned first to their left, then to their right, to move the stove wood for the stills from their piles in the brush to the piles behind the still shack.

And then handle them once again to stack by and around the roof behind that shack in order to make them available to be handled once again to feed the fires keeping the mash bubbling. To disguise what went on inside the perimeter woodpiles: Moonshining.

Did the blue-black mares sense their superiority? Or did the men, surely aware of the team standing idly, out of envy manufacture that possibility?

The difference: The horses were there at the beck and call of their masters; the men worked of their own volition.

Nevertheless, as the four men, wiping their sweating foreheads even in the middle of November in the Upper Peninsula when the degrees of Fahrenheit and latitude were often, on a sunny Sunday afternoon, not very far apart, trudged up the yards of the Mile Road spur, they nudged each other, hats in hand, at the ease the mares exhibited hauling the several cords ahead of them.

"Damn," grunted Jonas Amundsen, "look at that! They just walk up the road!"

Haywire chuckled. "Ain't seen nothin' yet! Wait til they git to that gate!"

August, the sweatiest, glanced at Aslak, walking with them behind the load.

"Shouldn't you have the reins in your hands?"

From that half-grin of confidence, Aslak answered, "No."

The team's heads now even, parallel with the near end of the gate, their ears turned backwards, though they kept going.

"Gee!" from Aslak, in a conversational tone; the mares took three paces to clear the near end of the gate with the front end of the sledge, swung to their right, dipped their heads a few inches to drag the sledge front end to the new direction, continued past the far corner of the woodpile's remains behind the still shack Stopped.

Shook their heads, blew, sagged their hips as before.

Hard to believe.

August put it into words.

"Seeing is believing!"

Jonas seized a chunk in each hand, roared, "I can smell the roast from the house!"

Herman: "Ja, we move to it!"

When the sledge was cleaned off, the four sat on the sledge. Aslak clucked twice, the team moved out up to the woods path.

At the barn, Aslak unhooked the double tree, the horses moved to the barn door, the four men helped take off the harnesses, hooked them up inside while Aslak brushed down his lovelies, sent them off to the pasture with a slap on those powerful, mountainous rumps.

At the outside, old-timey pump, they took off the worst of the sweat and grime, shared towels, moved to the front door where Eunice pushed it open for them.

The opening door blast of the roasting venison popped their salivary glands into production.

Work over for now. Now, EAT!

When the plates were empty, the table cleared, the dishes washed and stacked to dry, not much conversation distracted the feasters from the pleasantly comfortable stuffy stomachs in the various bodies scattered in a few clumps on the sofa, at the small table islands in their random spots on the huge living room and parlor floors. The names of those who for a few minutes were gone, then snapped back into consciousness, will remain unrevealed.

Decent, testing work, outside shoring up the still shack winter fuel, inside readying the roast, the potatoes, the corn on the cob—a sense of all jobs well done, good people to share one's comments about the day's weather, the near burning of the pies in the oven, all at ease in their own little worlds, from youngest to oldest, past achievers, hopeful strivers—what an uplift from the days of the now diminishing Depression, the soon-to-end Prohibition, the Upper Peninsula winter of inside comfort about to halt most outside activity.

August saw again, in his mind reflecting the mares' steady powerful pull of what was to be the still shack warmth and the boiling of the mash, that insurance of the future of man and moonshine for the winter. For the mares themselves, completely at ease in their domesticated slot, content in their work, receiving the admiration of their fellow workers and the praise of their master.

The wood, the horses, the men, he thought. No dark clouds of threat such as I have now. The price I pay for knowing the alphabet, for my schooling, for my success, for my home, for my love of Eunice, for my sense of achievement

How I thought I was helping Eunice walk a new path, being her sustainer and provider!

Jonas tried to tone down his stentorian call to Haywire, succeeded somewhat: "Time for us old bachelors to head for our own homes, leave the millionaires with their women to their own company."

Haywire, relieved to be up and moving, chuckled his agreement. They heard the usual demands not to be strangers, to come back when they felt like it, made the usual agreements to return, eased out the door.

Like two autumn leaves, the last off a tree, floating down a lazy stream, the two old men from Scandinavia these long years past were silent while climbing the hill, careful down the first few paces, then, the rest of the Mile Road in sight in the late afternoon, slowed down to an amble.

"How many times …" Haywire began.

"Ja, vi gar pa beinen vare hier," Jonas completed softly—for him. (We go on our own bones here.)

"Men enda er jeg glad i det, at jeg kunne gjor det," (I'm glad to be able to do it) Herman returned. Hardly ever given to regard, much less comment, on what he saw, he went on in English.

"First here we saw the timber all over, we saw it as something to cut down, earn our pay. Now the small we see" he waved ahead of them, "coming back, small now, …"

"Never see we the next timber," Jonas took it further. "Men det var vare arbeit a gjore, nu ma vi bruke det som er igjen." (That was our job, now we have to use what is left)

They stopped at the sagged open wide gate. Confronting them, the dead grassed, unused wagon way past a weathered white small house to an empty, graying, barn; a wagon with its tongue grass-covered a mere suggestion of the team he'd long since lost, the pump solid rust from rickety wooden platform to the end of its handle. Still operable, but barely.

"Not much, and cold inside," Jonas summed up. "But it is mine, and I can warm it with a match still. Better I come here, worse i Norge bakken!" (in the mountains of home)

Haywire watched Jonas force open his squealing front door, pull it shut. Shortly, a puff of smoke from the redbrick chimney released him toward his own house in the next forty, the last one on the Mile Road, touching M64.

Haywire's shamble picked up speed. The chill in the air, the remnants of Jonas' gloom he could not completely shake off, made his own shack a place to make haste for. Not as solitary as Jonas, well liked by all he met, to Haywire his black-tarpaper coated high roofed but single story house still echoed faintly of the Luna Light Gang meetings, before that the many Saturday night parties he'd hosted, all the neighbors their witness in sight and by sound.

He would bank his fire with some large chunks, half-cured ones on top, so that in the morning, there would be a few coals to build up when he returned from his night watch at the stills on Section Thirty. He was one-half of the moonshine making crew, Aslak the day watch-stander.

"Too busy to be sad, lonesome like Jonas," he told himself. The stove topped off and banked, the draft barely open, the stovepipe damper slowing down what little air that draft below the fire's base allowed, he turned back up the Mile Road in the gathering gloom to spend his night in the warmth of the still shack. That Jonas' time on life's turning wheel was short, that his own time was like the fire in his stove, he had no words for.

At the top of the hill he saw Aslak just rounding his barn on his way back from the still house via the woods path. The mares, who'd walked back with him, halted by the fence to which Aslak had just shut the gate behind him.

Aslak raised a hand high, looking at Haywire. Haywire chuckled to himself, waved back vigorously, turned right toward Kallaak's Corner.

The lines, were they from the Bible? Or a hymn from the old days?

'My cup runneth over.'

Life was good!

"Those poor old men," Cynara voiced the thought, her hands clasped in front of her adult life's desire, slowly rocking the end chair of the four in their semi-circle in front of the artfully joined stones framing the leaping flames.

"They never married, had children?" Eunice wondered.

What might as well be wondered of Sherman Pendock, late that Sunday afternoon the 12th of November 1933, standing, as often, on his porch, facing the timber not as a monarch toward supplicating or cheering subjects, nor as a fulfilled adorer of the thousands of acres of mature, virgin hemlocks and pines inching higher year by year, suggesting perhaps to a long-ago visitor from abroad the idea of green height for a children's tale for Jack and a Giant, to diminish Sherman's sensation of porch floor elevation.

He was quite aware that to sense their oft-felt communication with him he had to be out amongst them. Merely being looked at from even a short distance, the one hundred feet from the north end of his porch, did not open the line, begin a message.

Though he'd been among them countless times, sensed that message, as satisfying as it had been, they weren't his own kind.

He sighed, turned, sat in what he called his sundown chair, lifted his *A Shropshire Lad.*

'Oh, lads, at home I heard you plain,
But here your speech is still …'

At the Marsh home on M28 up past the rock crusher cliff and down the road, Floyd pushed himself away from the table. Annabel rose, began stacking the plates.

"I hope you had enough," she muttered, eyes on the knives and forks.

"If you and the kids had enough, I'm satisfied," he answered. "Let's see how the hunting, fishing goes for the cherry-pickers coming up here. Somebody around here might want another room added on, make enough money to hire Marsh Construction. Or I can try somewhere else, send money back here."

"Corn meal mush for breakfast in the morning." She carried the dishes, the turkey platter, into the kitchen.

Floyd stood at the picture window, looking over M28, the few empty cottages on the shore. Over Lake Gogebic the clouds, all rolled up in bunches, straight across the bottoms as if on a ruler-drawn line, showed just the bottom of the setting sun, enough to lay its orange-yellow glare on the still water.

When the kids come back in, be sure you look cheerful, ask 'em what they'll have to do for school tomorrow.

"Wonder how many will be in for breakfast tomorrow?" Anna asked herself. Not a sound from upstairs, nobody on the street out front.

Three singles for Sunday dinner. The total meals for today: Three.

Nobody but Eunice and I will sleep here tonight.

If August brings her back, maybe we can all share a brandy.

Hope what I've got in the bank will at least feed us, pay the electric bill.

Hope Randolph and his folks ask me there for Christmas dinner!

Is there an Avalon for old hotel restaurant owners or just for King Arthur!

Ed Erikson put up his hand, leaned against the corner maple tree, saw from the near corner of Center and Ash that he still had a block to go for his own front door on Railroad. Most of his old-bones kind of shuffle east on Railroad, begun an hour ago, had been past houses that in the good times had been lit up, young folks getting the most of the outside snow—a couple of snow-man starts near the edge of cleaned-off sidewalks, maybe a snow ball fight in progress ...

Now most of his walk had been out in the street—the only sidewalk clear of snow had been the ones on Pine, in front of Rosberg's Mercantile and, opposite, the Post Office and The Trading Post, Marko's Saloon, the Town Hall on the corner of Center.

Then this side of Ash, where the maples marked the inside edge of the sidewalk just done over after that town meeting, and the outside edge of the elementary school playground.

But there was no way he could get across the ditch this side of Center; he'd have to go left to Hattie Walker's, then come back along Center.

Maybe Warden Limpert would be at Hattie's, his mother-in-law, give him an arm to lean on back down Center, down Ash that block to his house.

While Ed figured all this out, Mrs Shankey, observant as always, didn't bother to get her old man out of his chair, sleeping under the comics section of the *Detroit News*. She asked the operator to ring Glenn Johnson's number.

So Ed had just straightened up away from the corner maple tree when Glenn Johnson, school superintendent, who lived just across the street from Ed, six feet three, the basket ball coach for Bergland, showed up, his unbuckled overshoes, his trademark, busting away the foot-high street snow, came over the ditch to put his left arm around the stooping, short stepping former final authority of Bergland Township's decision-making. Ancient.

Mrs Shankey saw the meeting, a pause while puffs of visible breath passed between the two, then watched the tall man amble at a pace attentive to Ed's up to Walker's corner, out in the middle of Center Street, shamble around her corner, finally disappear as they turned the corner of Ash and Railroad.

She let the shade fall to its normal level, strode past her still sleeping husband, picked up the Friday-Saturday *Ironwood Daily Globe*. No Bergland items there on the Localities News page.

Well, she'd seen something, anyway.

Peter was there to open the door; his father had taken his time, with Glenn Johnson's patient help, up the wide wooden steps, his searching feet crunching out his former coming down footprints.

"Maybe you ought to go out walking with your father," Glenn, in his precise lip movements forming all the letter sounds, "He had some difficulty with the snow banks today."

Peter nodded. "I offered. Next time I'll ignore his 'No, no, I can do it'"

A warm cup of coffee, fresh-perked Maxwell House, made its shaky way up to the old man's droopy mustache, back down to clatter on the saucer on the kitchen table.

"What's this big map doing all over the table?"

"There's money down in Lansing for a national forest; all the counties have to submit their recommendations for boundaries, available qualified personnel to survey, mark, and so forth by the first of the year."

"What's that got to do with you?"

"I'm a lawyer, Pa. I work in the county courthouse, not much law business lately. So I got together with Warden Limpert, Jim Demary and his son Clarence. We've got about a month to wrap it up, coordinate with Gogebic and Matchwood, and down to Lansing. I might just go down there, too, see who I can get to know."

Ed raised his hand, brushed his droopy white mustache. "Never hurts to get to know your boss, I know."

A brisk knock on the front door, Warden Limpert opened it, came in, got busy with Peter at the map.

Ed smiled a bit. Things going on. He didn't have to get involved. Nice for a change.

Jim Ferguson stood, dust cloth in hand, surveying the shelves in the pick-up room grown to a nearly daily meeting place, even for some of Bill Piper's old bench hangers-on.

"Don't need any restocking this Saturday, either, I guess."

Though his fellow-members were telling of a better, a more hopeful atmosphere in their customers' homes what with FERA barely holding its own, consumption, sales, were down. On the shelves, only the one for August's Applejack

Brandy had some empty space—about half its length, and the only jug tops needing no dusting.

"Maybe the first-and-only drink is becoming the first-half-and-only drink."

Jim's lips tightened as the irony of the drinking situation became plain.

"A bit humorous, in fact. The only thing making the consumption diminish below reason is not the act of Prohibition, but a Depression the government is doing its best to get over with!"

He plopped down in an easy chair beside his little potbelly stove. Idly, his gaze on the door, it occurred to him that the doorframe top bar, bare, could use a motto, something to talk about while enjoying one's ease in this relaxing, slowed-down gathering place for the Luna Light Gang—and anyone else!

The first one coming to mind brought back a real smile on the sober, quiet-spoken Jim's face. He rose, found a piece of board just short of the same length as the doorframe top. On the board he tacked one side of an empty white cardboard shoe box, four words with a broad-tipped pen, a screwhook above the door frame, a length of thin picture hanging wire looped around two nails tapped into the board's top edge became the motto over the doorframe top:

GRIN AND BEAR IT!

What August, Jim thought, with all his book learning, would call a thesis.

Chapter Sixteen

Preparation for the antithesis, more complex, was nearing its end in Milwaukee. Levi Skantz was not a man in whom resentment gradually wore away, to be replaced by good sense, or even common sense. Like a pot coming to a boil over a hot flame, in most people rage boils over, and even if the cause remains, the steam turns the water up into the air until the water is gone. The steam ends.

However, if the pot's lid is tight, air tight, the steam cannot escape. It forms beads inside the lid which eventually refurbish the amount of water to boil and boil and boil …

Such a lid was, in Levi Skantz' way of thinking, August's confrontation last Thanksgiving. To think he'd figured out a way to be aware of the scheme which he, Levi Skantz, that fat Germans's superior not only in the office but in every other way imaginable had worked on, investigated its possibilities, abused Gunlek Bergland's good-natured trust for years, had found evidence of it, had kept that evidence, flaunted it in his face, had bragged about how it had enabled him to come up with a business that was making him rich and waved that fifty-dollar bill in my face!

But I'm still smarter than he is! He'll be sorry he waved that bill in my face! When I'm done with him, thinks he safe because he's way up there in the UP!—I'll have every one of those fifty dollar bills!

"You put out the word, I'm here, let's get on with it," the hulk muttered, half to himself, not caring if Skantz heard. All this foaming at the mouth was bad business, not the way it was supposed to be done. I go, I tell 'em, they're scared, I come away after the job's done, if there was something I was supposed to get, I've got it.

That's business. I don't have to hear all about the reasons!

"Here's what you do," growled Levi Skantz, coming back from the far side of his tight little bachelor's room at the run-down hotel, where his fevered rant had taken him, reaching the Sphinx-like motionless mass, walking with that coiled up emanation of evil radiating that menace for which he was feared.

"Here is the key for the car outside. Take it up to Bergland, you have a sketch of the roads, where the Mile Road is. Schmidt's house is the third one on the right—no houses on the left, it's out in the boonies. Looks like a small barn with a silo in front."

"Get there just before dark, day before Thanksgiving. Don't be early, don't be a day late. He has to know that it's a full year since he was down here."

The hulk was impressed. "Yeah, we do that sort of thing, give the others something to think about, the date, something to worry about, themselves."

"I hear he has a car, a Ford Model B. If it's there, he's there. If it's not there, go up to White Pine—that's the next town up north on M64. Don't go back to Bergland. Stay away from Bergland, they know him there, they might connect back to you, to me, I don't want that, you understand?"

"Yeah, yeah."

"Wait, have a cup, a drink, come back. When the car is there, then you go in. Just knock, barge in!"

"I scare him, we go through forking up a bunch of bills, I come away, you pay me mine, that's it."

"You got it. You do it, do it right, there's extra for you, maybe; I put in the good word for you to your boss."

At the door, the hulk turned halfway back.

"How 'bout I rough him up if I feel like it?"

Skantz grinned, looking up at the hulk from his coil, like a rattler ready to strike.

"Tell him it's from me! Tell him it's his receipt!"

After Anna's brunch Thursday, November 23rd, Thanksgiving Day, they sat back in the Ironwood theatre seats to experience the pathos, poverty, senseless war in Erich Maria Remarque's *All Quiet on the Western Front*, thinking that this might be some curiously lyrical study of a period in WW I when, no attacks, no retreats, the newspapers would characterize it as the title of the movie indicated: all quiet on the western front.

True enough. No battles, nor artillery blasting away, machine guns mowing down ranks of advancing soldiers.

What they saw: Soldiers in deep trenches, muddy, trash-strewn, straggling back to spend some intervals with local wives and widows, some with little children, bereft as well by the war, finding what community, what meaning, they could create away from 'all quiet' except for a few snipers on both sides.

The scene in which a haggard young mother slices up a sausage one of the deserting soldiers has come up with somehow, several children scrambling around on the floor of the hovel behind the lines to pick up the rolling slices of sausage made Eunice's hands come to her face in schocked pity. The sequences of scenes in the trenches amidst the wet, muddy footing, the rats fearless of the despondent soldiers, kept the audience quietly horrified.

The scenes showing the deserting soldiers, caught while with the civilians, then being shot for deserting their posts—thus the ironic *All Quiet* in the title—made some of the viewers squirm in sympathy and distress.

Near the end, the scenes returned to show a young French soldier, an example of dutiful soldiering, though hardly a man in years. He found a few moments of delight while a sentry behind the sandbag parapet one afternoon, watching a fragile, aery butterfly flitting here and there just beyond the soldier's reach. His attention focused on gold and black beauty of the butterfly, indicated by the camera closing in on it.

The soldier's hand enters the picture. As it opens to capture the butterfly, a single shot rings out. The hand sags at the wrist, is still. The butterfly flits out of sight.

On the screen, the stark, bitter phrase:THE END

Eunice's grip tightened on August's hand. The lights came up to reveal the tears on her cheeks. August's throat disallowed any comment.

The noise of seats flipping back up as other viewers broke the grip of the ending helped Eunice come back to the present, end the image of the film's last scene.

She spoke haltingly as they neared the Ford Model B. "For a moment," she giggled nervously, "I wanted to shoot the sniper, punish him for shootin' that young soldier!"

August squeezed her arm in empathy. "Violence begets violence."

As they neared the turn-off away from Holiday Lake in Wakefield on their way back to Bergland, Eunice, who'd begun answering in few words, so that August, respecting her mood, apparently in reaction to the movie sadness, had fallen silent, suddenly put her hand fiercely on his near arm.

"Park here facing the lake for awhile. I have to tell you somethin'."

She faced the windshield, her gaze fastened on the lake, glimmering in late twilight.

Her face alternately clenching—eyes shut, mouth squeezed shut—then her shoulders sagging down, her face contorting—August reached to touch her.

"What's the matter?"

"We have to stop," she gasped. "I have to go away. I can't stay here anymore!"

August was speechless.

"Anna told me this afternoon, just before you picked me up," Eunice went on, her voice flat, still staring at Holiday Lake. "That man Cutler isn't just angry about you on the Mile Road, all your money. Jim told her what he's saying about me—all the horrible stuff I did and said before."

She twisted around to face him. "I can take it. I'll never, never be like that again! But it's not fair to you to have to have him pile that on you on top of what he's already doin'—callin' you ..." she broke into gasps, sobs, "if we stay together here ... reach for the butter-fly ... we'll be shot ... be shot by that evil man!" a heart-wrenching wail at her own words.

August, seeming far distant, sought to utter ... what?

What he had left his homeland to avoid was now present. Aimed at him.

All of what Frank Cutler was saying had the inescapable ring of truth. She had been what he now reminded everyone. I am a German, and he did Germans kill in WW I. Rich I am, the finest house have in the township. I do have an opinion of my stature as better than anyone else in ...

He saw again the Count Palatinate, his royal wear, his royal bearing, the man—yes, he was a man, mortal, ate, drank—but his sense of his position, his calm, positive demeanor, was that not what was needed now?

His sense of the here and now recovered, he leaned over, placed both hands on the now silent, grieving woman he loved.

"My dear, please look at me. Listen to me."

After a long moment, a handkerchief wadded in her hands, Eunice met his eyes.

"I was hoping for a moment it would be fitting for me to bring this matter of Frank Cutler up, for us to discuss, make a decision about ourselves. I have to say that I can see myself and hear myself well enough to think I can be thought of as a poor stick of a professor whose social skills are lacking or clumsy. Not worth your travail."

He paused, seeing understanding in her eyes.

"I have thought, and do still, that your past is exactly that, and no more, in spite of what anyone, especially Frank Cutler, may say. You are the best partner for me to live with the rest of my life; I hope the scales never fall from your eyes to see what a dull old fountain of quotes I am. A man whose idea of the greatest miracle is the alphabet, the Tree of Life, may disappoint you in your choice as those years still left to us wend their way."

She smiled, barely, as he added,

"Wherever we are!"

As they turned from the car to enter the Mile Road house, hand in hand, they saw headlights enter the lake forty next to them, then go out, heard a car door click quietly shut. "Somebody for some night fishing, I suppose," August said.

"Let's have a brandy, then you can take me back to Anna's!"

The door clicked closed behind them.

Eunice flinched slightly. Her face warmed. She squeezed August's arm.

"Excuse me, I need to," she reached for the bathroom door at her left. Then, suddenly, gripped his forearm with both hands.

"I'm a couple of days early—but it's what I've been hoping for!"

Purse in hand, she closed the bathroom door.

August, thinking he understood, doffed his coat, hung it and his hat on the rack to the right of the door.

"I see your dish is empty, mein hund! Just a minute while I tend the fire!"

Zwei rose from his rug by the cot at the far end of the room, trotted toward his master, tail a-wag, suddenly snarled to lunge past August as

A BANG! on the just-closed door!

The hulk burst in, the door thunking against the opposite wall as August swung to face the intruder. The poker dropped from his hands as the hulk pointed the dull black pistol, moved with big lunging steps to point it at August's belly.

"Okay, let's have all of those fifty-dollar bills, you fat punk! Or I'll let you have a couple from …"

In the split second of the frozen tableaux, August, hands in front of his body, facing the snarling menace of the man, the gun, Eunice, the bathroom door swinging open, stock-still in amazement Zwei acted.

He darted at the threat, sank his sharp teeth into the flesh of the hulk's ankle

The pistol went off as the hulk flinched, swung the clinging dog off the floor The surprise recoil bounced the pistol over the hulk's shoulder, August felt the burning sear in his left side Eunice sprang forward to pick up the pistol clattering toward her, squeezed the trigger as the hulk began his turn toward her in their deafened ears the three sharp pops doubled the hulk over, knocked him back and down in a heap of twisted legs, clutching at his gut A spurting fountain of red blood through his fingers, his mouth open, no sound except the *thud* of his head on the parquet floor.

Zwei let go.

Drenched in vivid red.

In the Ontonagon courthouse, the spectators focused on the coroner's answer:

"The cause of death was exsanguination from the several perforations of the abdominal aorta."

Peter Erikson faced the judge. "Your Honor, the prosecution moves for a directed verdict of justified killing in self-defense."

Judge Latvala rapped his gavel once. "So directed. The charge of homicide in the second degree is dismissed."

He gave Eunice a frosty smile. "You acted commendably, madam!"

In the week since the violence, August's through-and-through flesh wound above his left hip was healing, but the hug he gave Eunice as they stood for all to see and approve was a bit painful just the same.

So the applause for the verdict applied to the close embrace as well!

"Time for a celebration dinner," Aslak declared, as the foursome reached the warmth of the early afternoon sun that 11th of December, 1933. "The restaurant is right next door. I told them to save us a table on the way into the courthouse this morning!"

August turned to Eunice. "While we're here, let's see if we can access the records to find your ancestors."

The records clerk wrote down 'Lillian Eunice Ryan' (That's your maiden name?) and 'December 7th, 1892, Bucks County, Pennsylvania'.

"I'll have to call Lansing, they'll call me back when Pennsylvania calls them," the clerk advised. "And congratulations on the verdict! Is it true that no bail was ordered the morning after?"

"That is correct," August smiled. "Our word was good enough for Peter Erickson."

They turned to see Peter Erikson hurrying down the corridor.

"Thank you, Peter," Eunice said, shaking his hand. "It turned out just as you thought."

They roamed about the city, interested in what evidence remained of its having been, in its early years, a hub for lumber finishing and shipping, for copper mining up in the various tributaries of the Ontonagon River, the goal of millions of board feet of white pine clogging the West, South, Middle and East branches of that river.

In these days, what Ontonagon was known for was the acidic, sour effluvium of the pulp mill. What logs were shipped to Ontonagon now were not even logs—more like fence posts of mainly poplar, wood turned into pulpwood as the first stage of paper.

So Sherman Pendock's claim, with August's agreement, was true: The spirit of the woods lived on, the words carried on paper from that pulp just as the tall virgin timbers had carried the sails of ships, had formed the substance of homes, of factories, and what had taken their places was now the shelter and sustenance of wildlife in greater profusion than in the days and years and centuries of timber.

The sulphurous odor, carried by the winds all over Ontonagon County, in whatever directions the wind happened to blow, let none forget that wood was still a major element of that culture.

Five o'clock. Closing time in the courthouse. The records clerk handed August and Eunice a folder on her way out.

"There's quite a bit in this," she beamed. "When the word gets out, you will be one proud woman!"

Back in the restaurant, Aslak and August slid their chairs around to read over Eunice's shoulder the lineage of the former lumberjack, converted, lately become a woman, yet with the steel allowing her to shoot to kill:

Parents: Flora Rebecca McClellan b. Aug27,1859 m.John Ryan 1871

Grandparents: Eunice (Weeks) Avery McClellan b.May 5th,1827 great-granddaughter of

Eunice (Weeks) Avery, a descendant of John and Priscilla (Mullins) Alden—so all the descendants of this pair—including Lillian Eunice Ryan, now sitting at that table in

Ontonagon, Michigan, on the 11th of December, 1933, were possessors of Mayflower ancestry.

Eunice gasped, leaned back, face in her hands, while August and Aslak stared at this, this *woman,* one of the bearers of that desire for freedom, the will to work toward that freedom, that dogged persistence to plant the seed of the greatest country in modern times, now in this very day standing possessed of lineage equal to the stature she'd achieved this day in the eyes of all.

"You can be proud of your heritage," Aslak beamed.

"Even, too, would your ancestors be proud of you," August declared to Eunice. "I am humbled by your coming up to the mark in my defense. More, I am happy to have desired, and do so still, that you honor me by your love."

In the busy restaurant, peopled by courthouse workers, pulp mill workers, casual visitors, witnesses, August gently pushed his chair aside, knelt before the woman who had saved his life, asked her to share it with him:

> 'Come live with me and be my love,
> And we will all the pleasures prove,
> That valleys, groves, and hills fields
> Woods or steepy mountain yields.
>
> And I will make thee beds of roses,
> And a thousand fragrant posies,
> - - - - - - - -
> If these delights thy mind may move,
> Then live with me and be my love!'—
> Christopher Marlowe

'Tis said that 'Blood will tell', and so all who ceased their clatter and chatter as August knelt, and those who could not hear his words could still sense by the tableau what the kneeling man was asking, his right hand over his heart, his left, palm up, stretched out to the blushing but smiling lady were charmed that she placed her hand in his out-stretched one, lifting gently as she stood to face him, then freed his hand to place her arms around his neck and her lips to his for a long, long moment … until the waitress, beaming, started a rhythmic handclap soon joined in by all, no matter how their day had started, what it had held, how it now had ended, brought to share the evident happiness and joy of this blissful couple, whose delight by their sharing was not diminished but enhanced.

As they bowed their heads to the crowd, the two, arm in arm, moved to the exit, the clamor faded out.

To begin the Christmas dinner celebrating Anna's retirement from the Hotel to take up her duties as Gunlek Aslaksen Bergland II's nanny, she held up her small snifter of August's Appljack Brandy in the heir's grandfather's remodeled dining room.

"To Eunice, once knighted by me, and a worthy descendant of the Mayflower heroes!"

"To you, Anna, who after Yaga pointed, provided my path, and to you, August, who makes the journey a delight!"

"To my Adam, with whom I multiply in Paradise!"

"To Eunice, my better half, my own life-giver!"

"To you, Cynara, creator of our son; and to all here, may we inspire and nourish each other as the others did at the Round Table, this cup of kindness!"

The crystal snifters pinged together, then decanted the first sip.

"Anna," August announced after Cynara had invoked the Lord's Grace, "you may not be the only one to face a youthful challenge. The Northern Michigan University faculty Dean has asked me to visit them before February to interview for an opening!"

And the dinner conversation, genial, perhaps regretful at times, concerned his and Eunice's possible departure,

"But what about your new house!?"

Anna's response to the change in venue,

"Going up and down those stairs will keep me in shape!"

How Cynara would resume the mantle of Post Mistress if Sherman Pendock declined the post ...

"He'll have plenty of company in the Post Office!"

Just before midnight, Eunice and August went up and over and down the hill to their own door, where Zwei greeted them over the newly-laid oak parquet, then flopped again by the cot.

In the soft red glow of the fireplace, August and Eunice, standing, faced each other.

Each took one step, hands at their sides.

"I feel that we ..." Eunice began, "... are already wed," August completed.

She reached up, loosened his tie, slowly pulled it from around his collar, dropped it

unseeing at her feet. She continued with the top button, opening the collar.

"My dress buttons down the back," she murmured. "I want it off."

INITIUM

Acknowledgement:

My thanks to Marko Lulich and his *Akogibing,* the shore from which this set sail.

Made in the USA